The
Jinn and
the
Two Kingdoms

The Jinn and the Two Kingdoms

PETER W. BLAISDELL

Cover design by Heidi North
Interior book design by Andrea Reider

ISBN: 978-0-9992205-6-6
E-ISBN: 978-0-9992205-7-3

Library of Congress Control Number 2022903776

"Hell is empty and all the devils are here."

From *The Tempest* by William Shakespeare

"But I like my madness.
There is a thrill in it unknown to such sanity as yours."

From *Scaramouche* by Rafael Sabatini

The
Jinn and
the
Two Kingdoms

CHAPTER 1

Midnight in the Caliph's Library

Córdoba, Spain, mid-tenth century

I'm a woman among men, a skeptic among believers, a servant among princes, and a scholar amid the ignorant.

Which gets me killed first?

Lubna wondered this as someone rapped on her door.

Until the knock, she could imagine she had the palace to herself. It was late and dead quiet. She watched sand in an hourglass draining time from the night. Her study was dimly lit excepting an oil lamp to illuminate what she studied, an odd poem coupled with an odder map. Moonlight filtering in through a scrim covering her open window also lit the poem. The scrim kept bats out, but let the moon in.

The knock was deferential, respectful almost, but insistent.

Lubna rose from her cushion and walked to her study door. Matias, a courtier in the caliph's entourage, stood in the corridor with a dozen soldiers dressed in white cotton robes covered with chain mail. They wore scimitars in lacquered scabbards. Their clothing and armor didn't belong to any of the palace's regular guards; in the corridor's dim light, they looked like hell's emissaries with deeply shadowed faces and undulating forms in her oil lamp's shifting flame.

Matias saw her alarm at the sinister company he led and shrugged slightly as if to say things were not as bad as they appeared. He was just obeying a command, an unwelcome task. One day the tables might turn and Lubna's star could again be ascendant and she might knock at his door.

Like Lubna, Matias was a native Spaniard and a Christian, but she expected no sympathy from her fellow countryman and co-religionist. After all, she was a slave purchased to service the caliphate's endless need for labor while Matias was free and intended to rise far in the caliph's court; ambition oozed from every pore in his body, but nonetheless, tonight, he was deferential, no doubt remembering that Lubna, slave though she was, often had the caliph's ear and acted as his personal secretary on issues pertaining to the library and the quest to populate it with manuscripts from around the world. However, he was confident in his purpose, which meant someone influential was behind this visit—she wouldn't let herself believe it was an arrest.

"I need to come in," Matias said.

Again he politely shrugged.

Why? Why come at this hour? She replied to her own questions. *Many in court seem friendly, but aren't friends.*

No one had drawn weapons—she was a mere female. Ah, life's little fictions: as if Matias led a troop of escorts for a privileged guest of the court rather than guards for a prisoner possibly destined to be strangled in the caliph's dungeon. Lubna supposed she should be flattered that they had mobilized a squad of soldiers to summon her. Flattered or terrified.

"Who was the woman outside your door?" Matias asked.

Lubna didn't feign her puzzlement. "I don't know of any visitors at this hour."

"Aside from you, no women work in the caliph's scriptorium or library," Matias said. "Maybe she wants something you have."

"She was in the corridor?"

Matias nodded impatiently. "Dressed in a dark robe, rather pretty, though not as striking as you."

Lubna ignored the flattery and considered for a moment. Most thieves or assassins were men, but it was conceivable that someone had hired a woman to slash her throat. The night was heading in a very black direction.

"You're in demand at this late hour," Matias continued. "First, she was here. Now, we're here."

"Maybe a lost servant," Lubna said. "There would be no reason for someone I don't know to be here wandering around at night."

"A mystery, then," Matias said. "She was elusive. We saw her, but then she faded away into the shadows as we approached. We'll come back to who she was later, but now to a bigger mystery. I understand that you have a sort of scroll with a map or some verses. Somehow this gives directions to countless wealth."

"Everything I have has been collected on behalf of the caliph," she said.

"But that's the issue," Matias said. "The caliph, may he long reign, hasn't seen this document nor has the vizier. Actually, no one has seen it but you. And we only found out about it through indirect means. You haven't volunteered any information about this scroll or even told the court that you came to possess it."

"I didn't know what it was. I still don't. Its provenance is uncertain and its meaning is unclear—if it has a meaning. I don't inform the caliph or his court about every scrap of a document that comes into the library's possession."

"Not having seen the document," Matias said, "I'm in the dark as much as anyone, but it sounds like more than a 'scrap.' I see your writing table is full of books, scrolls, and writing implements—"

"That's no surprise, Matias," she said angrily. "I'm the court's scribe."

He paid no attention and spoke to the soldiers. "Search the table."

The soldiers barged into her study.

How humbling. The guards weren't here for her. They were here to help Matias ransack her office and the rest of the library if need be.

"Can they even read?" she asked.

"Don't be cruel," he said. "They can recognize a map."

She foresaw the clumsy destruction of her office and its priceless volumes, scrolls, and painstaking transcriptions in the surrounding rooms of the palace library, everything arranged and indexed to her exacting standards. Stacks of handmade books from the world over and rolls of parchments on wooden shelves reaching up to the ceiling lined the room. She had to summon a tall servant to access the highest shelves.

Most of the court was at best indifferent and at worst overtly hostile to this repository of learning, believing that too much knowledge undermined faith and generally created a cynical environment toward both religious and temporal authority. Lubna, however, loved the complex of rooms that she oversaw holding the growing collection of wisdom, her realm within Abd-al-Rahman's Andalusian Caliphate. She sniffed the dry, musty smell of the papyrus and vellum, and the sharper tang of the ink she used to transcribe the knowledge from any one of a half dozen languages she was conversant with into Arabic, the prettiest script with its beautiful curvilinear form. The smells implied a vast engine for the processing of knowledge.

Matias's guards would stumble on the scroll anyway so she said, "No need to look. I was working on it now. The poem is in the middle of the table. And, yes, there is a map of some sort on the parchment with the verses. I don't know how they're connected."

Matias picked up the scroll. "What language is this? Nothing that I recognize, not Arabic, Spanish, or Latin."

She'd been sipping wine as she worked before the interruption. Matias picked up her glass and drained it.

"You don't recognize many languages," she said.

"I recognize who has power in court—and in this room," he said.

The room was crowded with big men. She smelled their sweat on this hot night. One of the soldiers knocked into a shelf with neatly arranged scrolls, which fell to the floor in a cascade of papyrus.

"It's Aramaic with a few words in other languages," Lubna said. "I've translated it into Arabic."

"So the caliph and his advisers can read it?" Matias asked.

She nodded. "Translating poetry is slow work, getting the rhymes and meters right. I didn't want to show it to anyone before I was done."

This was partly true. She might eventually send the poem and map along to the caliph after she'd studied them. At the moment it was an intellectual puzzle she hadn't planned to share with anyone. Its verses described unrequited love, deeper than youthful lust, apparently written by someone used to spending time alone who had finally found a kindred spirit, and expressed their elation in an otherworldly sonnet that was pretty and lyrical.

The map didn't depict any region she'd ever heard of, but Lubna thought the verses were the key to the map's geographic coordinates.

"So there are several copies," Matias said sharply. "Who asked you to reproduce it? Where's the Arabic version?"

"Right beside the original Aramaic parchment on my table. See for yourself. Can I sit down? It's late and I'm tired." Lubna needed to reestablish her ownership of the library. Sitting while the others stood was a tiny step in this direction. Without waiting for consent, she sat cross-legged on her cushion by the writing table. She wanted wine to settle her nerves.

Matias held the lamp close and looked blankly at the original and the translation.

"What does this say about a cache of gold and gems hidden somewhere in Arabia?"

Lubna replied with a question of her own. "You came here earlier to find the map?"

The courtier looked startled. "This is the first time I've set foot in this room or anywhere in the library. It's a waste of time." He gestured expansively, taking in Lubna's study and the adjoining rooms and halls.

Lubna ignored his rebuke to a lifetime spent poring over and absorbing the learning of a world slowly dragging itself out of a mire of ignorance. She prided herself that she was doing her part to help the process by acting as the caliph's agent in establishing this repository of knowledge envied by courts in both Muslim and Christian kingdoms. Rare documents and new insights from across the span of human understanding made their way to Córdoba like water trickling downhill toward a reservoir.

However, Matias and his retinue were the wrong audience for this debate. She needed to remove them from the library before they damaged the scrolls and manuscripts, things Matias clearly held in contempt.

The threat of competition for the map might distract him from further interrogation. Ironically, someone actually had searched the library earlier today, Lubna recalled. It had been a thorough search and subtle, but she was so intimately familiar with how material was arranged that the slightest disorder from another's hand stood out.

"My desk and the scrolls were disturbed while I was away," she said. "I'd hidden the verses and map, so they weren't discovered. It seems you have a rival for it."

She didn't know whether this would work in her favor or not. She was playing with fire.

"I'll let the court know," Matias said.

Lubna noted that he'd said "the court," not "the caliph." This was a mistake on his part. Was he working on behalf of someone besides the caliph? Who was keeping secrets from whom? Most likely everyone from everyone else. She'd test the waters a little further.

"It's a pretty poem and a map to nowhere. Who else could want it?"

Matias kept his expression bland. "I don't know, the papacy or the Abbasids in Baghdad? There have even been sightings of jinn around Córdoba. Maybe there is otherworldly interest. Gold and gems appeal to most everyone."

Lubna heard suppressed laughter in his voice. She knew he was toying with her.

"One of you, stay with me," he told the soldiers. "The rest, look through the other rooms. Who knows how many copies of the map there are. Start at the top shelves and work down. No need to be careful. The librarian can put it back together when we're done."

She said, "We don't go among the books and scrolls at night to avoid the risk of fire."

Ignoring her, the soldiers fanned out into the surrounding rooms and reading galleries that led off her office. Lubna watched, furious at this further violation of her territory, but also mystified. At the beginning of the search, there was only one burning torch among the dozen guards. She watched this single point of light make its way ever deeper into the library's shadows. However, soon there were a dozen blazing torches bobbing about amid the shelves, turning the Stygian gloom into a brightly lit hall.

"Have your men watch out not to burn the library," Lubna said. "The material can't be replaced."

"Small loss," Matias said.

"If the library goes, so does the rest of the palace."

"Rest assured, they're good with fire, very good," the courtier said. "Lubna, who do *you* think might know about the map? You haven't told the court here in Córdoba, but maybe you've talked to others?"

"There's nothing to tell. Have learned men you trust inspect the poem and the map for whatever secrets you think I'm hiding. Your soldiers won't find more copies if they look all night."

Matias handed the original and the translation of the poem to the soldier at his side. Documents and illustrated manuscripts were piled about the office, works-in-progress that she labored over, transcribing them from a half dozen languages into Arabic. They covered her cedar desk in a snowy layer of cream-colored sheets.

"You worried about fire in this sanctum sanctorum," Matias said as he picked up the desk lamp and casually spilled oil over the documents, then held the lamp's flame close to the incendiary mess he'd just made.

The threat to the library's priceless rarities was clear.

"Anything else to tell me?"

"About the poem, nothing!" she shouted. "About burning the caliph's property bought with the emirate's funds, it will be Abd-al-Rahman himself who will talk to you—or his executioner."

Matias straightened up. Again she saw his small shrug.

"We're done," he called out to the soldiers. They filtered out of the adjoining rooms. Lubna saw no sign of the multitude of fiery torches.

"The rest of the rooms, lord?" one of them asked in accented Arabic. She didn't recognize its origin. "We didn't fully search them, just started."

"We'll come back. Bring her along."

"You're imprisoning me," Lubna said.

"Oh, no," Matias said. "I'm securing the court's valuable librarian for her own protection."

"Take me to the caliph," Lubna demanded. She had clout, and she would cut through the sinister ambiguity. She didn't know who was behind her arrest, for arrest it was. She would admit this to herself now that her circumstances made it impossible to deny. Abd-al-Rahman respected her work and the fame it brought to his palace from empires around the Mediterranean Sea and beyond. She would plead her case to him directly.

"It's night," he said. "I won't wake him for a librarian."

"In the morning, then."

"I suppose," he said lazily. "Depending on whether you keep your head."

All this for a damn poem? Lubna thought. *Where will they take me? The dungeon? Directly to the executioner?* She looked around at her office. It had been a sanctuary. She hoped she wasn't seeing it for the last time.

Matias and the soldiers bundled her into the corridor. Nobody laid a hand on her, but it was impossible to resist the company's impetus as they exited en masse. Matias blew the flame out in her lamp. Now the only light was a single torch carried by the leading soldier as they moved down the long, tomb-like corridors away from her office. Her breathing sounded loud.

Lubna glanced behind them, back down the dim hallway to see a tall robed man with a well-trimmed goatee observing them. No one else noticed.

CHAPTER 2

Ambush at the World's Edge

The Empty Quarter, Arabia, three months earlier

The jinn juggled emeralds.

He started slowly, but soon he had the jewels moving so fast they formed a seamless green circle. The gems were as big as hen's eggs, heavy, and expertly cut, a king's ransom that he casually orchestrated. Moonlight refracted through the jewels' facets, splashing the jinn with a green glow.

"These were mined in Egypt and buried with a New Kingdom pharaoh two thousand years ago," he noted conversationally to his companion. "I stole them from the tomb. They've got magical properties."

Jai shrugged. "Thiago, shouldn't you be planning an ambush?"

"I've done that," the jinn replied. "Now I'm composing poetry. Juggling focuses my thoughts while I create verses. It's a long, complex sonnet. Trying to keep the rhymes straight is challenging, so I've written most of them down on a scroll, but I need a perfect last line. They're for Lila."

"I guessed that," Jai said.

Thiago heard disapproval in his friend's tone directed at the poem or at Lila, probably both.

"With no false modesty, my poem is exquisite," the jinn said.

He slowed his hand movements to let the emerald circle resolve itself into individual stones, then deftly caught the gems one by one and pocketed them.

"I've drawn a map, too," the jinn added. "Of this exact spot, where we'll hide the treasure. We can't carry it all with us, not even a tiny fraction, so I'll bury what we don't take."

"You're a mapmaker as well as a poet. Splendid. But neither helps us steal Sheba's Treasure. Finish your sonnet; draw your map *after* we've got it."

"We're ready," Thiago said. "This is a fine spot for banditry."

"You'll slaughter them all?" Jai asked. "The rest of us don't want to take chances and have word get out."

"We'll see if that's needed," Thiago said.

From his vantage point, he looked far down at the moonlit desert floor. The stark setting inspired verses. Water had flowed here during rainy seasons long past, but no more. The heat was too intense and, as far as he could see in any direction, there were just the dry etchings of long-extinct riverbeds like creases on an ancient holy man's face. The place was as raw, sublime, and lifeless as any on Earth, and it was surely cursed, but the curse was so old that even God had forgotten what fate he'd once threatened.

The jinn felt at home.

Above it all, stars, galaxies, and a half-moon watched earthly affairs with disinterest. Coldly pretty as it was here on this side of the portal, the night sky was a thousand times more vivid on the other side. That world was a thousand times more malign, too.

Lit by the heavens' pale radiance, trackless sweeps of sand and rock led up to the rocky escarpment on which he and Jai stood. It was a long way down and they stood at the edge, careless of the drop.

And man's architecture had been built atop nature's castles. The jinn looked about at the broken walls and collapsed towers on the cliffs. The tall structures had been reduced by disuse and abrasive sand to crumbling, stony shards slicing into the night sky. Eternities ago, this Atlantis of the Sands had been abandoned. Who knew why, or who had built it, or how it came to be situated in the middle of nowhere. Perhaps the nearby caravan trails had drawn raiders who wanted a lair from which to sally forth and plunder the camel trains and then return to a secure fortress to savor their loot.

How appropriate to use an ancient hideout for his modern ambush.

"They're here," Jai murmured.

Thiago surfaced from his reverie.

"Their camels stink," he said. "You smell them before you see them."

Judging by the intensity of the stench, this was a huge caravan.

Thiago stared down at the valley beneath the cliff trying to manage his excitement. Right below him shimmered the portal between the world of demons with its capricious king and the prosaic world of humans with their tiny ambitions and small concerns. The portal looked like a morning mist over marshes at the sea's edge. And then a man stepped through the haze. By his bearing, he was more soldier than camel driver. The jinn saw a scimitar at his side. He held a staff in one hand and the other pulled a rope attached to a camel's nose ring. The leading beast emerged from the portal laden with packs, followed by other camels connected to it by ropes. Their baggage swayed side to side with the animal's gait.

The whole affair was well guarded. Shadowy warriors, some dressed in robes, some wearing chain mail and mounted on horses, followed the leader. The soldiers were armed with lances and shields slung to their mounts' flanks. They pushed through the diaphanous passage between worlds. The haze from the portal adhered to them briefly like a sticky cloud as they emerged, but neither warrior nor animal paid this any mind.

"Move on them," Jai said urgently.

Thiago held up his hand signaling patience. "They're not all through. Not nearly."

"Regardless, they'll sense us."

"They're still disoriented from the crossing," the jinn said. "No need to rush. You can see it by the way they move."

Transiting between the world of demons and the world of men was never smooth. Thiago remembered that a friend had lost a leg during a crossing and had to return home to grow whole again before making another trip. At best, one came through physically unharmed, but momentarily disoriented. Thiago intended to take full advantage of that confusion when he launched his headlong, hacking attack. And indeed, two of the camels below had collided, sending them staggering and spilling the contents of their packs into the sand, provoking torrents of curses from their drivers. One of the packs burst open, covering the sand with gold and silver coins. Moreover, the men were no better coordinated then the animals, and Thiago noted that both the armed guards and the drivers wobbled like they'd had too much wine.

"Why not just keep it on their side of the passage?" Jai asked. "Save themselves the trouble of crossing over. If I owned Sheba's

Treasure, I'd bury it beneath my throne with three dozen of my fiercest demons guarding it night and day."

Thiago laughed. "Because there are more thieves who hate the king in his own court than anywhere else. They'd find a way to get the treasure however he tried to protect it. So he thinks it's safer on this side. They'll see their mistake soon."

More and still more camels and men materialized through the passage, piling into the drivers, guards, and beasts who'd already arrived, adding to the muddle below.

Thiago said, "I believe there is another reason our dear king wants his riches here: He plans to invade the human world. Sheba's Treasure allows him to buy whatever support he needs."

"Who'd want this side of the portal?"

"I like it here," Thiago said with asperity. "As for the king, he's sucked everything he can out of our world, so he's got no choice but to come here."

The caravan's leader moved among the confusion, now prodding drivers and camels with his staff, now putting a steadying hand on a guard's shoulder, now directing several drivers to gather the spilled coins glittering in the moonlight over the sand and repack them. He was doing the best he could with a chaotic situation.

He must sense that his caravan is vulnerable, Thiago thought. *More guards than I expected. Can we overwhelm them with training? But my crew didn't really train like warriors do. They practiced like children preparing for a game. I lead a gang, not a unit of soldiers. And I'm about to attack the dearest possessions of the most powerful and crazed ruler on either side of the portal. Too late to change plans now. There are a million ways to die and I can imagine all of them.*

Below him, he watched his crew of jinn outlaws, the Fire Horde. They intently observed the confusion below. Thiago nodded to himself, fairly satisfied. There were close to a hundred jinn, males and females who'd grown bored by life regimented by extended family and tribal expectations on the demon side of the passage, and the need for endless obeisance to royal command. Here on the human side they could be free, and their talents stretched as far as their imaginations. Transitioning from human form to a whirlwind or a ball of fire was trivial in a world of demons where anyone could do this trick, but here on men's side of the portal, it made one supernatural—and able to undertake plunder on a grand scale.

Tonight, the Horde had hidden themselves among the ancient ruins and caves. Even knowing their locations, Thiago had trouble picking them out in the darkness. They'd be invisible to the caravan below except that occasionally, through inattention or impatience to get on with the attack, one of them would revert to their native jinn state, a blaze of smokeless fire, before catching themselves and morphing back into human form, clothed in long, black, full-body cotton robes with headscarves covering their hair and faces, leaving only a slit for their eyes.

The coin spillage below had almost set off a wholesale attack on the caravan ahead of his order. Fortunately, the guards and drivers below were so distracted trying to organize the jumble of people and loaded pack animals that they didn't notice. After the ambush, Thiago resolved to reprove his group for their lapses. A leader needed to instill discipline.

He watched a dark chariot amid the camels and confusion. It moved heavily and looked armored. The driver barely controlled the horses straining against their traces. Other guards kept well clear. Beside its driver, an archer stood with bow and an arrow already nocked. Thiago guessed he'd ridden in this position hundreds of times before, since he moved with practiced ease to accommodate his rolling, rocking platform.

Besides guards, is the caravan protected by magic? Thiago wondered. *Only one way to find out: attack.*

Jai felt the same. "Stop waiting! It's chaos. We're ready for a brawl. Take them."

"I want everything," Thiago said. "They're still coming."

There must have been two hundred camels below and at least that many men. They stirred up a dust cloud that drifted heavenward and almost obscured the portal, but still more figures emerged as if the passage between worlds birthed an endless procession of wealth.

"Move now," Jai whispered intently. "We'll be rich beyond counting."

Thiago didn't respond. He felt like he held back a stallion ready to charge; the urge to loose the reins was almost irresistible. But not yet.

Three more camels staggered through accompanied by a single small figure carrying a staff bringing up the rear. The man brushed dust off his robes and goaded the pack animals forward. A long hooded cloak enveloped him. Thiago observed his shuffling gait and bent posture. He was a liability to a caravan that needed to cover ground fast through harsh terrain. What purpose could he serve?

"Take them," Thiago shouted.

Jai surged downward before the words left Thiago's mouth. The Fire Horde burst from hiding and flashed after Jai, shedding their human forms as they went, to become streaks arcing in steep dives toward the caravan.

Thiago felt like he was in the middle of a lightning storm and shielded his eyes from the glare, then stepped off the cliff edge into thin air and started to fall. Halfway down and gaining speed, he morphed from his human body into an incorporeal shape—he had several, but chose fire. He felt no particular sensation during the transformation except that gravity no longer pulled him toward a crushing impact with the sand. His human form had such limited capability. Thiago flattened his dive and swept about searching for the guard commander amid the chaos, intent on disabling the caravan's leadership and ability to coordinate its defenses.

Surprise was complete. Thiago watched his outlaws race to come to grips with the guards. The camels and horses bolted from the living fire that raced about in their midst. Several fell kicking to the sand, pulled over by the weight of their packs.

Before he got to the commander, Thiago heard the man snap out orders to the drivers and guards to form a defensive circle. And then they transformed into the same fiery elemental forms assumed by Thiago's crew. Others became swirling tornados of sand and dust while still others sloughed off their human forms to become raging animals, desert cheetahs, eagles, and lions. Perhaps eager to join the fray, a few lost focus halfway through the transformation, resulting in odd fusions of human and animal. Eagle's talons extended from beneath the robes of a human warrior, a lion's head and mane topped the lower body of a human.

Thiago had expected as much; the guards were jinn themselves who had only assumed human form for convenience and to not terrify the camels they led between worlds. However, they would be far more capable of defending Sheba's Treasure in their elemental forms.

This was a fight between demons.

The commander transitioned into a glowing inferno and hurtled directly toward Thiago. The two fireballs smashed into each other in a soundless blast of heat and orange light. Reeling from the impact, Thiago tumbled sideways and shifted form to become a tornado of wind and dust. He enveloped the fireball that had once been the commander. Wind smothered and overcame the living inferno. The commander's light dimmed and then extinguished completely. Back in human form, the commander fell to the ground.

The caravan soldiers and drivers also were getting the worst of it from Thiago's Fire Horde. He'd relentlessly drilled his warriors to transition to whatever form gave them the greatest advantage in a pitched battle. If the enemy were human, shift to a fire elemental form and incinerate the opponent; if the enemy were themselves fire, transition to wind and snuff out the inferno's life in a storm of sand. Fire couldn't breathe without air. If the foe happened to be wind, change to a human form and cover mouth and nose with a headscarf and wait until the small tornado lost energy and dissipated of its own accord, then attack the remnants, covering it with robes to stifle its residual vitality.

These gladiatorial pairings were the riskiest part of the overall battle, as it was uncertain who would prevail in any individual combat; but, so far, his warriors were using his tactics brilliantly, able to morph more rapidly than their foes to seek advantage in their fights.

Still in wind form, Thiago soared over the battle seeking opportunities and threats. He smelled the charred odor of fireballs and felt concussive buffeting from wind elementals.

We're winning!

From a great height, Thiago saw the dark chariot surging toward the thickest fighting. It was ground-bound and couldn't touch the flying elementals, but given the energy it took for jinn to maintain themselves as fire or whirlwinds in life-or-death combat, much of the fighting had devolved to savage struggles in human form on the desert floor. And on the ground, the chariot was unstoppable as the onboard archer shot arrows with lethal accuracy and a madman's speed. Thiago watched three of his bandits fall in rapid succession.

This shouldn't be happening. Jinn were durable creatures tolerant of injury mortal to men. It took real effort to harm a jinn with arrows and swords unless the weapons were made of iron.

Directly ahead of the chariot, Jai dueled with three caravan guards. Despite being outnumbered, he was driving his opponents back. The chariot driver must have identified him as a champion among the attackers and deftly navigated between fallen camels and warring demons, lashing his four horses as the juggernaut tore through the melee toward Jai. Horde warriors who tried to intercept it were pushed back by an invisible force or fell beneath its crushing wheels.

The damned thing will turn the tide, Thiago thought.

He angled into a steep dive, swinging over a sand dune and gathering sand as he did so, then he flew toward the chariot's horses and released the sand in a blinding, choking cloud. Momentum carried the chariot and its four horses into the sand. Out of control, the driver rolled over two corpses, sending the vehicle up on one wheel and almost overturning. Somehow it righted itself, but not before ejecting the archer and driver.

Thiago exulted. He wasn't just a strategist; he was a leader.

But then he spotted the small, stooped figure he'd seen earlier advancing boldly toward the middle of the clash. The figure didn't hurry, but, intuitively, Thiago knew this was where the next threat would come from. He must be a magician. The king wouldn't have left his wealth without more subtle and potent protection than a troop of jinn disguised as camel drivers.

The figure grasped his staff in both hands and held it above his head, shouting stanzas. Instantly, the pace of the battle slowed. Thiago saw that his company of warriors could no longer transition from form to form fluidly. One of them froze halfway between fire and tornado. His opponent seized the chance to envelop the warrior and reduce him to a windblown puff of sand that vanished in a twinkling. The victor sped off to come to grips with another member of the Horde. All over the battlefield, Thiago saw similar scenes playing out. One of his warriors in the form of a leopard exploded in flames after being attacked by a fire elemental, another in the form of a cloud of sand was unceremoniously snuffed out by a squad of caravan guards wielding their voluminous cloaks to envelop her.

We're losing.

Thiago shifted to human form. Normally this transition could occur at the speed of thought, but now thanks to the magician's incantation, transitioning was laborious. If he was to be frozen as one form, being a humble human was the most versatile. He hit the ground running.

The enchanter turned to face him, his wispy dark hair not quite covering his balding pate. He'd grown vast and robust since Thiago had first seen him and he stood ancient, malignly wise, and supremely calm, as if no spell or supernatural attack could challenge him. However, spells and magical trickery weren't what Thiago planned; something crude was needed.

Before the magician could loose a curse to blast the skin off Thiago's bones, the jinn pulled an emerald from his cloak and hurled it at him. The gemstone flashed in a green streak at the magician's skull, stopping whatever blasphemous oath he intended before a syllable could be uttered. Being hit with the heavy jewel might itself have been fatal, but regardless Thiago lost no time in pouncing on the wizard's supine form and covering it in the folds of his cloak, both to stifle curses and to smother whatever life remained in the old man. When he was sure the magician was dead, the jinn retrieved his emerald, wiping blood off it on his cloak. Perhaps coming from an Egyptian tomb had enhanced the gem's potency. This world was inhabited by many gods, all of them prone to leaving their imprint on material objects.

Thiago collected his wits and looked around. The battle's momentum had swung back in his favor. Without the magician's stifling oath to dampen their nimble transitions between forms, his warriors resumed their attack on the caravan's soldiers.

We're winning again.

Then it was over. The sounds of the eldritch battle died away, and the surviving caravan soldiers—all back in human form so they could be managed easily—were herded together into a bedraggled mass sitting on the cold sand.

"We've done it," Jai said. He'd appeared at Thiago's side. His friend had received a long cut on his arm but otherwise appeared unharmed.

"Let's see if Sheba's Treasure lives up to its reputation," Thiago shouted at the Fire Horde. He gestured for them to rip into the packs.

He walked up to the commander of the guards. The leader looked shaken and defeated. He'd lost his scimitar and he no longer commanded his caravan or anything else. Purplish bruises covered his body and his facial hair was singed, but his robe and mail armor were intact. It amazed Thiago that whatever clothing a jinn wore while in human incarnation reappeared relatively undamaged despite the jinn's transitions to hellish fire or turbulent whirlwind or ravening beast. When jinns returned to their human appearance, there were never more than minor burns or tears in the most delicate fabric. The clothing's basic identity somehow preserved itself intact.

Living long enough to enjoy the treasure depended on staying anonymous, so Thiago tightened his black headscarf over his face. He'd demanded that the rest of his band be similarly secretive. He didn't need to push them on this; no one wanted word to get back to the king about who they were.

"The fortunes of war, commander."

"You'll find no fortune in this," the soldier snarled. He doubled over in a fit of dry coughing. "You didn't win here. You know who this belongs to?"

"The king," the jinn said. "That's why I took it. Spending it will be all the more fun knowing who I stole it from."

The guard commander looked angry at his flippancy. "You're Thiago, of course, a thief and exile."

"Why do you say that?" He wasn't going to admit who he was.

"Your whimsical arrogance gives it away. I saw you in court some years back. This is just your sort of stunt. You can pull aside your face covering. There's no need."

The man's judgment infuriated Thiago. However, there was no point in denying his identity against that certainty. Now there was a different issue at play: Should he kill the commander to keep word from getting back to the king?

"I'm Thiago, but I flatter myself that I'm more than a thief. And I'm only an exile if I want to go back. Otherwise, I'm at home wherever I sleep."

"The king's forces, jinn, ifrit, and every other demon in his service will come after you. And he'll hire humans in this world to help if you now call this home."

"How would the king know it was me?" Thiago asked. "Any number of groups would take Sheba's Treasure given half a chance. Whatever our king's other talents, he's good at making enemies. Besides, my biggest protection against discovery is that no one thinks I could conceive of banditry on this scale, let alone pull it off. I'm just a ne'er-do-well who likes a good party."

"He'll find out."

"He won't know unless someone tells him." Thiago looked at the soldier. "You wouldn't do that, would you?"

"Not if I gave my word." The soldier regarded Thiago. He'd shrunk a little as defiance drained out of him. "You don't believe me."

"Why would I?" Thiago pulled out a knife from a sheath and tested its edge against his thumb.

"I know your father, family, and tribe," the guard commander said.

"That doesn't help your cause. If you know them, you'll also know that there's no love lost between us. I'm my father's irresponsible offspring, supposedly firstborn, but he's probably not sure I'm his. My family and tribe—"

The jinn searched for the right word. He wanted to say they'd banished him, but that sounded too dramatic, like they cared enough to muster strong feelings about him. A better description was that his family and tribe had simply stopped talking to him when he'd gotten too headstrong. For his part, he hadn't tried to rebuild bridges.

"My family and tribe don't have much to talk to me about," he finally said.

"Whatever I do or don't do," the soldier said, "the king may determine that you were behind tonight's attack."

"But if you tell him, he'll know for certain." The jinn tossed his knife into the sand, just missing the soldier's leg.

"In which case, he'll come after you," the soldier said.

"Let them come," Thiago said. "I dealt with you and your guards, didn't I? And your magician, too. I can manage whoever or whatever comes along."

"Whatever comes along next will be more formidable than this lot." The soldier nodded toward his guards, most of their features blackened as if they'd sat too close to smoky infernos. Thiago's outlaws had blindfolded everyone. That seemed a pointless effort now that their commander could identify him. They sat forlornly mixed together with their camels and horses. Some of the beasts were still jittery from the battle; others phlegmatically chewed their cud with legs folded elegantly underneath them.

"Won't matter," Thiago said. He sat down on a bag of silver coins, some of which had leaked out onto the sand, not the most comfortable perch, but Thiago luxuriated anyway. It was the feel of wealth beyond counting.

"You're overconfident," the commander said. "Nonetheless, it won't be me who tells the king that you stole this."

"It's for all of us to decide how we play this," Thiago said finally.

Nearby, the Horde rummaged through the enormous haul. Mostly they stayed in their human form, but occasionally, overcome by the sheer scale of their pilfered prize, the boundaries between forms blurred and they shifted toward fire or wind before snapping back to appearing like men or women, the most practical option for looting.

It took a massive effort to pull his outlaws away from playing with their new riches.

"The guard commander knows me," Thiago shouted to his assembled band of outlaws, just get it out there, no point in hiding bad news.

"He knows who *you* are. He doesn't know who *we* are," a woman outlaw's voice called back. Thiago couldn't see who'd spoken in the darkness, just black forms surrounding him.

"If they know me, they'll eventually know who you are, too," Thiago shot back.

"There's a question here?" another voice shouted. "Kill them, kill all the guards, then nobody knows any of us and we stay happily alive and rich."

"Killing prisoners wasn't the plan," Thiago said.

"It was always *our* plan," a third voice from among the Horde yelled.

Thiago saw their eyes blaze orange, violet, and red through slits in their headscarves and knew there was no reason to put it to a vote.

The warriors returned to ripping open carefully tied packs to spill their contents about helter-skelter. The myriad of gems glowed as moonlight hit them. Silver and gold coins blanketed the sand and transformed the desert into a magical wonderland of burnished metal.

The guard commander had seen Thiago petition his warriors.

"When will you execute us?"

"Never," Thiago said quietly so that no one but the commander heard him.

"You wanted their decision."

"I don't always take advice well. Ask my family." With a sigh, Thiago stretched himself full length on the sand using a bag of silver coins as a pillow.

"I have your word that you won't alert the king. You know who I am, but your men are still blindfolded and, even if they saw me, they don't know me from a pile of sand. Our paths never crossed. Keep them in check. They heard my warriors' intentions for them. They may try to flee. I can't say I blame them, but that would provoke the Horde to slaughter all of you out of hand. There'll be a better chance for me to manage this in the morning. Meantime, I'll enjoy my moment."

Thiago looked about him. Besides gold and gems, there was clothing and fine weaponry, too. Thiago watched one of his warriors pull a scimitar out of a jeweled scabbard. Then she rummaged through a pile of loot and gently extracted a velvet robe, caressing the fabric to gauge its quality. She admired the sword and sheath and donned the robe after unselfconsciously throwing aside the cotton garment and chain mail she'd worn during the recent battle. A nude vision of exuberance, the woman twirled on her bare tiptoes in the dirt letting the robe swirl up from her body, brandishing the sword for the amusement of her comrades.

"I'm Aaliyah, the real Queen of Sheba," she shouted to the assembled warriors and the desert sky. Then she addressed Thiago. "Thanks to our leader, the first among equals from the jinn. He's a trifle vainglorious, but tonight he's made us all rich beyond belief."

She strode over to him and bent down to whisper into his ear, "You're not happy about killing the guards."

"I'm that obvious?"

"You're the sympathetic sort," she said. "I like that about you, but that's not the business we're in now."

"Even if we kill the guards, the king may still find out," he said. "Someone in our own group will talk."

"In that case, the king sends endless demons after you—and us. Any strategy for that?"

"Flee."

She frowned and threw her velvet robe over him, swaddling the two of them in a close and private embrace. "Usually you plan more intricately than that."

"Speed in leaving here is vital—and hiding the treasure so well no one can find it except me. Even I will only be able to locate it with a map."

"Some plan. Anyone can read a map."

"Not this one," Thiago said. "I've appended the map to a poem I've been composing. The key to understanding the map is in clues from the poem. The wisdom of a king can't decipher it without me."

He patted her cheek. "Second thoughts? There was always going to be risk. I made no secret of that."

"I live for risk more than them," Aaliyah said. She nodded at the rest of the outlaws capering about drunk with their gems and precious metals. "You've been honest with all of us about what we could gain or lose."

"Jinn are elusive when we want to be," he said. "And tough to kill even when you find us. And we have all this wealth to help us escape."

"It was brilliant banditry." She laughed. "The biggest theft in all of history on either side of the passage."

"So I'm the leader of a gang of thieves, Aaliyah?"

"You're more than a handsome bandit to me," she said and kissed his ear.

Thiago hugged her briefly—she was pretty and passionate—before gently, but determinedly untangling himself from her arms; he saved his love for another.

He stood up and addressed the assemblage. "The defeated commander and our own Aaliyah remind us that, whether we kill the prisoners or not, our dear king may send his minions through the passage if he ever suspects that I'm to blame for his caravan going missing. I don't know what form they will take, but I am sure they will be tougher than the camel guards we just beat. So, gather up as much of this stuff as you can carry for yourself with my thanks. It's yours for taking part in tonight's affair. Everything else, repack and put it in the building above us." He gestured far upward at the broken ruins of what must at one point have been an imposing hall dimly visible amid the other crumbling towers atop the cliff face.

"We need to move fast," he told them.

The outlaws grumbled at the exertion required to lug the trove to an inaccessible lair, but they were jinn and could fly it up to the top—though the effort significantly depleted their energy, like a human climbing a long flight of stairs.

Perhaps thinking the Horde was distracted by gloating over their ill-gotten riches, or not willing to face summary execution, one of the caravan guards sprang up in one fluid motion, transforming himself from human to fiery jinn form. He streaked heavenward in a green blaze of light.

"Bring him back?" Jai asked.

"Please," Thiago said. "Make an example or this will go on all night. We can't have them thinking they can run off to plague man's world."

Jai turned into a yellow inferno and launched himself into the night sky after the fleeing jinn. They became two bright dots against the stars. Then the fireballs collided and blended, washing the desert with chartreuse light. Ground-bound, Thiago watched. He couldn't observe who was winning though he had little doubt. Jai was powerful beyond belief and had never met another demon able to best him in combat whatever form the fight occurred in—fire, human, animal, wind, anything—so it was over quickly. Jai descended rapidly back into their midst pulling the escapee along with him, two incandescent patches of light descending to the desert floor. As they touched the ground, they both transformed from shimmering, smokeless fire back into human forms, Jai looking like a short, dark, muscular man with a black goatee. He arranged and smoothed his robes as if the whole affair was too inconsequential to notice. Conversely, his captive looked gaunt and battered. He collapsed unceremoniously among his fellows, who looked more deflated by their comrade's fate than after their loss of Sheba's Treasure. The caravan guard commander strode over to crouch at his side and inspect the damage to his soldier.

Charun, a Horde warrior, called over to Thiago, "Look at this." He appeared as a tall, lean human toughened from many battles with sun-darkened skin. "Two things for you to inspect."

Thiago first saw the chariot. Its driver and archer were gone, but four horses were still hitched to the vehicle. The night was chilly, but the equines sweated and stamped, as if they knew that the "men" surrounding them could transmute to other-worldly beings at will.

"Go for a ride," Thiago told Charun. "I saw it earlier—the archer riding it was using us as targets—but it's yours if you want it. Mind that you control the horses or they'll bolt. Some animals don't like jinn."

"I can't get close to it."

Thiago felt the chariot's aurora. "Iron. A war chariot of iron, a relic of an older time. It would be heavy for horses to pull with any speed, but unstoppable once under way, especially when loaded with archers. Useful in the king's army. It was protection for his caravan."

"Didn't work," Aaliyah said.

"It could have," Thiago said. "No jinn could drive it. They had a human driver to handle it and a human archer to fill us with arrows, but during the fight, I was able to distract the horses. Otherwise it would have cut a path right through us. Ask Jai."

"All true," Jai said. "Hard to admit, but our boastful leader actually saved me tonight."

Thiago took a step toward the war machine. Then another. As he drew closer, resistance increased. The chariot didn't want to be approached, not by his kind, anyway. He felt like he moved through ever thickening mud. Changing into another form wouldn't help. He was best able to face it as a human. Iron was the bane of entities like himself and every other demon, a formidable weapon for the king to wield against any company of supernatural creatures intent on doing him violence—or stealing his riches.

"Proving something?" Jai asked sardonically. He stood well away from the chariot watching Thiago's slow progress. Outlaws as well as their captives stopped their activities and stared at him, too.

"I'm proving that I can tame something everyone else is deathly afraid of."

It had started as a whim. Now he wondered if he'd taken on too much. Unfortunately, with this audience, Thiago was committed. Even after executing larceny on a massive scale, the Fire Horde was unforgiving about empty boasts, and several of them would readily usurp his role leading their war band if he lost face. In their eyes, he was the conceited son of an aristocratic jinn family more intent on his own aggrandizement than their well-being. It was Jai they really followed, and it was his friend's backing that garnered Thiago whatever loyalty they felt toward him.

"Pointless," Jai said. "Leave it to rust where it sits."

"Let's see if he's scorched to ashes," Aaliyah said. "He's always been suicidal."

The Horde laughed raucously as if Thiago's fate didn't matter to them one way or another, but they watched him struggle.

Thiago continued to push forward. Finally, he stood within touching distance of the wheeled conveyance feeling as if he'd struggled up a great hill. He ran his hand along one of the horse's flanks, using its warmth and strength to steady his nerves. Letting his long black hair blow free in the desert wind, he pulled off his headscarf to wrap it about both hands so he didn't have to touch bare metal, then he grasped the chariot's side rails and dragged himself onto the platform where the driver and archers had stood to harry anyone unlucky enough to come within range during a melee. An expert archer could slaughter supernatural beings at a hundred paces. He scanned the nearby sand. A little distance away, the bow and a leather quiver containing iron-tipped arrows lay half covered, the arrows scattered around the bow. The weapon must have been flung there when the chariot stopped.

With his dwindling strength, Thiago unhitched the chariot's stallions and loosed their reins. They bolted off into the sand dunes.

"No one else here could have done that," Charun said.

Enough showing off, Thiago thought. *If they don't respect me after stealing wealth beyond all imagining, nothing will convince them.*

He hopped off the chariot, almost falling to the sand. He hid his relief. Walking away from it, he felt like he was being pushed, but his strength returned with every step. The outlaws gave him a round of muted applause; he suspected they thought him reckless, but he didn't ask them to take risks he wouldn't perform himself and their affirmation felt good.

He looked over at Jai. "Yes, leave it to rust. It's impossible for us to use. Before we leave, we'll bury it in sand so the king can't turn it against us if he happens to come this way."

"Too bad it isn't steel," Jai said.

"Amazing that a trace of carbon makes base iron harmless to us," Aaliyah said.

"Steel holds an edge better than iron, too," Jai said. He pulled a steel dagger out of his boot and kissed the blade.

"And the other thing I was supposed to see?" Thiago asked Charun. "Hopefully this isn't another test of my manhood."

"I think not." The lean warrior nodded toward a black pile on the ground. "Pretty wood, heavy, ebony I believe, but it's just a stack of pieces. The wood has aged, but looks remarkably good. Why would it be part of Sheba's Treasure?"

"Pieces, yes, but they fit together to make something," Thiago said. "Hold that bit upright while I slide this part into it."

In a few moments, they had assembled a massive black chair, a throne. It looked out of place amid the glittering rubble of their recent attack beneath the cliffs and ruins looming over them. Several of the Horde strolled over to observe the otherworldly throne.

"It's the king's," Aaliyah said. "Sheba had it specially made as a tribute when she brought the rest of her treasure to our ancestors two thousand years ago. The wood is from the Kingdom of Anuradhapura."

"It's mine now," Thiago said.

"More comfortable than sitting on a bag of gold," Jai said.

Thiago settled into the throne, feeling its smooth, cool texture. One could rule from such a position. He understood the king's interest in it.

"I'm at home," he said. "I'd rest here till dawn, but we may have hostile visitors sooner than later and it's too heavy to transport far. Jai, help me lift this up to the hall above."

"A lot of effort for what?" Jai asked. "It's pretty furniture, but who sits on it in an abandoned fortress?"

"We'll be back from time to time," Thiago said. "The best parties happen in ruins. It's just you, your mates, and the universe on a starry night."

They spent hours lugging the riches to the ruins. Sitting on his new throne, Thiago watched the pile grow.

"Now that we have it, what should we do with all this?" Jai asked. Idly, he kicked a filigreed oil lamp in Thiago's direction.

Thiago picked up the lamp and admired the workmanship. "I did this to spite the king. And because I'm greedy, of course. Outlaws from our band who come through the portal to play can use it to buy anything that suits their fancy. That's what I intend to do. Now we have the wherewithal to indulge ourselves."

Thiago ran a finger along the lamp's surface from its handle to the tip of its spout. The craftsman who'd created it had obviously intended it to be more than a domestic implement to illuminate a home at night. Silver inlay like Arabic script looped and curled about the black enamel surface and all the way to the gold tip of the long spout.

"Another reason to capture this is because some of it is art," Thiago said. "There are pieces far better than this lamp in the pile we just stole. The king and his court wouldn't appreciate it; I do."

Two warriors kicked and chopped at a wooden chest nearby, finally succeeding in splintering it open with their swords. To their huge disappointment, it only contained papyrus and vellum writings.

"Words? All that work for words? I'll burn this shit," one of them laughed, beginning to transform into fire.

Thiago jumped out of his throne. "Not yet, Ajmal! Let me look at it."

He sifted through the written material amid the broken wood. "Verses, stories, histories from generations ago. Empires that came and went on both sides of the portal. We can learn from them."

"Who cares?" Ajmal said.

"I do." Thiago rummaged in his pocket and tossed an emerald to the jinn he confronted. "Fair compensation?"

Ajmal frowned, but strolled off with his companion examining his newly won gem.

"A bad trade," Jai said. "Besides, now you'll have fewer jewels to juggle."

"It's good writing," Thiago said. "Not as good as mine, but very good. Maybe there's more of it when I have the time to sort through all this stuff. Meantime, we can't let our crew burn everything they can't sell. Few of them read, so they don't recognize its value."

"I read only moderately," Jai said. "Everything I need to know, I learn by living life."

"You should read more. It expands the world beyond your immediate experience."

"My world was big enough already and I had everything I needed before this." Jai kicked at a pile of coins, sending up a spray of gold and silver that caught the moonlight. The coins appeared to fall in slow motion.

"This was just fun for me," he said. "Seizing the caravan, fighting the guards, nothing more, but now that you have it, isn't there something more you could do with it?"

"Besides spend it and admire the pretty stuff?" Thiago asked. "That seems enough to me, but I'm not as pure as you."

He stood up and shouted to the outlaws assembling Sheba's Treasure amid the ruins, "I'll hide what we don't take with us. We'll come back monthly to replenish ourselves with wealth, but careful how you spend it. Even on this side of the passage, the king will hear of it if you throw around coins and jewels or you try to sell ornaments in the bazaar."

This admonition cooled the frivolity.

"Everyone move away. Sheba's Treasure will be so well buried that the king and a thousand of his demons won't find it."

They left the ruins to cluster in the open air on the cliff top. Dawn had arrived over the ruins, tinting the broken stonework with purple and rose. The rising sun brought a hint of the furnace-like heat that would follow soon.

"Further back," Thiago shouted at his warriors. "Much further back and down into the canyon unless you want to be buried alive with the trinkets."

Jai asked, "Entomb the caravan guards and their dour commander along with our loot? It's the easiest way to be rid of them."

"One thing at a time," Thiago said.

He stooped and picked up a fistful of sand then stood up and let the grains fall through his fingers, whispering an incantation as he did so. The wind dispersed the sand in a thousand directions and he became one with the wind. The blowing grains grew rapidly into a tornado that towered upward to blot out the sun. The warriors' cloaks whipped about them and they covered their faces.

The dunes atop the cliff rearranged themselves to completely inter the ruins with Sheba's Treasure stored inside. Where once fragments of high towers and walls had stood flouting time, heat, and the elements, now a featureless heap of sand covered everything. It looked like any other pile of desert dirt. His outlaws would know roughly where the treasure was, but not precisely. The tornado dissipated as quickly as Thiago changed back into human form. His new wealth was better protected than a pharaoh's tomb.

"Impressive," Jai said. "Bigger than any whirlwind I could transform into."

"I practiced when I was alone in the desert," Thiago said. "I had endless time."

He shook sand out of his hair and fell to the ground, exhausted. It would take time to recover. He also needed to add critical details to his poem so that he could find this precise spot again. Hiding the treasure wouldn't do any good unless he could retrieve it.

CHAPTER 3

Ode to Fire

"You're here to plague humans," Thiago said.

"Anything for a smile," Lila said.

Ifrits were like that, he reflected. She was as much demon as woman—maybe more. That's why he loved her, but it wasn't blind love.

She'd strolled through the portal just a moment before. Unlike everyone else, Lila crossed between worlds with no signs of disorientation.

At her arrival, the camels and horses lurched about, trying to bolt, stamping and straining at their tethers. They didn't like Lila. The outlaws didn't care for her much either, those that knew her. Jai, Ajmal, Charun, and Aaliyah stared coldly at the ifrit.

"Not one for quiet entrances," Thiago said.

"Quiet isn't my nature," Lila said. She looked about at the evidence of the recent brutal fight. Smoke drifted skyward from charred patches of sand where fiery beings had died, and a burned, charnel smell hovered over the desert. The dust had barely settled from the storm he'd raised to conceal the treasure, and the chaotic collection of jinn and camels milled about in the heat, some exultant victors, some dejected captives.

"This caravan thing," she said. "I didn't think you had it in you."

"How did you find out?" he asked.

"I followed them. They tried to be secretive about how and when they planned to make the crossing, but they were over-confident and clumsy, really clumsy. You took advantage of that. Clever."

"I'm flattered," he said. "We *were* clever about how we captured Sheba's Treasure. We'll need to be wise to keep it. The battle's been over for hours, but you're only arriving now?"

"I wanted to see who would win," she said.

"That's blunt. You didn't think I could do it."

"Truthfully, no, but I'm thrilled that you did."

Thiago couldn't tell if her sentiment was genuine.

Lila's eyes always caught him first. They were black with no distinction between iris and pupil. They didn't show her soul, since ifrit didn't have souls. Further, her eyes rendered her opaque to anyone seeking insight into who or what she was, except for rare moments when they revealed that she'd seen everything and been impressed by nothing. Thiago intuited that she allowed these windows into her thoughts to mock her opponents. At the moment, she stared right through Thiago. This was disconcerting or beautiful, he couldn't decide which.

Black hair escaped from her headscarf. Besides the scarf, Lila wore a dark-gray cloak with blue trim which didn't hide her shape; even covered, she was sensual beyond measure, physically appealing and lethal; Thiago had seen her destroy a half dozen demons from a rival tribe without exerting herself. Truthfully, he didn't know what the ifrit was capable of—anything she set her mind to, he supposed, and once she'd decided to do something, she wouldn't have second thoughts.

"The king will hate this," Lila said. She looked over the ruins of the caravan. "Not only has he just lost half his wealth, he looks careless. The jinn and ifrit tribal leaders will wonder why he didn't just keep it secure on our side of the portal."

"He does look a fool," Thiago agreed. "He'll want to get it back and take revenge, but he won't know where to look or who did it."

"Too many know about this—the caravan guards, your own warriors, whatever you call them, the Fire Horde or something like that. That's hundreds. Someone will spill your story to the wrong ears. Simplify things. I'm surprised you haven't at least killed the guards already."

"My outlaws feel the same."

"I can help."

"I'm not going to kill them. Instead, I'm going to recruit them into my band. We lost dozens taking the caravan. We need replacements. And they've got nowhere to go. They'll be executed for losing his treasure."

"Kind, I suppose, but not wise."

"Practical," he said. However, he knew his logic wasn't going to convince her. It would be perceived as weakness.

"I have something for you," he said.

He pulled an emerald forth and presented it to her with a bow.

She cupped it in her palm, absorbing its history. "You killed a magician with this. Smashed his skull in, then smothered him. He was a jinn so he had a soul. I can feel his spirit and blood on the stone. You'd have sensed this while you murdered him, but you did it anyway."

"Him or me," Thiago said. He didn't want to dwell on the killing.

"You're ruthless when you want to be," the ifrit said.

"That's the first thing you notice about my gift, the blood?" Her reaction was in character, but he was disappointed nonetheless.

"It's a fine gem, as fine as I've seen. From Sheba's Treasure?"

The jinn thought she was placating him.

"From Egypt," he said. "I robbed a tomb some months back."

"Again, you have unexpected talents."

She leaned forward and kissed him.

"So where is the treasure?" she asked. "Wait. Don't tell me. I sense that you'd like to keep this little secret to yourself. That's wise. If everyone knows its location, it won't be your treasure any longer."

"I've hidden it. This desert keeps its secrets. I wouldn't be able to find it myself without making a map. No one among my outlaws or any of the caravan guards knows exactly where it is."

He swept his arms around him. "See for yourself. One pile of sand looks like any other."

"I'll do just that, look for myself," the ifrit said. Without waiting for his response, she began walking around the battleground, pausing periodically to inspect the terrain and the surrounding cliffs. Thiago wondered if her perceptive abilities would detect Sheba's Treasure buried beneath the enormous pile of sand he'd stirred up.

Lila had power, intangible but potent. The captive guards retreated before her. Members of the Horde gave ground more reluctantly but they too backed away, although Aaliyah looked ready to cut Lila to pieces with her newly acquired scimitar. The ifrit must have noticed their personal piles of the treasure that Thiago had given them as their initial reward for the caravan attack. However, she didn't remark on it and continued on her circuit.

Suddenly, Lila doubled over, clutching her stomach. Thiago heard her moan loudly in real pain and raced to her side. No one else moved to help.

The iron chariot sat well apart from the rest of Sheba's Treasure and partially hidden by Thiago's whirlwind. Its wheel rims, side rails, and yokes barely poked through the sand. The outlaws and their prisoners avoided it; but Lila, evidently suspecting that this indicated something special must be in this area, confidently strode forward, nearly tripping over the chariot's exposed bits.

Thiago again felt the iron's toxic force as he struggled toward Lila, but managed to interpose his body between her and the chariot, and then half dragged, half carried her away from the weapon's inimical power. Lila's robe trailed behind them in the sand.

"Water," Thiago shouted. "She's with me."

Jai tossed a water-filled gourd to Thiago. Then he backed away. He helped his friend, not the ifrit.

Lila lay prostrate on the sand. The jinn gently propped up her head and eased a little liquid into her mouth. Her eyes opened and she swallowed.

"Stupid," she murmured. "So stupid. I could feel poison in the ground, but I rushed forward anyway like a cow to slaughter. It hit me like an ax."

"I'd have told you, but you wanted to explore on your own."

"It's my nature." Lila sat up slowly, noted her disheveled condition, and modestly arranged her robe.

"Thank you," she said. "Why doesn't iron cripple you? Or kill you outright?"

"It can if I let it, but I practice relentlessly when I'm on this side of the passage, trying to get close to some source each day—of course there's almost no iron on our side. Because it's so deadly, I believe the king kept the chariot in case his subjects revolted."

"You're right," Lila said. "He worries about palace revolts, so he has a contingent of humans in his personal guard to drive it. I've heard he's immune himself, but who knows. You practice with iron?"

"It's agony. I showed off for my warriors to test myself and impress them. They think it's just boasting." He nodded toward a cluster of the Horde standing nearby regarding him and the ifrit impassively.

"I did it to prove that I'm not a complete dilettante at this outlaw business." He said this more to himself than her.

"How close did you get to the chariot?" she asked.

"I stood on it. Then it pushed me off. Can I impress you?"

"By standing on an iron chariot?"

"I had something else in mind."

"Show me." Lila didn't sound interested in the least, but he guessed she was still too weak to argue. Besides, he'd just saved her, so she felt a small obligation to humor him. The ifrit lounged on the ground and cocked one eyebrow.

"Well, show me."

The outlaws also gathered to see what he planned. Thiago saw that Jai sensed what he intended and tried to hide a smile at the hopelessness of moving Lila. Aaliyah looked angry that he would try.

"His infatuation is stupid," Thiago heard her tell Jai. She didn't try to keep her voice down.

Feeling uncertain that he would awe Lila or anyone else, Thiago nonetheless pulled the scroll with the poem and map from his cloak. He'd hidden them next to his heart. He began making writing motions in the air before him with his index finger. There were a lot of verses to remember, and, periodically, he referred to his poem. In synchrony with his hand's motions, enormous script materialized above them with the lettering in orange fire. He spoke the poetry as he wrote. Dawn made a perfect backdrop, and he inscribed his verses in the western sky for contrast before the sun rising in the east washed away his work like a child's designs in the sand erased by incoming waves. However, for the moment, his script shone vivid and brilliant.

"You're a poet as well as a bandit," Jai said, more in support of a friend than out of real admiration.

"A suluk," Charun said. "An outlaw poet exiled from his tribe."

Continuing to write, Thiago said, "What did my tribe ever do for me? They think I'm a rather bad jinn. And exile isn't all self-denial. Isolation has its uses, too. I spent my time alone in the desert well. It's a good place to plan robbery on a grand scale and to craft sonnets."

"Pretty," Aaliyah admitted. "When will you write one for me?"

Verse followed on verse until half the sky was covered with curvilinear lettering. He finished and sat down in the sand beside Lila, exhausted from the effort. Thiago thought he'd captured his feelings well with sublime meter and cadence and his imagery was good. He glanced at the ifrit. She'd watched his efforts silently. The outlaws clapped. He wondered if they were being polite. Aaliyah, at least, liked it. The words above began to fade.

"You copied all this from your scroll?" Lila finally said.

He nodded. "It's partly in Arabic up there because the script is prettier than any other human form of writing and a few of the warriors can read and appreciate it, but I wrote the original in Aramaic because none of my group understand it."

"You're being secretive, but why would you care? You've just proclaimed your affection for me to the universe." She paused. "Ah, I think I see. You have some other reason for keeping your scroll private. Your poem was surprisingly good, but words and rhymes were sometimes unusually placed."

"I'm a poet," the jinn said. "That gives me liberties."

"There was reason to your rhyme," the ifrit said.

She looked up at the waning remnants of Thiago's poetry. "It's a code. Those are coordinates buried amid the verses. Humans are so fond of this kind of thing, little tricks to keep the obvious concealed. This world has rubbed off on you. With a map and your sonnet, you'd know where Sheba's Treasure is. Otherwise the king would have to excavate the entire valley—if he even knew which valley to excavate."

"But he's got neither the map nor the poem," Thiago said. "And I'd venture to say that you weren't impressed enough with my literary skills to memorize the whole thing, so you've got nothing, either. Why not join me on this side of the passage? I'll share the riches and we could lead a fine life together, a grand life."

"Tempting, but I like my life on the king's side. He sees me as an ally. He has other qualities, too."

She could love who she wanted, but throwing in her political lot with the king bemused Thiago. The monarch was a dynast bent on consolidating his power over the realms of demons on his side of the portal and encroaching on the human side as well. Two thousand years back, his ancestors had ruled men. Now he ruled demons. With this pedigree, small wonder that he saw himself as heir to two worlds. And Lila admired him for this. She and the king shared ambitious ruthlessness as their defining characteristic.

The day's heat had begun to climb, and he didn't want to stay. It was time to disperse and enjoy his newly gained—and limitless—wealth. Lila's arrival hadn't changed that. She could stay with him—or not.

He knew it would be the latter.

He considered the former caravan guards and drivers sitting with their commander where he'd left them under guard. Time to finesse their survival. He'd need the help of his friends in the Horde, Jai, Aaliyah, and Charun.

As he deliberated, Lila moved nimbly and pulled out the emerald he'd given her and threw it with speed and precision at the caravan commander. The gem hit his eye and sent him sprawling backward to the ground, bleeding.

Thiago felt the world pause. The demon had brought fresh violence to the scene of his ambush. Then the world unfroze and guards and drivers lurched to their feet and fled in all directions, plainly expecting that they'd share their commander's fate. One collided with a camel in his panic. Some stayed in human form and simply sprinted away from the camp, others morphed into fire or wind and took flight upward into the sky.

"Catch them," Thiago yelled at the Horde. "Alive."

His warriors streaked after the fleeing guards with blazes of light. They would ignore his admonition to recapture the escapees and slaughter them if they could.

Lila is inspiring a massacre, he thought. *But she wants distraction.*

Faster than thought, she wrenched the scroll from his hand.

She had no soul to damn or he would have cursed her.

"You're with the king," he shouted.

"This is for me." She leaped into the air and flashed upward in a fiery streak, punching a hole through the airy letters of his fading poem.

CHAPTER 4

Above the Empty Quarter

Speed is easy if you're fire.

Thiago thought this as he flew far above the desert. Children of Adam and Eve would never know this feeling, but then, they wouldn't know the king's vengeance, either. His quarry was fast, too. And Lila was just as incorporeal as him, a fiery orange speck ahead of him, but he gained on her, murder in his heart. Amazing how love—even conditional love—could turn to disillusioned hate so quickly. He now knew she felt nothing at all for him. He should have known that all along. It was humbling that that she couldn't at least hate him back. However, the ifrit focused totally on her own ends. Recovering the treasure—with Thiago's poem and map—would be her goal pursued with monomaniacal energy.

Wind buffeted the jinn, threatening to tumble him out of control to the ground. Even elementals could meet their end as a smudge of blackened sand if they became drunk with freedom and quicksilver velocity and fell to earth in a death spiral, but he didn't slow down.

A dizzying distance below, the desert sprawled in all directions in the morning sun except to the west where he saw the Red Sea. The vista was of an endless expanse of sand colliding with the cobalt-colored water. A fringe of turquoise along the shore softened the transition. He smelled salt. The ifrit fled in that direction. He guessed she was making for Egypt. There was supposed to be another passage between worlds amid the pyramids. Or maybe she'd stay in this world, confident that her power and lack of scruple would overcome any human threat. And Sheba's Treasure was hidden on this side. That would be powerful incentive to remain in the vicinity.

They shared the sky with eagles. Birds of prey were revered by his tribe of jinn for their freedom and power. The raptors fled from the flaming elementals, sensing the supernatural quality of the creatures they met above the desert, though the jinn's and ifrit's sheer speed meant that sometimes they were caught by surprise and had to veer away sharply.

Thiago felt certain that he would overtake her, though they both were gradually losing speed. Unlike in the king's world where flight was effortless and he could forever soar above palaces, dragon-thronged seas, and trackless forests, on this side of the passage, gravity and wind resistance ground away his energy like a runner competing in a long uphill race. The arrows tipped with iron that he planned to shoot into the ifrit's heart slowed him further. Thiago carried a round dozen in a quiver along with a bow he'd pulled from near the chariot back at the caravan ambush site before he'd taken off after Lila. The quiver's thick leather shielded him somewhat from the iron arrow tips' poisonous effects, but he felt like he pulled an anchor.

Fleetingly, he wondered at the strange sight he must make to any human able to observe a flying amorphous patch of fire dangling a bow and quiver. However, he was at such a height that no desert tribesman below would be able to see him except as a bright dot streaking across the heavens like some daytime meteor.

Ahead, he saw the ifrit make a wide turn to come straight back at him, growing into a red-orange inferno as she drew closer. Normally, jinns and ifrits burned with a cold flame, but when they wanted to destroy an enemy, their fire became hotter than a smith's forge, and he could feel her incendiary, sunlike heat as she approached. She also presented a demon's face, with lolling tongue and fangs amid the flames in the fireball. Thiago wasn't mesmerized. This would panic humans or other demons, but he only saw it as confirmation of her essential nature. She hadn't bothered to change the eyes, which were two black orbs amid the fire.

Rage filled him.

Lila knew he followed and had clearly decided to avoid a protracted, tiring chase by simply killing him. He slowed and they circled each other like tribal dancers. However, their goal wasn't celebration, but incineration.

Time to attack before she hit him.

He had no intention of igniting his own furnace to counter Lila. The outcome of a clash of firestorms would be uncertain, perhaps mutual destruction in a pyre lighting up the morning sky. That wouldn't entertain anyone except the eagles. Thiago liked to think of himself as bold, but he wasn't rash enough to stake his existence on a chancy result. Instead, he notched a barbed arrow. The toxic iron tipping the missile meant that drawing the weapon was agony, but the ifrit would be finished if he could hit her. Shooting a bow was immensely easier in his human form; now, as an elemental being of pure energy, it was nearly impossible to firmly grip the wooden weapon and draw its string. His first missile flew wide and only grazed her. However, he sensed a soundless yowl of pain and anger and her red-orange furnace glow turned sickly green like gangrene suffusing an injured leg. Slowly the ifrit shifted back to her normal color, drifting in the morning sky, trying to recover, then she fled again, but in a more disordered pattern; he'd hurt her.

The jinn rejoiced, not just at injuring his adversary but because she'd had to drop the poem during the fight to avoid burning it when she'd become an inferno. No doubt she'd meant to recover the fluttering poem after quickly disposing of Thiago before the poem hit the ground.

The jinn saw it drifting downward, a little cream-colored dot buffeted by air currents, now lifted on thermal updrafts, now pushed downward by gravity, twisting and turning like a snow-flake misplaced in the desert sky. Lila flew downward after his poem.

He followed her—it was *his* sonnet—and shot another arrow after the ifrit, but this one arced earthward and came nowhere close to striking its target, though the errant missile galvanized her to greater speed and evasive maneuvering and she spiraled and barrel-rolled away from him.

Suddenly, he saw an explosion of feathers as the frantically turning ifrit slammed into an eagle that had had the misfor-tune to stray into their gladiatorial arena. As a being of pure energy, Lila was unaffected by the collision, but the injured rap-tor dropped downward like an anvil, unable to save itself. The eagle's descent paralleled the path of the fluttering papyrus.

What do I do? Catch my poem containing the map? Shoot another arrow at the ifrit? Rescue the eagle?

Thiago angled down into a steep dive toward the raptor. It was alive, but, besides feeble flutters, the bird fell helplessly. While watching it, the jinn also saw his poem. He'd catch them both and then deal with Lila. However, the ifrit wasn't working to his plan and swirled about him weaving a helix of inferno-like heat and blinding light.

Thiago caught the eagle just above the ground and deposited the panicked and disoriented—but living—creature on the sand. He felt the ifrit's heat almost on top of him and rolled away, working to gain height and a good vantage point to aim another arrow at her. Meantime, the poem tumbled past both of them. They were in an area of endless dunes and blowing sand blasted into the air by their conflict. Amazingly, the jinn saw that the scroll was intact and hadn't been singed or torn, but it was quickly getting lost. Lila swept past him after the poem.

Deciding he'd have a better chance to accurately aim his bow in human form, Thiago dropped to the sand and transitioned. Endless practice with his outlaws made the process almost instantaneous. He cast aside his headscarf to see better, notched an arrow, and sent this at the ifrit. This arrow came close to impaling his adversary, just missing her eyes amid the fire. Again he heard a scream of rage and pain. Wounded, the ifrit struggled skyward and away from him. She was severely tattered but managed to flitter off, losing herself in the desert sky.

Thiago stared about. The poem was nowhere to be seen. After an hour of unsuccessfully looking amid the ever shifting dunes, he gave up and sat down. For several moments, he simply breathed deeply. Partly this was exhaustion at the chase and his duel with Lila, partly it was black despair at losing the map and poem. His friends in the Fire Horde would turn on him once they learned that he'd lost the location of their wealth. Without its exact coordinates, he and the Horde could scour the valley for decades and never stumble on it. For just a moment, he considered pulling out one of the remaining arrows and ramming it through his heart. The barbed iron would kill him, which would be a fitting end to what had only last night been a phenomenally successful theft.

He lay back on the searing sand and didn't feel heat, one of the advantages of being a fire elemental even when he was in his human form. Anyway, it was near evening and the temperature was beginning to drop. He began considering his circumstances.

He wasn't completely without hope. He couldn't pinpoint the precise location of his poem and map, but he could sense its general location. He'd written it. It was part of him like his writing hand. He knew it wasn't that far away from where he sat. If it were found and moved, he'd know roughly where it went to.

Still, it was laughable that he or any wandering tribesman would stumble on the map however large it was. This stretch of the desert was aptly named the Empty Quarter, though it wasn't completely barren. Humans were scarce, but they existed. Witness the ruins he'd used to hide Sheba's Treasure in. However, the caravans that had once transported frankincense had ceased to traverse this region centuries ago, and any nomadic tribes currently living in the area would be intent on survival, not searching for lovelorn scribbling even if it was embellished with a fine map. And, if by some wild chance they did stumble on his poem, most likely they'd throw it in their evening cooking fire.

He gazed around him. As far as he could see in any direction, there were dunes and nothing more. Sheba's Treasure was gone forever. Best to think of himself as an exile and fugitive—who had once been rich beyond measure. Thiago had only his arrogance to blame. It had all been a lark, but he'd let infatuation with Lila mask her essential nature and the risk she posed to his enterprise; he'd planned and coordinated an epic theft, but left hundreds of witnesses alive who might alert the king about who had taken his most precious belongings; and he'd hidden the treasure so well that even he couldn't find it without the fragile assistance of a pretty poem and an artistically drawn map. The one durable outcome of his effort was that he'd struck a blow against the king and the demon tribes that he ruled including Thiago's own family, but this was a juvenile gesture. Oddly, what he regretted more than losing Sheba's Treasure was losing his poem, a silly gesture of affection, but one with subtle alliteration and perfect structure that he'd never be able to fully remember or re-create. He marveled that he could admire his poem but despise the muse that inspired it.

Thiago shook off his lassitude and stood up. The area might be barren, but someone or something could be drawn by the recent pyrotechnics that had lit up half the heavens as he and the ifrit dueled.

The jinn heard rustling nearby.

Lila returning for a second attack? The king's agents already on my trail and bent on ripping me to pieces? My own warriors out to kill me for losing their wealth?

He picked up the bow and quiver. He peeped over the dune top and spotted the golden eagle who'd been an unintended casualty of his fight with Lila. The raptor looked bad with disordered and scorched feathers, but still alive. He picked it up gently. It was heavy and tried to slash at him with its talons. Thiago carefully wrapped the eagle's claws in his headscarf to control its struggles.

There was purity in the desert away from human ambitions. The eagle represented that.

He'd nurse it back to health.

CHAPTER 5

Verses from the Netherworld

"We saw a fight between demons in the sky," Adil said.

"No. A star drifted low and challenged the sun," Jabir said.

"We saw mirages during the midday heat," Rahim said. "And we still have not found Father's camel. So, shall we save the wild stories for the campfire later tonight?"

This closed the argument, as Rahim was the oldest and knew the most about their world. He tended to favor straightforward explanations to life's mysteries.

"Let's spread out and continue looking for the stupid beast," Rahim said. "Stay in sight of each other. I don't want to find a camel but lose a brother."

The three youths fanned out across the dunes pushing westward. From time to time, Rahim looked over his shoulder at where his tribe's modest campsite lay. Intervening dunes blocked sight of it, but he prided himself on an excellent sense of direction. By periodically checking the bearing they traveled against the sun's position above them, he kept himself oriented. Certainly, their footsteps quickly blew away so it would be his tracking skills and intuition that got the three of them home safely. At least, the approaching evening took the edge off the day's heat. However, it stayed light enough to spot a camel even at a distance.

"Is that a mirage? That white thing?" Jabir called over to the other two. They slogged through the dunes and gathered together, looking down at what Jabir had found.

"It's a scroll of some sort," Rahim said. "Rarely, Father handles them if a merchant from the coast happens to bring one to trading gatherings. The lines are drawn on the scroll and they hold memories. They also count who owns how much of what. Sometimes scrolls settle arguments, sometimes they start them."

"That's pointless," Jabir said.

"Pick it up, Rahim," Adil said tauntingly.

As much to prove to his brothers that he wasn't afraid of this alien and potent object as out of any real curiosity, Rahim did just that. He'd never touched one and was surprised to find out how light it was. He ran his fingers over the edge, taking care not to touch the lines inscribed on the scroll, though it didn't look like they would smear if he did. He wondered if any of the knowledge contained in the scroll would pass through to him via touch. The edges were charred, as if someone had held it too close to a campfire only to rescue it before it burned entirely. However, most of what it showed was clear enough. Besides the cramped, curving, orderly lines, the scroll also contained pictures like he might idly draw in the sand to amuse himself by the fire at night. His father never took much interest in his markings, but didn't discourage him, either. Rahim thought he recognized at least some of the tiny diagrams as representing places, hills, ruins, valleys he'd seen when the tribe traveled south on trading business. It took a mental adjustment to think that the scroll depicted familiar, tangible locations. He would look at it further tonight and show it to his father, who read just a little and might understand some of the markings. Rahim carefully rolled up the document, which seemed made for such usage, and placed it inside his cloak.

And then, just like that, they weren't alone. Five horsemen cantered over the dunes and loomed over the youths. They'd almost materialized from the desert air so sudden was their arrival. One of them led their camel. The beast pulled at its tether strenuously enough to almost rip the nose ring out of its nostril and stamped and rolled its eyes at the five figures who led it.

Rahim noted that they were tall, lean, and carried bows, scimitars, and sheathed daggers. One had a lance. Unlike the camel, their horses were at ease with their riders and looked sleek and untroubled by riding through rugged desert in the heat. The warriors dressed in white robes wafting about in the wind, common enough in the Empty Quarter, but they didn't look like any of the local tribes that Rahim had seen if for no other reason than they were armed to the teeth. He couldn't see much of their faces, as scarves and headdresses covered their features; but, Rahim reflected, neither could these mysterious arrivals see the three brothers' features, which were also covered against the blowing sand. Maybe this would be an advantage.

There was a pause long enough to be awkward. Rahim guessed that this was intentional to allow the three boys to be intimidated by the five heavily armed strangers. He wasn't intimidated though he was curious. He noted that the riders had positioned themselves with the sun directly at their backs and blazing into the three brothers' eyes, so Rahim walked up the flank of the dune they stood on to be out of the sun's direct line. He needed to think nimbly to counter whatever advantage these intruders sought over him during the ensuing negotiations. He hoped his younger siblings would follow his lead; all their lives depended on it.

The horseman with a lance shifted about to face him and finally said, "You've seen two beings." It was a statement, not a question. Rahim noted that he spoke proper Arabic, but not the local dialect. "They are magical and could have shown themselves in various forms, fire, men, or the wind."

"We feel wind, but how can we see it?" Adil asked.

Rahim glanced at this brother then addressed the lancer, "We've seen no one magical or otherwise. You have our animal." He nodded at their terror-stricken camel, which had just lost bowel control and deposited a pile of dung on the ground.

"If they showed themselves as humans," the lancer said, "one would have been a tall man dressed as we are. The other would likely have been a woman, a strikingly pretty woman. That isn't who they are. The man is a jinn. The woman is an ifrit. They don't come from anywhere near here and they're demons who prey on tribesmen like you."

"Jinn are said to haunt everything including our family's cooking fire," Rahim countered. Careful. He didn't want to show these warriors so little respect that he goaded them into killing the three brothers for insolence.

"We truly haven't seen another soul of any description excepting yourselves," he said. "Harming us won't change that. We have no reason to lie. Our tribe is to the south not far from here. If we don't return—with our camel—they'll look for us."

One of the riders drew his scimitar. Rahim heard the steel rasp against its sheath as the blade came out, but the lancer motioned restraint.

"If you've seen no one," he said, "have you come across a scroll—that's thin papyrus or animal skin with lettering . . ."

"I don't read, but I know what a scroll is," Rahim interrupted. "I'm from a desert tribe, but I understand a bit of the world. Anyway, it's a big place out here. Finding anything is next to impossible, even something as large as our camel."

The lancer nodded to the warrior holding the camel's lead. The figure dropped the lead, sending the animal surging off into the dunes.

"You may well see us again," the lancer said. Then the five wheeled about and moved over the top of the sand dune and out of sight.

"Burn the scroll," Jabir said.

"I will," Rahim said. He exhaled and realized how tense he'd been. "I'll throw it in the cooking fire. What possible value can it have? Let's collect our camel."

"You did well today, brother," Jabir said. "Things could have gone very badly for us."

Later that night sitting by the tribe's fire, Rahim pulled the scroll out of his robe and studied it. The images and lettering looked more vivid in the firelight and shadow with the lettering capering about on the page. Seeing the unusual object, his father stepped to his side.

"What is it?" Rahim asked him. He'd already told his father and the tribal leaders about the five eerie warriors who'd questioned him and his brothers out on the dunes that afternoon. That had set the tribe to debating whether to mobilize all the men and scour the surrounding region. However, ultimately they'd decided that a search would be pointless as no harm had been done and this was a fight the tribe didn't need—particularly if the intruders were somehow supernatural. They'd gotten their camel back, after all. The tribe set more guards that night around the perimeter of their camp, but likely the five warriors had moved on.

"It's verses," his father, said looking at the scroll. "It's not Arabic, not mostly anyway, maybe Aramaic or Persian. I can't make out more than a word or two, but it rhymes like the verses we tell each other at night."

"Supposedly, there was a suluk living among the ruins three days east and south of here," Rahim said. "Maybe he thought his poetry should be preserved? He lost his poem, we found it."

His father shook his head. "Why anyone, even an outlaw poet, would commit such a thing to letters, I don't know. Verses are best spoken to listeners who sit before you and can respond directly."

"But a solitary exile would have no audience for their work," Rahim pointed out. "Putting his thoughts into writing would be the only way to preserve them."

His father remained skeptical. "I've only seen scrolls tallying what merchants send on caravans."

"So, into the fire?" Rahim asked. "Whatever it is, why invite more attention from the men—or whatever they were—who questioned me today? They said they might come back. Maybe others are after it, too. We should be well rid of it before that happens."

With self-conscious drama, Rahim stood and held the scroll dangling over the fire between his thumb and forefinger. Red embers spiraled upward in the velvet night past the papyrus. The youth let it drop toward the flames.

His father intercepted the scroll before it hit the fire.

"However useless it is to us, it has value to someone. Your experience today tells us that. Yes, there is risk in keeping it, but we cross paths with a caravan in about three days. Maybe one of its traders will show an interest and, just possibly, there is some silver in it for us. Strangely, there are merchants, scribes, and rulers who collect such things in cities."

~

"Sarah reads more languages than me and has a good eye for appraising works of unknown origin," her father, Yonah, said. "Better than anyone among us, I think."

"Better than anyone here?" Aharon said. The mildness in his reply didn't hide his condescension. "You want her to stay while we do business?"

"And why not? You can't be threatened by a young girl."

"I'm nineteen, Father," Sarah said. "Not so young."

"Not so married, either," her father said.

Sarah frowned. Her family was intent on finding a suitable match for her, but she rather liked being unmarried for the time being until someone appealing came along. And someone who appreciated learning as much as she did. Regrettably, her unattached status couldn't go on forever.

"I digress," Yonah said to Aharon. "Today isn't about personal business. It's about a particular and special poem. Besides, there's a certain symmetry here. There are two of you including your son, Lior, representing the House of Wisdom and, if you'll allow Sarah's presence—she'll stay quiet as a cat—the two of us will represent my little shop. One pair of eyes and ears can miss things that a second pair will catch during valuation of this item."

As if this business can only be done by men, Sarah thought.

"Where is 'this item'?" Lior asked. "You graciously allowed us to see it before competitors, very kind of you."

Sarah didn't think the young man sounded grateful, but he must feel obligated to mouth platitudes to facilitate the tense bargaining that would ensue.

"It doesn't sound that impressive, really," Lior added. "It's not even a collection of poetry. My understanding is that it's just a lonely scroll with a single sonnet from an unknown."

Ah, the negotiating is starting already, Sarah thought. *These things always have a rhythm to them, but Father is a master at sensing opportunity, detecting the buyer's needs and turning it to his own advantage.*

However, Aharon and Lior aren't sheep going to slaughter. They'll be braced for hard negotiating and for Father's inflated prices, since they represent Baghdad's premier collection of written matter, though now Córdoba's library is rising fast to challenge them.

"Sarah, bring the scroll out," Yonah said. "I sense doubt from our esteemed guests. Let's get to this business."

Playing the dutiful daughter, honored beyond belief to join their august company, Sarah worked her way back into the shop through a warren of shelves and alcoves piled with books that represented the part of her father's business customers never saw. From the street, their shop appeared modest—this was intentional, why attract thieves or tax collectors?—just cushions strewn over a Persian carpet surrounding a low table suitable for examining the shop's wares under an awning, sun faded from too many decades shading seated buyers of printed matter and illustrations during endless dealings to sell the world's knowledge and imaginative strivings. The output of all that brilliance was distilled onto papyrus, vellum, or, recently, paper which was supplanting other materials.

The shop's back rooms were labyrinthine and cloaked in Stygian darkness without windows, entrances, or any other source of light. Why place lamps there when not needed and waste expensive oil and risk burning the whole place to ashes? The rare books exuded a musty smell curiously mixed with spice fragrances. She guessed this was because printed matter often made its way to Baghdad via spice caravan. Only Sarah knew this part of the shop well enough to locate the document in question, though she had to hold her lamp high and search carefully.

Finding what she sought, Sarah returned to the front area and unrolled the scroll before the three men. She placed sandalwood chess pieces at the four corners to hold the scroll open. The miniature elephants and horses seemed fascinated with the verses, but, if she'd expected a collective input of breath and appreciative exclamations from Aharon and Lior, she didn't hear it.

"Its condition isn't ideal," Aharon said. "Though I'll credit the scribe with fine calligraphy."

"Those are sooty fingerprints near the upper left corner," Lior said. "Rather an odd hand; the prints look elongate and large."

"It's passed through many hands," Yonah said. "And, overall, the work is reasonably undamaged." Sarah watched her father work to redirect attention away from the scroll's defects.

"Well, let's read it," Lior said. "If it has value, that's where we'll see it."

The young man began scanning the scroll with his father peering over his shoulder.

"Mostly Aramaic with words in Persian and Arabic," Aharon said. He pointed out a word for his son.

"Yes, I see," Lior said. "Hebrew, too. Once in a while a Hebrew word is inserted, almost as if the author wanted to make it impossible to fully appreciate the work without being a polylinguist, although the different languages are used for maximum effect as if the poet chose the very best possible word for a given verse to capture an emotion and used a full palette of the world's languages to do that. And the whole thing is embedded in some sort of strange map that the poem obliquely refers to."

Sarah couldn't resist. "The poem is a key to understanding the map. Maybe it contains directions to someplace important."

"Or directions to some shepherd's winter cache of grain for his flock," Lior said.

"A very talented shepherd with a fine sense of rhyme and meter." She didn't keep the sarcasm out of her voice.

Yonah jumped in to prevent an unseemly argument between his daughter and the House of Wisdom's agents who were also their guests.

"Sarah, can you bring our esteemed visitors tea?"

"I was wrong to joke," Lior said. "There is something to what the girl says. This is a puzzle as much as a poem."

Sarah smiled at the young man. At least he acknowledged that her perspective on the scroll had value.

As she again moved to the back rooms in search of the shop's tea service, she saw a veiled woman closely observing the inspection of the poem from behind a tall shelf overflowing with books. However, before Sarah mastered her surprise and challenged the intruder, the woman deftly moved further back into the heavily shadowed stacks of shelves and alcoves. Shaken, Sarah considered calling her father away from the front room discussions to help her investigate, but decided that this would interrupt things just as the two buyers were becoming intrigued with the scroll. Certainly, she wouldn't tell the visitors that their transaction was being spied on by an unknown interloper from within the shop. That would hardly strengthen her father's reputation.

Sarah lit an oil lamp and edged further into the shop's interior rooms where the stranger had retreated. She had moved with fluid swiftness. Sarah had no weapon; nothing like that existed in the bookshop; her father was a learned and unaggressive man. She looked about hurriedly and grasped a Torah pointer from a nearby shelf. Though small, the pointing finger at its tip was at least sharp. This was absolutely not its intended use, but under the circumstances, it was all she could find. Unlike many of the pointers she'd seen, which were crafted in silver, this one was cheap and made of some other metal, probably base iron.

Despite her fear, Sarah was conscious of the irony of using a Torah pointer as a stiletto, but she edged into the shop's depths holding both the pointer and the lamp before her to ward off the mysterious intruder. She had no idea how to use any sort of weapon, and the shadows among the narrow, overflowing stacks looked threatening. However, she methodically checked every part of the back room and found no one. Nothing appeared disturbed, but given the general clutter, it was impossible to say for certain.

"Sarah, tea for our guests." She heard her father call back to her.

She emerged with the service and set cups out before the three men, not bothering to provide a cup for herself. Wondering if the apparition had been some figment of her nerves at this important potential sale, she unsteadily spilled water into the pot and sometimes on the carpet, and lit a small oil cooking stove to heat the water for steeping tea leaves.

Her father looked at her closely, sensing something wasn't right, while their visitors continued to pore over the document. Aharon occasionally looked up in exasperation at the slow delivery of refreshment and Lior nodded encouragement at her shaky efforts to prepare tea. She hoped he assumed that she was simply nervous at the potential sale and the windfall it would bring her family's shop. She also caught his interest in her. As the afternoon progressed, Lior spent as much time glancing at her as at the poem. Maybe she'd inadvertently worn her robe tightly enough to accentuate her form. He seemed cosmopolitan and handsome enough in a diffident sort of way, and Sarah decided to allow herself to feel flattered by his attention.

"There is value in this document," Aharon admitted. "No, no, spare me, Yonah." He held up his hands to forestall a flood of praise for the scroll from the bookseller.

"I won't play coy to help my negotiating position," Aharon continued. "The sonnet is original, almost otherworldly. We have nothing like it. I'm admitting that the House of Wisdom may have an interest in it, if—and this is a big if—we can agree on a reasonable price. Of course, I'm not of the caliph's religion, making my position and that of my son precarious. The caliph and his vizier trust me, but only up to a point. My office is secure as long as the individuals I serve believe I'm not spending the caliphate's money rashly."

This prompted a bout of negotiation. With half her attention, Sarah followed its ebb and flow. Normally, she loved these transactions, how well her father could read the other party's interest in the book under discussion, how well he could gauge at what price his opponent would turn tail and stalk out of his shop, how well he would tiptoe back from that precipice and close the deal with a handshake, an exchange of silver, and a round of tea for everyone.

But today Sarah couldn't focus on this and kept glancing behind her toward the darkened stacks. She saw nothing, but had the distinct sense that whatever had watched them before, watched them still.

Finally, she bolted upright and hissed into her father's ear for him to retire for a moment to the back of the store with her.

Aharon and Lior looked stunned and baffled at this interruption, probably suspecting that it was some distraction planned to give Yonah advantage during the haggling. With profuse apologies, her father bowed himself out of the front room and strode after her.

"Sell it!" Sarah told her father once they were alone. She kept her voice low, but the strength of her feelings came through in her tone. "Sell it now at any reasonable price. Sell it even at an unreasonable price."

"What are you saying?" Yonah asked. "They see its strange originality."

"Strange, yes, it's strange," she said. "It's a love poem from a peculiar being to another peculiar being. None of this is entirely human. No poet or sage that we know could compose such verses. You've read it. You know I'm right. The map makes it stranger. I don't know where it would direct whoever tried to follow its lead, but I doubt any good would come of it. It may be a map to nowhere. Or to hell."

"Such emotion," her father remonstrated. "I should not have let you join this business. Between Lior paying attention to your breasts rather than the poem and your own childish behavior, the shop stands to miss an opportunity that could make my whole year profitable as well as cement our relations with the House of Wisdom's buyers for future commissions."

"I saw a *shedim* or a *dybbuk* or some other demon in the form of a pretty woman among the shelves and books back here," Sarah said. She nodded toward the shelves behind them. "This person or thing was entirely focused on the scroll." She told her father more about sighting of the veiled woman.

Yonah listened carefully and restrained himself from interrupting her.

"We're a small shop and don't have the resources to defend this poem—or defend ourselves if we kept it," she concluded.

"Let me get a word in, daughter. Our goal is the same: dispose of the scroll. I don't know what you saw, if anything, but I respect your caution nonetheless. The only difference we have is what bargain we drive. Let me try to thread this needle and get a good price for it, but ensure that it goes out the front of our stall before the afternoon is done."

~

"Why bring me something from the House of Wisdom?" Lubna asked. "I know of your father by reputation. He's a loyal servant of the Abbasid caliph's library. Is he aware of this plan?"

Lior shook his head. "If that troubles you, I'll walk away now and find another buyer in Córdoba or perhaps one of the Italian city-states or the Byzantines. I'm sure there will be other interested parties."

Lubna sat back on her cushion considering the young man. "Let me at least see the poem."

Her visitor reached for a worn leather satchel at his side and pulled out a large scroll. Everything about his nondescript, dusty clothing suggested someone who preferred not to attract attention and traveled discreetly. After surveying the room and seeing nothing but Abd-al-Rahman's court attendants and palace guards some distance away, Lior unrolled the scroll before Lubna on the carpet. She leaned forward.

"I'm intrigued," she acknowledged after a moment.

"Before we go forward," Lior said, "there is something I need to ask you and another thing that I need to tell you."

Lubna repressed a laugh at this odd approach to negotiating a sale. The slight young man with already thinning dark hair looked earnest, but callow. That might be to her advantage if she decided to buy the scroll.

"Ask whatever you want. If it's reasonable, I'll try to answer."

"If we negotiate a price, do you need anyone else's approval to close the deal?"

Lubna was offended. "I speak for the caliph's library. No one will argue with my decision or what price I pay."

She almost added that no one else in court, excepting the caliph himself and visiting scholars, cared enough about Córdoba's growing library and center of cultural learning to pay much attention to her activities. And the caliph's acquisitions budget was large so she would have to spend lavishly today to attract awareness and unwanted oversight. However, Lubna was wary by habit; she worked hard to preserve her island of autonomy within the snake pit of the Caliphate of Córdoba's court politics. Making enemies or drawing attention to oneself was a fast path to the dungeon or execution. She was just the harmless librarian and court scribe catering to Abd-al-Rahman's eccentric interest in building a prestigious collection of the world's best written material. The Christian kingdoms in Europe had no repositories of splendid books to compare with Córdoba. From what she knew of them, they were barely civilized.

Lubna and Lior sat in an anteroom off the caliph's hall for receiving foreign visitors and supplicants. Lubna reflected that Lior didn't really fit either of those categories, not important enough to be a bona fide foreign visitor to the caliph's court subject to the attention and honor that would entail and not needy enough to be a supplicant. He had something to sell to Córdoba's collection of rare books. If she as the librarian for this august collection had no interest, he'd go elsewhere. She would bear in mind that he had other options while arguing about price.

In the main hall, Lubna saw the vizier sweep past accompanied by his retinue of courtiers and advisers, everyone dressed in sumptuous headdresses and long-sleeved robes. She noted that Matias gave her and Lior a searching stare. He was oddly curious about a transaction that would ordinarily be far beneath notice to a seasoned politician like himself. She recognized a second man, Ahmad, a regular attendee at court gatherings with an uncertain role, in animated discussions with the vizier, who also looked her way, but then he resumed talking to the vizier. The big hall echoed with their footsteps. She moved to stand up in a gesture of respect, but the vizier glanced incuriously at her and Lior and gestured at them to stay seated. The eminence wore a look of profound weariness and boredom. Excepting Matias and Ahmad, none of the two dozen officials and ministers appeared to care about their activities. The group briskly passed in a haze of murmured conversation and perfume.

Politics and foreign affairs only interested Lubna if they affected her role as librarian, though the caliph regularly engaged her reluctant services as translator and scribe for court proceedings and sought her discreet advice, secure in the knowledge that her disinterest made her a more objective adviser than the dozens of sycophants and ambitious minions that populated his court.

But today, no one sought her wisdom on governance and the librarian again immersed herself in the purely intellectual effort of valuing the literary quality of a set of rhymes. She regarded the scroll. Marvelous verses flowed across the papyrus. Just skimming the opening passages held her rapt. Whoever had written it balanced profound passion—it was a love sonnet— with a deep grasp of meter and rhyme. Also, she had to admit that acquiring something of this character out from under the House of Wisdom's grasp for her own caliph's collection added a fillip to today's bargaining. Abd-al-Rahman might approve, given the animus between Córdoba and Baghdad.

In their unsettled world, pitting empire against kingdom, faith against faith, and progress against reaction, culture was a weapon.

"You were going to tell me something?" she asked. "That was the second thing you needed to say before I determine whether I'm interested in the poem and, if so, at what price."

Lior waited a moment. Finally, he said, "This poem has a complicated history."

"It's old," Lubna said. "Of course its history is complicated. Who knows how many hands it's passed through?"

"Yes, many hands have touched it—see the finger smudges near the top. But it's not that old. Inspect it carefully."

The librarian looked at the scroll again, this time paying more attention to the condition of the papyrus than the text. She held it up to the light filtering into the visitors' hall through open arches far above.

"You're right," she said at last. "It's new. So what? It's the literary merit of an item that gets it into Córdoba's library, not age."

"After we acquired it, someone tried to steal it from the House of Wisdom," Lior said. "Guards prevented that, but not before several were burned down to their skeletons. Also, a book dealer in Baghdad's souk held the scroll before we bought it. Just after selling it to us, his stall burned to ashes. It was a very intense blaze that took half the neighborhood's citizens to put out or the main marketplace would have burned as well."

"This is connected to the poem?"

He shrugged. "My father doesn't think so, but his opinion is clouded by the fact that he paid a lot for the scroll and he doesn't want to believe that he acquired a cursed poem at great cost. I was part of that negotiation, so I hold myself to blame, too—I was distracted. I'm married to that distraction now. Anyway, our rashness wouldn't reflect well on our positions as buyers for the House of Wisdom."

"Maybe the unfortunate bookseller's shop simply caught fire. It can happen without sinister intent. And if it was arson, why would this unknown criminal burn the stall *after* the bookseller delivered the scroll to you and your father?"

Lior looked embarrassed. "Maybe it was an accident. Or maybe it was a message."

"What was the message and who sent it to whom?"

"I don't know," he said. "I didn't tell you this to create a puzzle, but because I felt it wrong to hide the malign circumstances that follow the poem. And then there's the map. That may have something to do with all this."

"I respect your honesty about this enigmatic sonnet—and map," Lubna said. "But, if you're right that demons or something supernatural chases it, why would I buy it? My position in

Córdoba is as complicated as yours in Baghdad. Bringing trouble into this palace won't make me friends."

He nodded. "But Córdoba in Andalusia is many weeks journey from Baghdad and the Abbasid court."

"Whoever or whatever is chasing the poem may not be deterred by distance," she said. "Another question is: Won't it be missed? Your father will be none too keen on losing it whatever mystical baggage follows the piece."

"Eventually it will be missed," her visitor admitted. "Baghdad's library is huge but well ordered, and we're careful about indexing our material. Things don't stay lost for long. But no one will know where it is or who took it."

Lubna leaned forward again to peer at the poem. "Aramaic mostly, but a mix of other languages, odd meter and rhyme, but very evocative despite that, a poem about love in a strange world, and, you're right, there is some peculiar connection between the words and the pretty map that surrounds the poem. It would be good to take time to examine it more closely. It will be secure within our library. As you say, why would anyone think to find it here? And Córdoba's palace guards are less prone to spontaneous combustion that Baghdad's."

CHAPTER 6

Show Trial

Thiago entered the portal and felt as if he peeked over God's shoulder during creation. It was blasphemy, but what he saw during crossings inspired his poetry.

Transitioning the portal was like entering a dream, neither a good dream nor a nightmare, but a weird, brilliant reverie.

The portal was the iciest desert dawn he'd ever experienced, before sunrise and before the desert awoke and remembered it was a desert and thought it was something else, something cold.

Every nerve in his body felt as if it had been dipped in ice water.

As Thiago moved through the portal, he felt like he'd drunk many glasses of wine without dulling his senses. Or he'd sampled a desert plant's elixir that expanded his aesthetic perceptions and heightened his awareness of pain.

Passage affected everyone differently. To him, it was a realm between worlds with visual effects rivaling the aurora borealis and where travelers were serenaded by sounds made by musicians performing on instruments that hadn't yet been conceived and might never be played. Even smell was altered and amplified; the aromas he sniffed were from a kitchen tended by demons cooking meals for angels and using the most savory spices available in heaven or hell.

It could be a deadly dream; there was always risk when entering a passage. One might not come out the other side. It didn't happen often, but he knew individuals who'd vanished into the portal's maw forever. A cousin had had this misfortune the previous year. The family had mourned once it became apparent that the passage had swallowed another traveler and blamed bad luck. Enemies of the family ascribed it to his cousin's poor character and not showing enough respect to their lord, the king. Thiago thought his cousin had intended to kill himself and simply chose a portal crossing as the exotic setting for his final act of defiance against fate.

However, despite their hallucinatory nature and physical dangers, portals were touchpoints between the human world and the netherworld of assorted demons and a very long-lived and insanely ambitious king. As such, they were traveled by supernatural beings intent on exporting malice and magic to a realm beyond their own. However, there was minimal traffic in the other direction; mortals occasionally stumbled upon their side of the portal and wandered through, but access to the demon world was in the middle of the Empty Quarter amid a searing, trackless desert, so it took a particularly determined explorer to find it and brave the transit. Sometimes these individuals prospered in the king's court or served as bodyguards since they were impervious to iron. Sometimes they were fed to monsters.

Completing today's passage intact from the prosaic human world, Thiago emerged into a park near the king's palace and throne room. The contrast between the Arabian desert's blasting heat and the well-watered park's shade shocked him. He ran his hand over indigo-colored ferns with a texture like satin.

Thiago pulled a frond off the plant and, for a time, held it, drawing comfort from its smoothness and nerving himself, then he threw the leaf aside and strode up the marble flagstones to the king's palace on a hill overlooking the rest of the capital city. It was a long walk because he took his time. He wouldn't have approached this lion's den except that the wrathful king had imprisoned his father and threatened horrific torture followed by execution unless Thiago returned home at an appointed hour to stand before the throne and explain his role in the disappearance of Sheba's Treasure.

He was uncertain what the king knew, but the very fact of his summons suggested that someone had crossed the portal to accuse him of the crime. However, none of the Fire Horde could have charged him with the theft without implicating themselves. Besides, they loathed the king and his court. Further, with considerable acrimony, Thiago had persuaded his outlaws to recruit the surviving caravan guards to replenish the Horde's depleted ranks. As they'd failed to protect Sheba's Treasure, the guards were exiles from the demon world and well motivated to stay shut about the banditry.

So, by elimination, it would be Lila who'd leveled charges against him. However, what proof did she have of his culpability? Had she fanned the king's suspicions of him by suggesting that Thiago harbored seditious thoughts toward the throne? It would be a short step in the monarch's distrustful mind to believing Thiago was the outlaw behind the outrage, and even being the scion of the realm's most prominent jinn family with a long history of steadfast loyalty and service to the realm wouldn't shield him from prosecution.

Anyway, not answering the summons would damn him and condemn his father to a horrible death. Thiago held his family in some contempt, but he wouldn't let them be liable for his actions. Besides, if the king had anything at all, it was just accusations.

However, Jai had advised him that it was a thin line between accusations and execution. His friend had wanted to attend the trial to show support, bear witness, but Thiago had told him he'd go alone to be held solely accountable. And if the king and his court were convinced that he was behind the theft, his best defense would be that they would never retrieve it without his map and him alive to decipher it. Kill him and they would have nothing. That loss might be enough to undermine the throne. The king would know that.

Empires were built on illusions as much as raw military power, and one of the demon king's conceits was governing with an open, welcoming style. However, despite efforts to give his palace the appearance of being accessible to any citizen at any time, the jinn had to pass through ever bigger clusters of guards. Today, the soldiers waved him along, watching him as he went. As he neared the throne room, a quartet of royal guards fell in behind him.

"An escort?" Thiago asked. None of the soldiers responded.

"I know the way. I won't get lost." He almost added, *I won't run*, but decided this wouldn't be taken as levity and would look a lot like an admission of guilt. He didn't need to make the situation more brittle.

He sauntered into the palace projecting confidence he didn't feel.

He'd seen the throne room as a youth when he'd accompanied his father to court functions, but his parent had stopped inviting him as Thiago became less diplomatic about showing his disdain for palace life and politics. Still, he had to admit that the hall was grand beyond belief and built on a scale so large that he could barely discern its far corners.

Fluted columns lined the throne room and supported a ceiling so high that birds comfortably flew about untroubled by supernatural and human beings below. The hall's hues were garish with gold and maroon dominating the color scheme, contrasting with the searingly white marble floor. Gods and giants could comfortably inhabit the hall without feeling cramped. Thiago reflected that the room's occupants, particularly the king, had godlike drives that spilled beyond the throne room's confines and had inspired the creation of the surrounding city of towers, parks, and delicate palaces visible through arched windows along the throne room's walls.

The capital bordered the Erythraean Sea visible through stone arches. The body of water was close enough so that surf sent spray past the arches. Little rainbows materialized and vanished as sunlight hit the mist. Periodically, enormous, brightly colored creatures broke the sea's surface in leaps that sent fountains of water reaching up to the clouds. This wasn't play. The beasts, all scales and teeth, spent most of their time preying on one another and sometimes hapless victims of the king's mercy. Thiago recalled watching members of the court who'd fallen out of favor get put out onto this ocean in small boats for the general amusement of the audience to bet on how long it would take before they were devoured. Occasionally, the poor individual would be torn to pieces as competing predators pulled in different directions. The court wagered on the victim's fate—assuming they weren't themselves the individual consigned to the boat.

Looking at the urban expanse, Thiago noted a discordant sight: a distant burning structure, an aristocrat's castle, its smoke smudging the sky and drifting in their direction. He smelled charred wood and perhaps flesh. Thiago wondered if the blaze was accidental or the king had torched some treasonous offender's home, or perhaps laborers had been pushed too far and retaliated against their tribal lord.

This was the only ugly note as he looked far and wide. A broad beach lay beneath the window, and grand palaces and manor houses of the nobility were situated to enjoy the view. Pretty as it all was, the jinn knew that the king's hubris and acquisitiveness stretched beyond this supernatural world and through the portal into human domains.

The king was the center of this world. Only he sat, black bearded, complete unto himself, and as solid and immutable as the prophets of old. All about him, shuffling uncomfortably at being forced to stand for what promised to be a long trial, officials, warriors, and priests packed together, intent on getting the best views of the interrogation, but arranged so that those favored by status or royal indulgence clustered nearest the throne. Included in that group were the eleven jinn and ifrit leaders who served on the king's council and ruled the demon tribes that formed the realm's foundation. Thiago knew them by reputation and also knew that each of them felt that they could more capably perform royal duties than the sitting monarch. There should have been twelve tribal leaders, but today his father was in the palace dungeon.

Besides the realm's aristocracy and palace society, the hall had been thrown open to anyone wanting to witness the king's judgment against the miscreants who'd stolen Sheba's Treasure.

Examples would be made.

Blood was in the air.

Palace guards watched the throng closely and some unsheathed their swords. A crowd of this size could be hard to control. However, the king seemed calm and pleased with the scale of the gathering, chatting with courtiers beside his throne and occasionally nodding at a favorite. Despite the monarch's certainty about his ability to hold the people in thrall, Thiago wondered if he could turn this unwieldy mob to his advantage if the need arose during the trial.

The king's edict was that whatever type of being they were, mortal or supernatural, they had to appear in their human forms in the throne room to avoid unhealthy competition between species. Overt tribalism needed to be suppressed for the realm's unity. Occasionally, however, emotion overcame someone and they transformed into bestial or elemental forms before remembering themselves and returning to their mundane human incarnation. Their neighbors affected not to notice such lapses.

The monarch's wives and concubines stood near the throne arrayed in a myriad of gowns and diaphanous dresses. Their rainbow of hues contrasted with the room's gold and maroon. Thiago hadn't bothered to count the king's consorts and he wondered at the distinction between wife and concubine, not to mention the many casual, royal bed partners. Without doubt, the monarch's appetites were huge. Amid this harem, Thiago speculated about how Lila would describe her amorous circumstances with the king.

Careful, this is the wrong time to show jealousy over someone who never liked, let alone loved, me, he thought.

Ignoring the strange splendor surrounding him, Thiago strolled forward toward the monarch sitting up a dozen steep steps on a dais before him. *This will be unpleasant business; I might as well get on with it.*

The case had begun already. A supplicant bowed before the monarch face to the flagstones, but this witness wouldn't testify. Shocked, Thiago saw that it was Jai prostrating himself for the last time before a royal audience with a spear protruding from his back. The iron-tipped weapon had transfixed his friend with enough force to burst through his chest and send the point several feet beyond the body. Jai looked like an animal spitted for the king's feast.

Thiago started forward to tend to his friend, but two bronze-helmeted guards blocked his access. After a moment, another soldier strode forward, placed a sandaled foot on Jai's back, and wrenched free the spear, sending the corpse onto its side in an awkward slump on the stairs leading to the dais. This guard was human and unaffected by handling an iron-tipped weapon. Maybe he'd been the one who'd hurled the spear. Blood pooled on the marble and stained the body's white cloak. In life, Jai had been supremely athletic and graceful. Dead, he was anything but.

A peacock moved past the corpse and paused to spread its tail plumage. Now a hundred blue-green eyes looked at Thiago, accusing him of Jai's death. The audience laughed and applauded. Folding its plumage, the bird ambled down the steps and back into the crowd.

No one else moved to care for Jai's remains even though Thiago saw that members of the Fire Horde mixed in with the audience.

I didn't invite them to come. I'm the only one who needs to be here.

Word must have gotten around about his peremptory summons. The Horde were dispersed so as not to attract attention. Jai had been popular with the Horde and most of them looked as stunned as Thiago by this demonstration of raw monarchical power. Thiago had no idea whether the king knew of the existence of his group of brigands or who comprised it, though obviously he'd known that Jai and Thiago were friends and assumed that Jai must understand Thiago's role in stealing Sheba's Treasure. Thiago also didn't know whether the Horde's warriors were discreetly armed; if they were, he wasn't sure whether they'd take his side in this showdown. However, if they chose to coalesce and fight, they'd be a handful to deal with despite the king's many guards.

Thiago caught Aaliyah's eye. She looked furious about Jai's sordid end. Thiago could count on her support, at least, but she was one among a multitude of onlookers.

"Loyalty," the king said. "Your comrade had it. He didn't utter a word against you or implicate you in any way for stealing my possessions even when I pressed the point with a spear." The king gestured at Jai's body. "But you don't show loyalty toward me."

Though he didn't exert any obvious effort, the king's voice carried to the far reaches of the throne hall.

"Too stunned to talk?" the monarch asked Thiago. "Did you think your whims would drive my actions and I wouldn't react to having everything I hold dear stolen? Sheba's Treasure came to this kingdom two thousand years ago. Generations of monarchs before me have venerated it. During my reign, I loved every gem and coin. There are things in that trove too extraordinarily beautiful to describe with histories that no one alive remembers. I want it back."

So my guilt is a foregone conclusion, Thiago thought.

"At least see to his body," he said.

"See to his body," the king mimicked. "I am your king. Use my title. And I'll see to his body whenever I get around to it. Meantime, let's hear from someone who might know the treasure's whereabouts and who's never at a loss for words, the soulless one, my favorite ifrit. Last night, in my bed, she had a lot to say about this thieving jinn who stands before us today."

Lila stepped forward respectfully from the audience to stand beside Thiago.

Some of the throng clapped. She had her tribal contingent of ifrit sprinkled among the crowd, one hundred or more. Thiago couldn't guess what guises they would assume if given free rein outside the king's throne room, but now they all appeared as sleek and elegant humans. Both men and women were preternaturally beautiful, powerful, and poised. On a discordant note, all the ifrits' eyes were identical: coal black. Despite the crush of attendees, Lila's tribe stood subtly apart from other demons, particularly jinn, maintaining a superior distance.

Thiago didn't see anyone from his own family.

He hadn't expected them.

The king ran his fingers through his beard. "Ifrit, tell us how you pursued this renegade jinn—"

"My name is Thiago."

"—to get my treasure back for me." The king ignored the interjection and addressed himself to the ifrit. "You have a thing with our 'Thiago' here, a dalliance, but you set that aside for my greater good."

The audience tittered at the reference to the supposed romance between Thiago and Lila which the entire court knew had duped Thiago, but no one else.

Thiago also knew that the king's ultimate sympathies in this trial were with Lila, but the king never resisted taunting any of his subjects, particularly his bed partners.

"Yes, my king," the ifrit said. "I'll say my piece, but it's simply put. First, I never had any sort of 'thing' with Thiago despite his fantasies; and, second, there is no case for him. He seized your treasure, endless gems, gold, and an ebony throne from the Kingdom of Anuradhapura. He's a clever and callous thief— and arrogant, too. He's renounced your rule. He consorts with humans on the far side of the portal. Is there more to say?"

"Succinctly put. You have a response, jinn?"

"My name is Thiago. Her name is Lila."

"Shut up," the king shouted. "You're whatever I call you."

With visible effort he collected himself. Thiago had ripped aside any pretense of equanimity and judicial objectivity.

You're not a judge, you're a tyrant, he thought.

Thiago sensed the ifrit bristle at his reference to her human name. She used Lila only on the other side of the portal and even then only when disguising her demonic nature to humans.

Thiago intentionally worked to anger the king and the ifrit. If he was to have any hope of surviving the hearing and freeing his father, injecting doubt and chaos into the proceedings might help this purpose. Further, he could barely control his emotions with Jai's body lying directly before him turning cold. Still, he needed to temper his feelings. If he pushed the king hard, he'd wind up like Jai.

Accusation is enough.

"Ask Lila where your lost treasure is," he said.

The ifrit jumped in, "Sire, I only know roughly where it is— near the other end of the portal hidden in some sort of ruin."

"The best parties are in ruins," the jinn remarked.

Lila's ifrit contingent hissed, but there was muted laughter from the rest of the crowd which the king affected not to notice. Lila turned to stare through Thiago. The laughter stopped.

"Intimidation won't work," Thiago said.

"This dissenting jinn has hidden its precise location," Lila continued, still watching Thiago. "Without a map he doesn't know exactly where it is, either, so he created one specifying where he buried it."

"So find the map," the monarch said as if speaking to a cretin.

The ifrit ignored the rebuke. "The map is in a city called Córdoba under the rule of a prince who fancies himself the leader of the western end of a great sea in their world. I was after that map when you summoned me."

"My favorite ifrit, this gets me no closer to retrieving my wealth."

"My case is simpler than Lila's," Thiago interrupted. "I took your treasure."

No point in hiding it and nobody else dies because of me. My strategy isn't denial any longer; it's attack.

The crowd murmured at his confession, anticipating summary judgment against the jinn and his prompt execution. He'd be fed to the sea monsters or an iron spear would be thrown into his guts. There were more-inventive options. Then they could all retire to someplace with comfortable chairs and sit down, libation in hand, to savor memories of the spectacle.

The king leaned forward. "When my dear ifrit told me you'd orchestrated the mad scheme to take my wealth, I wouldn't believe her. How could a frivolous, lovesick puppy have done something as ambitious as this?"

"It took some planning," Thiago said. "But others would have taken it if I hadn't. As for getting caught, I'm cynical, but apparently not cynical enough. I hadn't guessed Lila would be your agent. Yes, the stupid lust of youth made me think that she'd be on my side. Besides banditry, I stand guilty of being a jilted lover, may that amuse your court."

"If you could, would you have sacked a city for her?" the king asked sarcastically.

"No, but I'd steal a treasure to stop a war."

The crowd murmured, puzzled by this revelation. Thiago would exploit that confusion.

"Ah, so there's a noble motive behind your thievery?" the king said. "Not just simple greed? Or banditry to impress my pretty demon bedroom acrobat?"

"*Your* demon?" Thiago asked. Now he was sarcastic. "Is she really? She's not mine—I see that now—but ask yourself whether you trust your favorite ifrit to return your treasure once she finds the map—if she finds it."

The audience went silent.

"That's a ploy to pit us against each other, sire," Lila said urgently. "I'll bring it all back to you."

"I don't doubt you," the king said. "But I've sent detachments of my palace guard, jinn, ifrits, and humans through the portal to help you look for the map. One group rounded up some boys in the desert. The boys of course claimed to know nothing about anything. As it turned out, they had the map after all. Then it went to a human city called Baghdad. More drama ensued and the map then traveled to this Córdoba place where you were about to get it, but that didn't happen somehow—"

"Sire, many thanks for your offer, but I don't need your help," the ifrit said. "I can do it on my own."

Thiago knew Lila had just made a mistake. By trying to exclude the monarch from the search, she'd only made him more suspicious of her intentions.

"All on your own?" Thiago asked. "Get it all on your own? Even with the map, you won't find Sheba's Treasure."

"It's part of a poem," a voice from the crowd shouted.

The entire throne room audience looked around to find the speaker.

"Show yourself," the king demanded.

Thiago saw Ajmal push through the assorted dignitaries as if he were their equal, leaving a trail of angry spectators, all of whom thought they were superior to him, before finally emerging between Thiago and Lila to stand in front of the king. In his human form, Ajmal cut a striking figure in a wild, unhinged sort of way with a full, blond beard longer than the king's and braided red hair that refused to be coiffed. It angled off his head in odd directions. A scarlet headband did nothing to civilize his mane and, indeed, Thiago knew that he wore it not as a nod to style but as a mocking comment on his betters' dress. He wasn't Thiago's friend, but a stage this big must have been too tempting to pass up.

Several guards surrounded the insolent intruder, uncertain what sort of threat he represented if any. Thiago had to credit Ajmal's boldness—or stupidity—at inserting himself into the tense hearing. Would he say anything helpful or simply confirm the king's intention to ram an iron sword through Thiago? And Ajmal, too.

Not appearing the least unnerved by the king, his scores of retainers, or the grandiose hall, Ajmal said, "He's a poet, our Thiago is. Can't judge his verses 'cept to say that they rhyme. I can say that the poem and the map go together like fingers in a glove. I think learned folk call that a simile since I used 'like.'"

"Can you understand the map using this poem?" the king demanded.

"Can't read," Ajmal said.

"You're mocking me?" the king said. His tone was smooth on the surface, but white-hot lava flowed underneath. A dozen guards took the cue to level spears at Ajmal.

"Not I, sire. Mockery is beyond my poor faculties, but I'm capable of threats. In fact, I do threats really well."

Thiago watched incredulous at this challenge to royal authority, but then noticed that other outlaws had filtered forward to get close to the throne. Aaliyah winked at Thiago. So, some of the Horde were loyal to him after all. Many could care less about him, but were enraged at Jai's murder. In any event, they all hated the king.

The rest of the audience sensed that an unexpected body of spectators of unknown origin and strength had decided to interfere with today's proceedings. Uncertain what force Thiago could mobilize, some began to turn into their various essential forms ready to fight or flee as circumstances required, here a petite concubine turned into a pyre of fire, there a modest-looking court official became a leopard.

Chaos threatened. Thiago had a counter to the king's power, at least for the moment.

"We can turn this into a bloodbath," he addressed the king shouting over the commotion. Then he turned to the room at large.

"I'm on trial here brought before you under threat to myself and my father. Many of you know him and think fondly of him. He's not the brute I am and had nothing to do with any crimes I've committed, but he'll be dinner for the fishes in our sea if the king has his way. Threatening a respected and loyal elder in the realm's biggest jinn tribe, is that fair? The king has always liked ifrits better than jinn."

"Clear the hall," the king said urgently to the nearest soldiers. "Especially the Fire Horde. 'Fire Whores' fits them better."

"Now they're trying to insult us," Ajmal addressed fellow outlaws. "Do we let him do that?"

A chorus of outrage from the Horde surged over other noise reverberating through the hall.

Thiago was impressed. Ajmal had unexpected gifts as a rabble-rouser, but he needed the audience's attention for another moment before slaughter started.

"Let's put this question to the king," he shouted. "Whose treasure is it, anyway? His? Or yours?"

Plainly, this question had occurred to many in the throne room, but no one had dared raise it. During the pause following his query, the jinn pulled a handful of emeralds from his pocket. No need to mention that these were from an Egyptian tomb, not Sheba's Treasure. They would serve his purpose. Thiago was after maximum effect.

"Here. Take them. They're yours, not the king's, not mine." He threw a half dozen of the gems into the crowd, setting off a violent scramble among those closest to where they landed.

He had their attention.

"Why send Sheba's Treasure through the portal in the first place? No doubt there are plenty here in the realm who'd have been happy to try taking it. And who can blame them? It's yours, after all. But the king has endless guards, supernatural and human, to protect it. Sending it to another world where an outlaw like me might steal it is imprudent to say the least."

"Tell me," the king mocked as if letting the throng in on a private joke. "Why would I send it to the other side?"

The crowd quieted in anticipation of an answer.

"It's funding to conquer humanity," Thiago said. "You control everything on this side. What's left? The human side. You'll use Sheba's gold to hire mercenaries, suborn rulers, pit kingdom against kingdom."

"If true, what of it?" the king said. "Many on the human side don't believe we exist, so surprise works for us. We'll simply materialize out of a portal and massacre them. If I invade—if *we* invade—the realm of humans, there will be more for all of us. I'll share it with all of you."

"Like you shared Sheba's Treasure with your subjects," Thiago said. "I've just thrown away more wealth in emeralds than you've ever given away."

The jinn sensed unrest in subjects that had been cowed by the king's authority for time beyond counting. Cynically, he assumed that a need for freedom didn't motivate them. Rather, it was getting a share of Sheba's Treasure that stoked the latent violence in the room and the crowd's ambivalence toward their king.

"There's a word for what our king plans," Thiago shouted. He paused just long enough for his question to sink in.

"Tyranny," someone responded.

"That fits perfectly," Thiago said. "But I would have chosen 'distraction.' By invading the human side, he's hoping to distract you from the pretty, but miserable, existence many of you lead here. Our dear king happily extracts massive taxes, conducts summary executions—my friend Jai is just the most recent— imprisons individuals for no cause whatever, pits tribes against one another for his own aggrandizement. I could go on, but we'd be here for a week."

"Sire, there's no need to win this argument," Lila said. "We start by getting your riches back and we do that by convincing him to tell us where it is. Torture him or his family. You have his father here in prison. Bring him out now—"

"Tear me to pieces," Thiago said. "It won't do you any good. Tear my father to pieces. I don't like him anyway. Without the map, I'm as ignorant as you are. While you ponder that, I and my warriors will see to my friend, Jai. He was one of us and we respected him. There are eulogies to say and ceremonies to per- form to send him off properly."

Thiago moved toward Jai's body followed by Aaliyah, Ajmal, Charun, and dozens of the Horde. Many of them had drawn daggers that they'd hidden in their robes. Several dispensed with weaponry altogether and transformed into their most potent elemental forms. True to their namesake, this was fire and Thiago felt the heat of their flames.

The king's closest guards formed a perimeter about the monarch while others pushed from the room's far reaches to assault the Fire Horde. Some were human, some were jinn or ifrit. The supernatural members of the guard transformed into fire to match the Horde's pyrotechnic prowess.

The rest of the crowd milled in confusion about whose side to take, but at least half of them had defensively completed their own transformations into fire, wind, wild animals, and other entities from a madman's nightmare.

Thiago watched the seething mass sardonically. So much for the monarch's carefully orchestrated show trial. He noticed that Lila had disappeared. They'd confront each other sooner rather than later.

Things teetered on the edge of war in the throne room.

"Let them have the body," the king said to the guards. "The fish have had enough to eat today." Thiago knew that he postured for the court. The monarch relaxed on his throne as though none of the court's simmering revolt threatened him.

Then the king said quietly just for Thiago, "You wouldn't have come back for this trial unless you loved your father. Wherever you go, I have that over you. If my agents get my treasure before you do, you and your father die; if the ifrit finds my treasure before you do, you and your father die; if you return it to me, you still die, but your father goes free."

"This is the king's wisdom?" Thiago taunted.

"And you will be consumed by fire," the monarch concluded. "My word on it."

"I am fire," Thiago replied.

~

"Hello, Father."

"Can you get me out?" his father asked.

He must be desperate, Thiago thought. At any other time, there were endless formal greetings and pleasantries before his parent got to the point.

They had him locked in a cage with iron bars on four sides. The enclosure sat in the middle of a courtyard in the king's open-air dungeon.

He was a spectacle as well as a prisoner.

Periodically guards passed, shepherding other captives to and from cells. Whenever the mood struck, jailers threw rotten fruit and vegetables at Thiago's father. They cheered lustily if they scored a hit. The prisoners found this funny, too. His father sat amid a pile of garbage in a stained robe dead center in the cage and as far from the bars as possible, but there was no place to position himself where the iron wasn't close enough to hurt and weaken him. The enclosure kept the elder jinn from changing form to fire or wind and slipping through the bars. Thiago saw that his father was deteriorating. A few scraps of bread sat next to a small bowl of rancid olive oil. Maybe the jailers intended to starve his father and save themselves the effort of executing him.

Like every other part of the city, peacocks had the run of the dungeon and meandered about preening as they nonchalantly swept past the cage. His gaunt father watched them hungrily like he would have wrung their necks and eaten them raw if given a chance. There had to be a malign intelligence at work in this avian behavior, and Thiago was reminded of the peacock's mocking display by Jai's body. The jinn fantasized about cooking and eating one of them. He thought sage and salt would be good seasonings.

"I can't get you out now," he told his father. "There is no enchantment I can conceive, no magic I can make, no form that I can take that releases you from an iron cage. But I will get you out somehow."

He moved as close as possible to the bars. The king had permitted him an audience for as long as he liked to drive home that he had control over his father's fate. Nobody monitored their conversation and, in fact, the guards ignored him. Plotting escape was unimaginable.

Nonetheless, hoping against hope that he'd have a chance to return and somehow spring his father loose, Thiago discreetly inspected the open-air dungeon. Iron was everywhere, in the cell doors, in the barred windows, and in a rusted, woven mesh covering the entire structure. Bright, cheery sunlight filtered through, creating dappled patterns on the floor.

On three sides of the courtyard, rough-hewn stone walls stretched up toward the sky. Cells honeycombed them. The fourth side was open to a stunning view. The structure was as much amphitheater as prison, and built for spectacle as much as incarceration. The courtyard fronted a cliff that dropped a long way down to a thin sliver of rocks, sandy beach, and the Erythraean Sea. The vista must have been designed to mock inmates who had views rivaling aristocrats in their palaces in the nearby city, but no way to access the beauty. If a prisoner somehow managed to escape their cell and climb down the sheer cliff, sea creatures would make short work of them at the bottom. If the escapee took to the air, the iron mesh would ensnare them, or flying demons circled waiting to pounce. Their forms were fluid, shifting from birdlike and substantial to beings of pure energy. They would eat a jinn as quickly as a seagull. In their corporeal form, the flying monsters reminded Thiago of much larger, gaudier versions of raptors he'd seen on the human side of the portal.

"You played with those creatures once," his father said. "Ordinary games didn't interest you unless there was risk."

"I haven't grown up much," Thiago said.

As a child, he'd tested his luck and skill by swimming near the sea creatures and teasing them to catch their attention before fleeing to shore with the beasts snapping at his heels, some lunging after him onto the beach. At first, his friends admired him as a daredevil. However, as they all got older and he kept at it, they decided he was a reckless attention seeker and he had fewer friends.

He liked friends, but he liked fun more.

"Hurry getting me out," his father said. "Or there won't be anything left to release from this wretched place. There won't even be enough to feed the monsters. Or maybe they'll be more creative when they kill me."

"Don't think that way," Thiago said sharply. "You're not dead yet." His father would die of despair before the iron's toxic effects did him in.

"I've heard the king complain about not having inventive executioners," his father said. "The old standbys aren't amusing: pitting two condemned individuals to fight by promising that the winner lives, but then killing both anyway; chasing a prisoner with an iron chariot before crushing them."

Maybe his father wanted to show his son that he was still someone to be reckoned with and not afraid of these fates. He transformed into an incandescent yellow-white sphere of fire as pure as a star's center. The fire burned true. Its radiance was so bright Thiago's eyes hurt. In that moment, Thiago saw what his father was capable of—once upon a time. However, the flames guttered out quickly, leaving the caged man more deflated than ever.

Several of the guards clapped.

"Brilliant, old fellow," one of them shouted.

"Save your strength," Thiago said. "You're trapped."

"They simply throw dead prisoners' corpses over the cliff," his father said, breathing heavily from the failed transformation, "Or throw them living over the edge or impale them on spikes up above the walls so the airborne beasts are primed for fresh meat. I've asked our tribe to intercede, but their influence is weak given that my eldest offspring is a traitor to the realm and a thief."

"I haven't made your situation easier after today's drama in the throne room," Thiago admitted. He described the trial and the ensuing chaos. "I instigated the disorder. The king barely kept an insurrection from brewing up in his own throne room. He may despise me for grabbing his treasure, but now he's afraid of me for throwing oil on a political fire that's been simmering for years. The only reason I'm alive is because he needs me to find Sheba's Treasure."

"He made that bed for himself," his father said. "Still, he is the king and has been since time immemorial. We owe him allegiance."

"Do we? That's forgiving of you. In your circumstances, I wouldn't be so charitable. He's hell-bent on using the kingdom's wealth to fund invasion and pillage in the lands of men. It didn't take me to tell the court this. Most already knew and were angry about the strategy."

"As I am," his father said.

"You should have protested with the rest of our tribe," Thiago said. "We and the rest of the jinn will bear the brunt of this; any casualties will be ours. The ifrit will strongly shout their support of the cause, but do very little. This side of the portal has enough factions and furies. Do we need a clash in another world, too?"

"I did protest," his father said with as much anger as his weakness allowed. "I represented our tribe and other jinn tribes. No one listened, especially not our king. Why do you think I'm in this cage? Not just because of you, though your insanity hasn't helped."

"Good to know that I'm not the sole reason for your troubles," Thiago said. "Thinking practically, how will they move an army through the portal without losing many in the process? I don't pretend to understand how passages work, but I think they can only tolerate so much traffic. They may be fragile and treacherous in ways we don't understand. Would a hundred thousand warriors passing through at one time disrupt their architecture? Besides, I've traveled in the world of men—more than most jinn—and they've developed martial skills with their endless warring on each other. They're as bad as we are. We'd be in for a fight. Probably we would prevail since we can become the elements that govern their world and the animals that prowl outside their cities at night when torches burn low, but it might be a near thing. We wouldn't win without losses."

"If you hadn't taken the treasure—" his father began.

"This whole business would have started anyway," Thiago interrupted. "I simply ripped the bandage off a bloody wound in my own admittedly childish way."

"It *was* childish," his father said quietly. Thiago sensed that feebleness was all that kept his father from shouting at him through the bars.

"You're young and careless of others. You think your life can't end as suddenly as your friend Jai's did. You're careless of consequences, too. But what you did affected me and your family."

"It might have stopped a war," Thiago said.

"I'm sure that was your only motive." Sarcasm dripped from his father's tone. "The fact that it made you rich beyond counting had nothing to do with it. In the future, look to your essence before you act. The wind and the sands and, above all, fire are your best teachers, not chasing wealth or some sultry ifrit who plays you for a fool."

Thiago almost retorted but held himself back. Everyone had known Lila for what she was, but him.

His father's lecture continued; Thiago had heard it before. "Don't read men's words or visit their libraries. And your poems are inconsequential."

"Not to me," Thiago said.

"They brought you—and me—suffering."

"Do you read, Father?"

Thiago felt incredulity emanate from the older jinn. "Human writings? Whatever can they tell us?"

"They tell us about things beyond our own world."

There was a long pause, then, "Other worlds don't matter much. We exist in this one for better or worse. It is beyond magnificent in its own strange way."

Thiago looked where his father pointed out toward the sea. Somehow everything looked brighter on this side of the portal. A scaled, crimson creature with black stripes along its back breached with a gargantuan splash of water. It was savage with teeth longer than scimitars currently impaling some lesser monster in its jaws. It arced back into the water, whipping its neck violently to dismember its prey before disappearing into the depths to savor its catch. Above this primal demonstration of power, fat amber clouds backlit by the afternoon sun scudded across the sky as if some celestial giant had left toys scattered above the Erythraean Sea. Purple-tinted, translucent palaces with delicate towers on shore commanded views of the ever-changing panorama. The structures soared up to touch the clouds untroubled by gravity. His father owned the prettiest palace. Maybe the king would seize it as recompense for Thiago's aggravation.

"Where else could you see that?" his father asked. "And your family and tribe are here."

"It's impressive," Thiago admitted. "But there's more beyond this."

"What can you do there that you can't do here?"

"My magic goes further on the human side. Here, I'm an ordinary jinn with capabilities certainly, but nothing remarkable compared to everyone else. There, I can move mountains."

"I take it you read and write human script," his father said.

Thiago nodded. "I captured a ship once on the other side of the portal. One of its passengers was a court scribe from Baghdad returning home from India by sea."

"These are human places?" his father asked. "I don't know them."

"They are human, not as sumptuous as here, but significant nonetheless."

"So you are a pirate as well as a caravan robber." This came out as a statement, not a question.

"The only difference between piracy and robbery is where the theft happens," Thiago said. "This won't make you feel any prouder of me, but I rob tombs, too."

"An all-purpose thief."

"A successful thief," the jinn countered. He pulled one of his remaining emeralds out of a pocket. He was down to two now after tossing a half dozen into the crowd earlier.

"From Egypt," he said.

"Fine workmanship," his father said with no apparent interest. Thiago remembered Lila's dismissive remarks when he'd made her a gift of one of the stones.

"Anyway, the scribe taught me several human languages before I let him go."

"How useful," his father said. "Your family would be proud."

"You always show contempt for what I do," Thiago said.

"When contempt is deserved."

His father lurched to his feet. "That came out badly. I'm sorry." He took a step toward Thiago, reaching toward his son. In turn, Thiago moved closer to the cage, but they both came up well short of grasping each other's hands. After a moment, by mutual consent, they gave up. His father was exhausted.

"Do they have dungeons on the human side?" his father asked.

"None as pretty as this one, but, yes humans have many dungeons. The two worlds are similar that way. Too similar."

"Trapping one's fellow beings for sport or punishment is universal," his father said wearily. "The cells around me are packed with the king's enemies. He has a flair for creating enemies. So far, it hasn't caught up with him. There must be thousands of them here. If they ever got loose—"

"I'll be back to get you out if I have to use the treasure to bribe every guard here," Thiago said.

"Some of them are jinn from our tribe," his father said. "They may listen."

"There's a bit of hope, but to pay off any of them, I need to free someone who may help me find the treasure, a librarian of all things. She's in a prison, too."

The jinn began to walk away from his caged father but stopped.

"We shouldn't part arguing," he said.

"We disagree," his father said. "Parents often disagree with their children, but I don't deny you. I'd persuade you to behave better if I could, but I'd never deny you."

CHAPTER 7

A True False Flag

S omeone screamed in a neighboring cell. Though muffled, the noise cut through the thick stonework and heavy cell doors. Lubna couldn't decide whether this was the caliph's executioner at work or an inmate who'd gone mad. Besides his vocalizations, there was a background cacophony of prisoners' cries and shouts contending with the guards' commands and harassment. Even the dungeon's massive structure didn't mute this. The librarian realized that prisons weren't quiet.

Odder still, she heard an animal's wail from within the dungeon. Excepting Bradan of Normandy's pet, she'd never seen or heard a wolf, but this must be what they sounded like. Were they feeding prisoners to beasts? The caliph, Abd-al-Rahman, could be entirely ruthless and lethal, but he'd never struck her as sadistic. Like breathing, killing was simply an integral component of ruling a growing imperium in a turbulent time with enemies around every corner. When needed, he accomplished it as efficiently as possible. However, she'd heard that others in court weren't just motivated by expediency and enjoyed assassination, imaginatively performed, for its own sake.

Lubna felt that she had a good grip on her emotions, especially fear, after surviving in the complex, violent crosscurrents of the caliph's court. However, that confidence eroded as she sat in this hot dungeon cell serenaded by sounds of pain and terror.

They'd brought her down during the night, but the cell was nearly lightless as well as airless and had no window to the outside world, so she didn't know what time it was now. There was ever so faint illumination coming in through a tiny, barred portal in the cell door. It limned the cell's walls but nothing else. There wasn't a bucket to piss in. The room stank and she breathed shallowly and tried not to think about the stench and squalor. She would lose her senses soon enough in this hellhole with no certainty of her fate. Lior was right that vile events followed the scroll from owner to owner.

Idly, Lubna noted that her cell, awful in every way, was larger than her office in the palace's library where she willingly spent most of her waking hours—life's ironies.

The librarian heard voices approaching in the corridor outside the cell, quietly at first, and then louder. She heaved herself upright and groped her way to the portal. Either her entreaties to be presented to someone powerful enough to free her had finally been heard, or they'd come to strangle her. She guessed strangling was a bad way to go.

"This is the prisoner," said a man outside her door. His voice sounded like a wire brush on a dirty metal pot. "The Sardinian will have no trouble squeezin' away this one's life. Her neck is slender. The last one in this cell took forever to choke. He was big, so his neck was big. Executioner finally took his head off with an ax, blood everywhere. See why we shouldn't use the ax? Strangling's cleaner—"

"There's no mark on the door," a second voice interrupted. This slurred voice sounded like its owner had just downed several mugs of wine to ease the tedium of selecting the executioner's next victims.

Lubna saw an oil lamp move about outside her cell and come close to her door.

"Enough light?" the second voice asked. "See, no mark. Even a fool like you can understand that."

"I'm the fool? Who's been down here for eternity?" the first voice countered.

They both sounded drunk. Lubna took them to be the caliph's jailers. "Does Abd-al-Rahman, may his name be blessed, know I'm here?" she shouted through the door.

The jailers paid no attention.

"After the Sardinian has practiced his craft," the second jailer said, "I search the bodies for coins and valuables. Surprising what you find. Also, I plays a bit with the corpses."

"You disgusting shit," the first jailer said. "Clean death—even on false charges—is one thing, but perversions have no place in the caliph's dungeon."

"If you're dead, you don't got no say in the matter," the second voice snarled. "It ain't perversion if they ain't aware. Reason enough for me to stay down here—"

"The women, they're kept elsewhere," the first voice said. "Got to keep 'em separated. There's rules to follow. This is a cleanly run dungeon 'cept for you. So why's this girl here?"

"Don't matter," the second voice stated. "She's a goner soon. Someone didn't want us to wait."

"How about the one in the next cell?" the first voice interrupted.

"The screamer? I'll strangle that one myself, no need for the Sardinian."

"There's no mark on his door, neither," the first jailer said.

"Chalk markings on the door," the second voice remarked. "It's a poor system to pick prisoners for our humble executioner to finish off. I'm sure the Sardinian wanted them both done for. He told me himself."

"One way to settle this: Ask the Sardinian," the first jailer said. "Chalk is stupid—"

"What is Sardinia?" the second voice asked.

"The place where they get the best executioners," the first voice said. "That's obvious enough."

"Ever been there—Sardinia, I mean?" the second voice asked. "The land of executioners, it must be quite a sight."

"I need to travel," the first voice responded. "Don't get out of the dungeon enough."

The guards were right outside her cell.

"Bring the wretch Matias," Lubna shouted. "He'll answer for this."

The voices dwindled as the jailers walked back down the corridor still mulling the utility of chalk for identifying prisoners selected for execution and the location of Sardinia. Lubna grasped the bars in the cell door's portal and hung on to them for support.

"Faith."

Lubna thought she imagined the quiet, deep voice in the corridor. Had the jailers come back to toy with her? No, this voice had a different timbre.

"Have faith in whatever god or gods you believe in. This will all come to a good end. I'll try to get you out of here. That's a start."

She heard a key inserted into the door followed by strange, vivid curses as rusty tumblers ground against each other and with some effort the door opened. Still hanging on to its bars for support, Lubna tumbled out of the cell into the corridor.

"You'll have a thousand questions," said the tall man who'd released her. "There's time for answers later."

Lubna doubled over and threw up on the stone floor. Everything in her stomach from last night's dinner and wine came up in an acid-tasting rush.

He held on to her arm so that she didn't pitch forward into her own vomit.

Wiping her mouth with the back of her hand, she regarded him in the light of the lamp he carried.

"You were outside my office last night," was all she could think to mumble.

"Yes," he said. "Let's move." He pulled her upright.

"You're after the poem? You're a demon."

"Friends call me a jinn, and, yes, I'm after the poem. It's mine. I wrote it. You have it?"

"I had it. Matias has it now. He's in the caliph's court."

"Whoever Matias is, I'll find him," Thiago said. "Can you help?"

"Not so easy," she said. "I don't know who supports him, maybe Abd-al-Rahman himself or his vizier, maybe someone in court I don't know. Matias has his own squad of soldiers, too."

"There's a way around every obstacle. Now, let's leave."

"How did you keep me from being killed? Magic?"

"Hardly. That takes energy and I'm rather tired after searching the last several weeks for my poem. I used a wet rag to wash away the chalk markings on your door. I'll support you down the corridor. Can you walk on your own? We'll move away from the guard station. They'll be back soon. And before you ask, I'm Thiago."

She caught pride in his tone as if she should know the name or, if she didn't know it now, she'd soon learn of his fame. He didn't sound modest.

"Why did you set me loose?" she asked.

"Because you had my poem until recently and I think you can help me get it—and the map. I don't know this world well, but I need to understand how things work here to locate my poem."

"Besides gratitude, why should I help you?"

"Gratitude isn't good enough?" Lubna heard sardonic humor in his voice. "Then how about this, because you want your position as court librarian back and knowing who's after my poem also tells you who's behind getting you executed sans trial."

"Let me out, too." A man's voice came through the door of her neighboring cell.

Despite his urgency, Lubna saw the jinn stop outside the cell door.

"You'll never get out without me," the man in the cell said weakly. "The place is a maze."

"We'll release this bastard if I can do it quickly," the jinn told Lubna. "Sometimes screams are answered, not often. I couldn't get someone out of a cage recently, so I'll do my bit today. If anybody's keeping score, maybe my good deed will count." Then he added, "Probably not."

"Cynical?" Lubna asked.

"Sure. You should be, too. You did nothing wrong, but you'd have been strangled if I hadn't shown up. Also, if we believe him, there's a practical reason for freeing him: He may know the way out better than me. I had a hell of a time finding you. This place *is* a maze."

Holding the metal key chain wrapped in a thick cloth, he struggled to jam a succession of keys into the lock. Despite the cloth's protection, Thiago handled the keys as if they were a white-hot fireplace poker.

"I'm not good with iron," he snarled. Again Lubna heard a stream of vulgarity describing odd combinations of human and demonic anatomy. Though she'd read extensively, the librarian was unfamiliar with the acts Thiago described.

"There we go; finally the right one." He wrenched the door open and threw the key chain far down the hall. "Gods, it feels good to be rid of that."

"How'd you get them?" Lubna asked. "A spell?"

"I go for simple solutions when I can. Magic isn't so simple. Wine, I plied the jailers with wine, stronger than they're used to. Wine opens more cells than battering rams—or spells. Help him out into the hall, will you? Yes, he's smelly; so are you. I'll grab his other arm and I'll carry the lamp, too."

"It's Ahmad," she said.

"You know him?"

"He's a court official, doing what, I don't know. He's everywhere in court except my library and he's got everyone's ear including the vizier's. He's interested in my poem."

"It appears everyone is," the jinn said. "And it's *my* poem, not yours."

Together, they dragged the weak prisoner down the narrow corridor as fast as they could, finally meeting a larger hallway. This one was better lit with a regular series of torches in wall sockets.

Behind them shouts erupted.

"That would be your jailers, who aren't fond of chalk, discovering that you're gone and so is this Ahmad fellow. They'll be faster than us. What we need now is a distraction—"

A howl reverberated throughout the dungeon. The stone halls amplified this primeval, bestial sound. The prison's other sounds, sobbing, curses, banging on metal bars, ceased for an instant. Something was loose in the dungeon.

"Very timely is my new friend Bradan and his wolf," Thiago said. "Though the animal won't tolerate me."

"Bradan from court?" Lubna gasped. Everything moved fast in a kaleidoscopic whirl.

"The same," Thiago said. "Besides me, you've got at least one ally here. Interesting fellow. When he realized that you were in the dungeon and I intended to spring you, he decided to help. He'd heard courtiers whispering about how the arrogant Lubna had finally been brought low and which part of the dungeon they were holding you in. Bradan's a good man to have at your side in a tight situation. I wish he'd join my Fire Horde, but his wolf would object at consorting with jinn. I think we go through this arch here and then down the alley."

The wolf let out a second unearthly howl. Sounds of alarm resounded throughout the prison.

The man they carried wasn't that big, but he felt muscular and heavy, and hard to drag. However, she sensed that he was recovering and beginning to move under his own power.

"Not the alley," he mumbled. "Right back to the guard station if you go that way. Instead, up these stairs—careful, part of the steps are missing—and across the courtyard."

The three of them edged up a long flight of stairs to emerge into a courtyard surrounded by stables and palace kitchens. Lubna and the man closed their eyes at the sudden assault by the noontime sun. However, Thiago didn't react to the brilliant light after the dim underworld they'd just left.

"They won't see us," Ahmad said. "Duck into the cooking quarters here."

Lubna was surprised to note that he was familiar with the palace's more obscure corners. She'd never seen the kitchens before and only vaguely knew that they existed because she dined well. She smelled the meal preparation and felt famished and parched. She'd just thrown up her last solid meal and no one had bothered to feed her or provide water while she'd been in the cell, probably because they intended to execute her quickly.

"Where's the nearest gate out of the palace into Córdoba's streets?" Thiago asked as the three of them huddled behind a pile of flour sacks. "We can lose ourselves among the city's shop stalls."

Just beyond them, cooks and servants made the midday meal, but they'd stopped in their tracks listening for the atavistic howls coming up from the dungeon below. Several of them began running for the far gate across the courtyard as a trio of palace soldiers moving in the opposite direction pushed through them and headed down the steps into the prison. None of the soldiers looked happy at having to confront whatever demon was loose.

"Use the gate the cooks are running through," Lubna said. "We look like dirty servants ourselves and maybe no one will recognize us as escapees in this crowd."

Ahmad had recovered unexpected energy or he was motivated by not wanting to meet the executioner.

"Let's run for the gate now," he whispered. "It's unguarded at the moment. Can you go faster?"

"Oh, I can fly," the jinn said. "But that leaves you two in a bad way."

Thiago froze as if he'd revealed too much.

Lubna thought she'd misheard. "What?"

Ahmad looked oddly at the jinn, too.

"I misspoke," Thiago said, sprinting toward the gate.

The flood of panicked servants and kitchen staff became a stampede and the three allowed themselves to be carried along with the crowd out of the palace. No soldiers tried to stop them or even noticed them amid the press.

Outside the palace walls, they separated from the kitchen servants milling about, uncertain whether the threat inside the palace was real. A marketplace packed with shoppers and stalls crowded up against the palace walls. A guard captain shouted for them to get back to work. However, Lubna, Thiago, and Ahmad mixed in with the crowd and worked to distance themselves from the gate as they wandered into the crowded souk.

The librarian stared about her at the bustle and color. She rarely left the library's confines excepting court appearances, and when she left the palace, she was always accompanied by several servants who mediated her interactions with Córdoba's citizens. Though she could value a rare book accurately and drive a hard bargain to gain it, she didn't know what a fair price was for a pomegranate or a handful of cashews. Today, she had no silver for them anyway. It wouldn't do her any good to escape the headsman, but die of starvation.

Thiago seemed equally intrigued by the novelty of the souk. He sniffed deeply.

"Amazing spices," he said. "There are ten different languages spoken here and hundreds of colors. Every sense is engaged, a little like a portal crossing."

"Where and what is this portal?" Ahmad asked, looking narrowly at the jinn.

"I forgot myself—just rambling. It's been an exhausting week."

"I haven't thanked you for saving me from the executioner," Ahmad said. "Who are you?"

"An outlaw occasionally and a poet always," Thiago said. His tone was flippant, but again Lubna noticed vanity in his tone. "And you?"

"Ahmad, lately an honored member of the caliph's court, but I made the wrong enemies and had worse luck with my friends—or people I thought were friends. I never knew who I offended to end up in the dungeon, maybe Matias."

He turned to Lubna. It was the first time he'd addressed her directly. Was it because she was a woman or the librarian, a position of little importance in the palace's hierarchy of functions? Probably both; she was used to it.

"We were neighbors in the cells," Ahmad said. "And both of us almost enjoyed the caresses of the executioner's silk rope around our necks. I recognize you as the custodian of the caliph's collection of written matter. I know a bit about such matters. I wouldn't have thought that was a dangerous occupation."

"Nor did I," the librarian said. "Circumstances changed."

She had to restrain herself from lunging at a table piled high with fruit.

"We can talk about Córdoba's politics in a bit. Can we eat now? I have no silver. Do you, Ahmad?"

He shook his head. "They don't tend to give prisoners much to spend," he said dryly.

"I don't know the first thing about food markets," Thiago said. "But I can pay what they ask."

He pushed through the press of shoppers before the fruit stand and addressed the shopkeeper.

"What will this buy?"

The jinn rummaged through a deep pocket in his robe. "Ah, good, I haven't lost them." He pulled forth a large emerald and held it in his open palm over the fruit before the merchant.

The shopkeeper stopped for a moment looking at the deep-green gem glittering in the sunlight. Other shoppers realized what Thiago showed the merchant and stopped talking to gawk at the emerald. The crowd around the drama grew quickly and pressed in on Thiago, Lubna, and Ahmad.

"It's a fake," the shopkeeper finally said. "I won't give you one cashew for it."

"Someone in the marketplace deals in jewels?" Thiago asked. "Bring them over to assess it."

"We'll make ourselves known to all of Córdoba including the caliph's court," Lubna hissed. "Put it away. Be discreet. Don't you know a thing about people?"

"Only a little," Thiago admitted. "I come to your world when mine becomes unbearable. When I'm here, I spend most of my time in deserts not marketplaces."

Fleetingly Lubna marveled that she was talking to someone who claimed to be a jinn who could fly. She didn't know whether to believe him other than he had the damnedest habit of arriving in spots that a mortal shouldn't be able to access—the palace library late last night past hundreds of the caliph's guards and the dungeon today through an army of jailers and executioners. Casually pulling huge emeralds from his robe also made his assertions more believable. It made him conspicuous, too.

"Let's leave," Lubna said. "I can go hungry and thirsty a little longer." She backed away from the fruit stand pushing spectators out of the way.

"Quietly mix in with the crowd if we still can," Ahmad said. "Displaying your emeralds will attract the caliph's guards and gangs of thieves."

The three of them worked through the press. Several passersby shouted questions at Thiago wondering where he'd stolen the gems from, maybe the palace treasury.

Ahmad knew the city well and led them away from the market. Eventually, after wandering through a dozen neighborhoods, doubling back on their path several times, and doing everything else they could think of to throw off any pursuit, they found a quiet square situated in a prosperous residential area far away from the souk and palace. The three sat down with their backs against a bubbling fountain in the shade of olive trees. It was a miniature park. Occasionally, a hot breeze sprayed cascading water beyond the fountain's basin, leaving a rainbow halo that evaporated almost as soon as it hit the flagstones.

Statues of Roman equestrians were positioned around the square. The soldiers and Caesars looked muscular and permanent on their prancing stallions. Lubna wondered if the caliph's city planners had done this to convey a sense of continuity between the Andalusian caliphate and past empires that once ruled the Iberian Peninsula. All the current elegance and glory would revert to dust soon enough, but she hoped the collection of rare books she'd laboriously assembled would somehow be preserved. However, it was hard to be optimistic in a violent, disordered era.

"We might do better by splitting up and going our separate ways," Ahmad said. "But you've brought me luck so far. May I stay with you while we're in Córdoba?"

"Let's hope our luck holds," Thiago said. He reached into a pocket and pulled forth a handful of dates and tossed them to the librarian and Ahmad. Oranges followed.

"A little confusion goes a long way," the jinn said. "We'll call this our well-deserved meal, not up to your palace's standards, but fresh from the market."

He nibbled at a date.

Evening came and a call to prayer emanated from a small mosque across the square. City attendants strolled about lighting the oil in streetlamps with candles atop long wooden poles. The lamps' illumination gradually replaced sunlight, and shadows colonized the flagstones. Nightfall cooled the square only slightly from afternoon temperatures, and a hot moon rose to add wan, white light to the lamps' glow.

Ahmad dozed slumped against the fountain amid a pile of date pits and orange peels. Lubna wanted a nap herself, but instead moved closer to Thiago. She'd been ripped from her scholar's existence and pushed into a world of jinn and executioners where no one's motives were clear including Thiago's. She had questions about him, his poem, and their survival.

"Do you have faith in any gods?" she asked.

"When things go my way, I believe," the jinn replied. "When things don't, I curse and refuse faith. No one notices either way."

He stretched long legs out before him.

"I believe in poetry," he said.

"Who was it about?" Lubna asked. "The poem?"

"Someone I loved. I wish I had wine. I'd feel less silly talking about my verses if I were drunk."

"You're bitter."

"A little," he said acidly.

"She's a jinn like you?"

"She's an ifrit. I have a soul. She doesn't."

"That matters?" Lubna asked.

"Mostly, no. Except that I'm bound by more rules than she is."

"This ifrit, she's a demon?" Lubna asked.

Thiago nodded.

"Not someone to cross," Lubna said.

"Not someone to love," he said.

Night had fallen and streetlamps were now the only light besides the moon. The librarian looked at boulevards radiating off the square into the neighborhoods. The lamps illuminated the broad boulevards like golden spokes centered about the hub where she reclined, the center of a little universe. Through open windows, she heard soft conversations and occasionally children's shouts as the palace city fed itself behind thick, white-washed walls and drowsed getting ready to sleep in the heat. Smells of Arab and Spanish foods blended harmoniously. Lubna desperately wanted to return to her former life in the palace and a cup of wine, though now that she roamed the city—however unwillingly—she realized how confining the library had been and how circumscribed her life was.

"You're a demon?" she asked.

"I've toned it down since visiting your world."

"I thought jinns were ugly," Lubna said. "You're presentable enough."

"Thanks," Thiago said dryly, but he seemed genuinely flattered by her compliment. "If you want ugly, I can be ugly, animal features, horns, bad skin, goat's ears, a tail. Or I can take on a green aura. But I'm trying to fit in to find my poem. Besides, I like this world. Why look like a monster in it?"

"What does the ifrit look like?" she asked. "A monster?"

"Only beneath the surface. On the outside, she's the prettiest, coldest dream you've ever had. She's after my poem."

"I thought your rhymes were exquisite," Lubna said. "Does she want it as a memory of what once was between you two?"

Thiago laughed heartily. "Nothing was between us as far as she's concerned. It was just my puppy love for her. So, the verse's literary qualities aren't important. She's interested in it because it's a map as well as a poem. It's a map *and* a poem. They talk to each other. The map makes no sense without reading the poem for clues. I crafted it that way."

"You can find this poem-map?" she asked.

"In a general sort of way. I put raw emotion into the poem when I created it, so there's a connection between me and it."

"Where does the map lead?"

"To all the wealth in the world."

"But that's in my library," Lubna protested.

"What a sweet sentiment! You have the world's learning. I have its wealth, Sheba's Treasure—if we can find it before other entities get it. I've lost count of how many competitors I have, but the ifrit is one of them. And you say this Ahmad may be chasing it, too?"

The jinn looked at their sleeping companion.

"Separating ourselves from him would be smart," the jinn said. "But he knows Córdoba very well, better than either of us. For the moment, let it be, but we'll lose him when a chance comes."

"I know roughly where I buried Sheba's Treasure," he picked up his train of thought. "Though not precisely. That's where the map comes in. I could chastise myself for hiding it too well. I could chastise myself for stealing it in the first place."

"Your ifrit has been close to the poem already." Lubna described the woman she'd heard of from Matias.

"That's her when she's in human form," the jinn agreed.

"She tracked the poem and map to my library?"

"Unlike me, she has no affinity for them since she didn't create them, but it doesn't matter. She can follow me and I'm after the poem and map, so I'll lead her to them unless I'm clever and evasive. It's been just beyond her reach across half the world from desert nomads to Baghdad, then across the sea to Córdoba."

"She has a name?" the librarian asked.

"In her world, no. She doesn't need one to live and communicate with other ifrit and jinn. I don't either, for that matter. We're known by everyone who needs to recognize us. I can sense other jinn and ifrits well before I see them and I know exactly who they are. That doesn't work in this world. Here, I'm just like you or other humans; unless I see or hear you, I don't know who you are. However, the ifrit can sense other supernatural beings—jinn, ifrits, whatever from a distance—even in this world. She's different that way."

"She can follow you?"

Thiago nodded. "Different rules for her."

"What's she called when she visits the human world?" Lubna asked.

"Call her Lila," Thiago said. The librarian thought that Thiago worked to control his emotion. "That's what she styles herself when she deals with humans. Or call her nothing at all. She's a demon, so she doesn't deserve to be identified in your world or mine."

"Lila," she said. "That means 'dark beauty' or 'woman of the night.'"

"That's her," the jinn said.

"You seem happy enough with your name," Lubna said.

"I do like Thiago," he agreed.

"It's Spanish," Lubna said. "I expected something from some far-off demon world."

"It's a human name, but then these days I'm spending more time in your world than my own. It's a curious rule that I can't explain, but jinn and other demons need names on the human side of the portal to identify themselves to each other let alone to humans. My group of warriors had a hilarious time assigning themselves names when we set up our ambush. All they could think of was vulgarities until I told them to behave. Then they came up with rather pretty names using local culture for inspiration. Most of the time, they forget their names anyway unless I remind them. For me, it wasn't a chore. Having a name makes your folk less likely to wonder at who I really am, so I picked something familiar to locals like you."

Lubna caught the jinn's condescending tone.

"I've made enemies on the other side, and I may be stuck here for a while so I'll be Thiago for a while—though there is someone I urgently need to free from a worse dungeon than the one you just left. I've also troubled myself to learn several of your languages—Arabic, Aramaic, some Norse, a bit of Latin, and the Spanish and Frankish tongues—to get along here."

"I know those tongues, too," she said, not to be outdone by this strange being.

"Your world has too many languages," he said. "A veritable Tower of Babel. No wonder you have so many wars. In my world, we all speak the same language whatever our tribe. Names and languages aside, we have business: Can you get me to Matias? He's the last person you know who had my scroll.

We'd have to get back into the palace unless he's already fled the city with it."

Lubna tensed at risking summary execution again. Her instinct was to flee beyond Córdoba, maybe beyond Andalusia, not reenter the palace. However, it was *her* library, *her* collection of scrolls and books, and she hated the thought of its stewardship passing to someone else or, worse, having the collection scattered or destroyed. She needed to clear her name and that meant finding the peculiar poem and understanding its even more peculiar author.

"Matias refused to let me see the caliph or the vizier last night," she said. "I was scheduled for a speedy death. That argues that he and whoever sponsored him wanted me gone without the caliph or vizier knowing about it."

"Sheba's Treasure would motivate anyone to do anything," the jinn said. "Including people you thought were friends and valued your learning."

"I'm just a humble slave," she said. "I take nothing for granted, but one thing I'm sure of is Matias. He wants me dead. I don't know whether he's working on his own behalf, or for some court faction, or an outside power, maybe the Abbasids, or one of the Christian kingdoms in the north. He's got his own band of bodyguards," she said. "They aren't natural."

Lubna described the soldiers who'd invaded her office last night.

"They're from my world," Thiago said. "The king sent them. If Matias thinks they're under his orders, he'll be in for a shock."

"Your king wants to steal the treasure, too?"

"He's not the thief. I'm the thief. He wants it back."

Lubna digested this. "So, you're a poet and an outlaw."

"That was romantic until just recently," he said. "He's king of the jinn and ifrit and other tribes of demons too numerous to count. Supposedly he's descended from the king of Judea. His ancestors may have been worthy and blessed, but he's a prick. Sheba gave his family all that treasure two thousand years ago and it's been passed down over the generations to this unworthy bastard."

"He doesn't rule you, it seems."

"He doesn't rule me," the jinn agreed.

"Does he control Lila?"

"I don't know. She'll play whatever game gets her the treasure. She likely fancies herself the next Queen of Sheba. Regardless, I need my poem back. I can't walk through walls, but I can fly both of us over them. If you can tell me where Matias's room is, let's wake him up."

"He won't be in his chambers," Lubna said. "It's too early. He'll be out whoring and drinking with other young courtiers. They don't hide their vices from the rest of the court."

"Everyone loves a party," the jinn said. "So we wait and sleep for several hours. This is a quiet neighborhood and no one's noticed us yet. We'll enter the palace and search out his room when he's sure to be back."

The librarian could only agree. She hadn't slept in a day and life had become a hellish adventure that had drained her dry. Lubna wondered if blood still flowed within her. She took comfort from routine and schedule. These were conducive to her intellectual pursuits and exploring the works in the library. They told her everything she needed or wanted to know; she could live in her mind and discover the world at a safe remove. Even love and erotic attraction seemed something better read about than experienced firsthand. The fountain's stonework felt like a pillow and she slept.

Hours later, when she awoke, the fountain still flowed, but children's voices had stilled and savory food smells lingered only as an afterthought. The streetlamps still shone, but the nearby manor houses were dark. The moon had shifted. They were deeper into night. Lubna looked about. Ahmad was gone. Instinctively, she searched her robe for anything missing, but then realized she had nothing to steal anyway. Well, good riddance. He'd led them unerringly out of the dungeon and through Córdoba's streets. However, his motives were uncertain and suspect. Thiago had done a commendable thing in freeing him, but if she never saw him again, that was all to the good.

"He's left," the jinn said. "He took nothing. I checked."

Thiago had apparently just awakened, too. Or maybe he hadn't slept. Lubna wasn't sure what mortal rules applied to jinn. He looked rested and alert.

"Do jinn sleep?" she asked.

"Do jinn sleep or does *this* jinn sleep?"

"Do you sleep?"

"I sleep when I can't help it. I don't like the nightmares. Those started recently."

"I think Ahmad didn't sleep much, either," Lubna said. "He feigned slumber and listened while we talked earlier."

"Then he'll know we're after Matias," Thiago said. "As you say, he may be yet another player after the map. I'm not sure if he's friend, foe, or something in between. He seems capable of fending for himself. For us, it's best to keep things simple in this drama. So we enter the palace."

"I fly, too?" Lubna asked unhappily. "Over the ramparts?"

"It's fairly safe," the jinn said. "It's tiring with two of us, but I've done it before, and it's just a short hop. Here, grab my hand. And don't let go," he added dryly. "That would be bad."

He didn't wait for her acquiescence. In an instant, the fountain, square, and Córdoba dropped away beneath them. Panic gripped Lubna. They flew higher than birds and, with a god's-eye view, she saw the nighttime city's streetlamps outlining boulevards through neighborhoods. She saw fires too where the city's residents had escaped their cooking quarter's stifling heat to prepare evening meals outside. The diners were now asleep and the fires had been left to gutter. With her in tow, Thiago made for a huge, well-lit structure before them with torches everywhere flaming beneath arches and shining through windows. The palace stayed awake all night and the structure glowed against the dark city and surrounding hills.

"Where does Matias live?" the jinn shouted to her over the air movement.

"Over there." Lubna pointed. "Courtiers live in that complex next to the visitor's hall." She'd say anything to get them back on the ground.

Thiago and Lubna alighted deftly in an open-air courtyard surrounded by rooms with no more impact than if they'd stepped off a low stool.

"Now what?" Lubna asked. She took a deep breath and reached down to touch the flagstones, confirming that they really were back on solid ground.

She looked about. She'd lived in the caliph's palace for years, but there were whole sections only vaguely familiar to her including the quarters where the caliph's numerous courtiers lived.

"There must be two dozen rooms here. I've no idea which one Matias is in. He's probably back by now, but that doesn't help us. We can't pound on every door."

"Then we wait out of sight where we can watch the rooms," the jinn said. "He'll appear sooner or later. If he drinks, he pees and I see chamber pots outside doors." He settled himself behind a lemon tree. Dozens of the fruit trees had been artfully arranged about the courtyard.

"You may need this later." He pulled a knife from his cloak and passed it over to her. She noticed that he was careful to present it to her so she could grasp it by the handle without cutting herself on the blue steel blade.

"For me?" she asked, stunned.

"Everyone is armed in my world," he said. "Your world isn't any safer."

By accepting the knife she sensed that she had changed and not for the better. It was a night for new endeavors. Uncertainly, she hefted it. This was a proper weapon with a long blade honed to razor sharpness. It was heavy but well balanced. She'd never touched anything pointed beyond what she needed to feed herself. Others handled weapons.

"How will I use it?"

"It's not that hard. Think of it as an extension of your arm. Don't bother with slashing someone. That kind of wound isn't necessarily fatal. Also, it exposes you to counterattack. Keep it simple and push it into your opponent's guts. That's what the point is for."

Feeling less inclined than ever to hold the weapon, Lubna wondered where to put it. There was really no place to conceal the knife on herself so she sat down next to the jinn and placed it in her lap.

She also wondered what sort of world the jinn came from that he could so casually explain how to kill with a dagger. Then again, was his world that different from Córdoba?

"I thought you didn't do iron," she said.

"The knife is steel. I'm fine with steel. Iron and steel, similar, but not identical. Yes, I know, another silly rule for demons, but I have to abide by them."

"Won't you need a weapon for yourself?" she asked.

Thiago pulled a second dagger out of his cloak.

"I keep spares. Besides, I'm a jinn. Among other things, I can become fire or a whirlwind or an animal when it suits me. That makes me reasonably formidable."

Then he pulled an orange out of his bottomless cloak. "Have another piece of fruit. I kept several from the market. Use the knife to cut it open. That shouldn't be too difficult."

CHAPTER 8

Among the Lemon Trees

"That's our man?" the jinn asked.

"No, he's another minister, not Matias," Lubna said. "He's more senior in the pecking order and I believe he reports directly to the vizier. His name is Salman."

"Everyone needs a name in your world," the jinn said.

They hid on the opposite side of the courtyard from where the minister knocked on a door. It was a peremptory knock. The caller wore officious authority as easily as his silver-embroidered kaftan. He reminded Thiago of the king's officials from his home world and he disliked him for that.

He and Lubna had concealed themselves behind lemon trees planted around the courtyard clustering near the columns where they could get sun during daytime. A gentle nighttime breeze wafted through the leaves and fruit. A few lemons had fallen to the ground. Tonight, the courtyard was citrus-scented and shadowed with its flagstones bleached white by moonlight. A trio of bats fluttered through the branches and columns and out into the night. Thiago reflected that if the scene before him wasn't as surreally sublime as the gardens in his family's aristocratic property in the kingdom of the jinn, the interior citrus grove was at least meditative and pretty. And sinister.

There was no response to Salman's knocking so the man pounded insistently. Thiago watched as he twisted the door handle and entered holding a candle high for illumination and stepping over something on the room's threshold. He didn't stay long and Thiago saw him urgently back out of the room into the middle of the courtyard but never take his eyes off the open door until he stepped on a lemon and sprawled onto the flagstones, losing the candle in the fall. He sprang to his feet, whirled, and raced away in a flurry of multicolored robes down the corridor he'd arrived from. His slippers made almost no noise. He'd entered the courtyard an influential figure in the caliph's court and departed a timorous boy.

"We'll look," Thiago said. "I've no idea whether that's Matias's room, but something badly shocked your minister and drama follows my map, so it could be there. Matias may be dead."

"Small loss," the librarian said. "The court is well rid of him."

"He visited you in your library with a contingent of guards, probably ifrit from my king. They may not have been his henchmen as much as his murderers once he'd obtained the map. Or someone else may have killed him. Be ready for the worst."

"If he's not dead already, I have a knife. Is killing someone hard?"

"You might get the chance to find out," the jinn said.

He looked at the small, determined woman next to him radiating barely contained rage. How far would she go to exact vengeance on Matias?

"Killing is easy once you get used to it. Don't get used to it," he said. "Don't take up outlawing, either. Stick with scrolls and books."

"I could tell you the same: stick with poetry rather than stealing a king's treasure."

"Point taken," he said.

As the jinn and librarian left the concealment of the columns and trees, another figure materialized in the courtyard opposite them and moved in on the open door. Unlike the minister, this individual didn't have the confidence of authority and crept toward the room hugging the wall. He looked carefully about the courtyard, but didn't see the jinn or librarian in the shadows.

"That's Ahmad," Lubna said softly to the jinn.

"The man is more than he seems," Thiago whispered. "How did he get here? If there was any doubt, that confirms that he's after my poem, too."

"Half of Córdoba chases it," the librarian said.

"We'll confront him." He glanced at Lubna. "For his benefit, I'm just one more interested party in the poem. Don't breathe a word about what I can do. Having unsuspected abilities may be helpful later. In the meantime, I don't want half of Córdoba chasing me as a demon."

"Buying fruit in the market with emeralds made you pretty conspicuous."

"It happens all the time where I'm from," the jinn said. "I'm getting used to your world's customs."

Ahmad moved toward the door unaware that he was observed. He had no candle, but moonlight hit the courtyard at an angle that partially lit the open room. Thiago saw that Ahmad nerved himself before edging into the unlit room. Like the minister, he glanced down at something in the doorway, but ignored it and entered. After a moment, he backed out. However, unlike the minister, he didn't flee, but stood centered in the courtyard apparently deep in thought.

"You look like a man who knows he's in over his head," the jinn said. "What's in there?"

He'd moved quietly until he stood behind Ahmad. The man jumped and blurted a curse.

Thiago placed a hand on Ahmad's shoulder. He was slight, but the jinn felt wiry muscle under his cloak.

"Quiet or we'll have the whole palace on our ears and you'll be back in the dungeon," Thiago said.

"The fellow Matias is dead, throat cut," Ahmad said. He'd turned to face the jinn and pointed toward the dark doorway. "I don't know what happened in there. I do know he's dead."

Keeping his hand on the man, Thiago asked, "How did you get here? We all slept at the fountain. When we woke up, you were gone."

"I could ask you the same. How did you enter a well-guarded palace with an easily recognized escapee from the caliph's dungeon?" Ahmad nodded at Lubna standing beside the jinn.

Thiago tightened his grip on Ahmad's shoulder and flashed his dagger.

"You answer first," the jinn said.

"There's a sally port," Ahmad said. "That's how I got in. Did you use it, too? They need to conceal it more cleverly or guard it better. I've been a part of the caliph's court for years so I knew of it from exploring the further reaches of Abd-al-Rahman's palace, may God bless his name. It's not at all obscure. Everyone in court must know about it and I've seen all manner of 'guests' smuggled in through that entrance for high officials' nighttime pleasure, including farm animals. Pardon my coarse descriptions, madam." Ahmad again nodded at the librarian.

Then he noted, "Not a good night for a pretty woman to be out and about. Surely there are more appropriate places to be."

"But I'm armed." Lubna held up her dagger, twisting it so that moonlight flashed on its blade.

Thiago smiled to himself. Having a knife had changed her.

"And I can't go back to my library," she continued. "Until I find out who had me imprisoned, my best choice is to be out and about."

Ahmad shrugged. "I think what you're after isn't there anymore."

"What are we after?" Thiago asked.

How much does he know? the jinn wondered. *Who does he represent? Is he an agent of the king or some human government that's caught wind of my poem and the treasure?*

"A map," Ahmad said. "There are apparently verses on the scroll, too. It connects to wealth beyond counting. How, I don't know."

"You're more than you let on," the jinn said. "Which means you keep secrets. I don't need that. You're good at appearing open, but hiding things. I freed you. You helped us navigate the dungeon and Córdoba's neighborhoods without blundering into a squad of the caliph's guards. We'll call that an even trade, but we part company now. Go in peace, but go."

"I usually work alone," Ahmad said. "That's served me well over the years, but this is more than I can manage on my own. It's to our mutual advantage to be partners."

"What are you trying to manage?" Lubna asked.

"Recover the poem-map, of course. The one you stole from Baghdad's House of Wisdom—"

"I did no such thing," the librarian said. "I paid honest silver for it, a lot of silver."

"Call it what you want, but you got something, this poem, that was taken without the knowledge or permission of the Abbasid caliph, long may he reign, who wants it back. And then we learned that it may be the key to endless wealth, so it's not a library curiosity any longer, but a tool for our survival.

"Word came to me that it was en route from Baghdad to Córdoba. Once it arrived here, I had instructions to follow the young scholar who sold it to you. It's quite an affront to have upstarts in Córdoba's library acquire something that took us considerable wealth to get. In fact, the whole Caliphate of Andalusia is an affront to us. For Baghdad, things are unsettled with threats on all sides—Turks, Persians, tribes from the steppes. It's all a cauldron waiting to boil. If the scroll leads to wealth, we'll use it to defend ourselves."

"You're a spy from Baghdad in Abd-al-Rahman's court," Lubna said. "I've seen you for years in Córdoba."

"I've been successful for years," Ahmad said.

"Yet you were imprisoned?" Thiago asked.

"I was successful until I wasn't," Ahmad said. "That's why I'm not hiding anything from you now. What's the point? If I survive, I'll go home to Baghdad where my family lives, may God smile on them. I got careless searching for this poem. There are many individuals after it. However, I was determined to get it first, as my caliph has placed a bounty on it—actually, I'll sell it to anyone who can beat his price."

"Loyal to a fault," the jinn said.

Ahmad missed the irony. "All this for some trivial verses, may the author rot in a cold hell."

Thiago murmured, "It's a good thing the poet isn't here to be offended."

"Who cares about the verses?" Ahmad said. "It's the directions to this supposed Sheba's Treasure that count—if it exists. Maybe it's a legend."

"Let's find out," the jinn said. "Into the room. For the time being, having a spy on our side who knows the obscure corners of the palace intimately may be to our advantage. Regardless, the minister that just ran off will be back with soldiers and none of us wants to be standing next to a body without a throat telling them what we're doing here at midnight."

The three of them slowly approached the open door. Lubna extended her dagger before her, holding it in both hands. Ahmad pulled a small ax from his robe. He'd somehow armed himself after his stay in the dungeon—a man not to underestimate, Thiago thought. He noticed that the ax had a serrated blade that looked like it could deliver a savage slice.

As they were about to cross the threshold, the jinn stopped in his tracks.

"Iron," he said. "Half the damned palace is made of it."

He stared down at a thin, rusted chain carefully stretched on the ground from one edge of the doorframe to the other. It looked like a viper.

"Who cares?" Ahmad said. "It's an odd piece of jewelry or some other curiosity that has nothing to do with the dead man."

Thiago glanced at the librarian and nodded ever so slightly. From his earlier experience unlocking her cell, he saw that she understood: Iron and jinns didn't mix. She reached down to pull it aside, but the jinn stopped her.

Fighting weakness and a strong urge to throw up, Thiago wrapped his headdress around his hand. He told himself that the chain was thin. Before he could think about it further, he grabbed the chain with his bundled hand and tossed it into the middle of the courtyard with a metallic jangle.

"Unusual effort for a trinket," Ahmad said.

Thiago ignored him. He was glad the librarian had been there to encourage him.

He pulled his dagger out.

The three of them looked across the threshold into the room. Aside from the open door, there were no windows or other openings. The moonlight backlit them, sending their three shadows boldly into the center of a sumptuous room. Several carpets covered the floor and incense still smoldered from holders. Silk cushions were haphazardly strewn about on cedar chests and chairs. Thiago, Lubna, and Ahmad's shadows made themselves at home and weren't repulsed by recent, violent death.

Matias's body lay on its back, sprawled on the bed, and seemed at ease amid the luxury in death as much as in life. One arm was positioned awkwardly underneath his torso with its hand out of sight. The other had been flung out toward the door as if importuning a visitor for assistance getting into bed. He'd returned from a riotously good time in Córdoba's brothels with his companions and wanted to enjoy a well-deserved rest. However, a bloody gap existed where his windpipe had been and there was a smear of dark red on the pristinely whitewashed walls. Thiago guessed that the courtier had used his dying breath to cough up a fountain of blood. Edging closer, Thiago noted an expression of rude surprise on the young courtier's face.

The jinn moved further into the room and sensed copper. He'd smelled it before when humans bled out. Matias hadn't been dead that long and the killer might still be near. Supernatural beings were different. Depending on their form when they met their end, he would smell fetid rot, charred wood, seawater, and caramel.

Matias's eyes were wide open. Thiago reached down and shut them. He didn't know if this was a custom here on the human side of the portal, but it seemed appropriate even for an utter pig meeting the most squalid of deaths.

Likely his killer had been a man; the iron chain, thin as it was, would have been proof against a jinn, ifrit, or some other imp from slaughtering the hapless Matias. Thiago flattered himself that he was the only supernatural entity who could have removed the barrier. There were demons from his side of the portal capable of smashing their way into this chamber through a wall to avoid the door's iron barrier, but that would have attracted the attention of the entire palace and, moreover, the chamber appeared to be intact. Nonetheless, the fact that Matias or someone had thought to create such a barrier meant that the courtier knew he was being stalked.

"We haven't long before the minister returns," the jinn said. "Whatever we can learn needs to be learned fast. Who came for him?"

"Lila knew that Matias had visited the library." Lubna murmured this into Thiago's ear.

But Ahmad's ears were excellent. "Who's Lila?"

"A library patron," Thiago said. "And someone not to meet. The scroll is nowhere obvious in the room. Let's search his body and his clothing. Help me roll him over so we can see what's in his hand under his stomach."

"Search a man's corpse?" Ahmad asked. "Don't ask a woman to do that."

"Who else?" the jinn asked. "In my country females do what males do, however repugnant—"

"What country is this?" Ahmad said with shock.

Don't be too revealing, Thiago warned himself.

"In a far-off country," he said. "With unusual customs."

While Thiago dissembled, Lubna ran her hands over Matias's body.

"Nothing," she said. "Except wine stains and still-wet blood."

Thiago pulled the corpse's arm from under his body. Crumpled in Matias's hand, he saw his poem and map. Gently, he extracted the scroll from the courtier's death grip.

"Half of the poem," the jinn said it quietly, but he felt like screaming. In one movement he launched himself at the wall and smashed his hand into it as hard as he could, sending a spider web of cracks in the plaster up the wall.

Ahmad and Lubna stared at him. Someone from a room several doors down called for quiet.

"That's pointless," the jinn said.

Boot clatter approached at the run.

"And that would be our minister returning with the caliph's guards," Thiago said.

Tenants in the rooms neighboring Matias's chamber had been roused by the commotion and shouted questions in the courtyard just beyond the open door.

"Ahmad, can you lead us to the sally port and then out of here?" Thiago demanded.

"Follow me," Ahmad said peering outside the room cautiously. "We've got a few more hours of night and this part of the palace isn't well lit."

They sprinted out of the death chamber. Behind them, shouts erupted. Matias had been found.

Ahmad was fleet and familiar with where they needed to go. Clearly, he had no intention of being caught and visiting the dungeon again. He opened up a gap between himself and the jinn and librarian and didn't look back.

"Fly us out of here," the librarian gasped. She slowed.

"If needed," the jinn said. He reached out to grab her hand. "But the minister and his soldiers are way behind us. And they don't know where we're going."

"We didn't get what we wanted," she said.

"Half," he said. "Better than nothing, but not enough. We'll get the other half. I can generally sense where it is."

"Generally," she said. "That's strong magic."

"Don't be cruel. It's the best I can do. At least, we can chase it."

"So—generally—where is it?"

"Leaving Córdoba, probably heading to the coast."

"If I'm slowing you, leave me," she said.

"Very altruistic," the jinn said. "But you helped me find Matias—what was left of him and half my map, so stay with me—if you want. I'm learning this world's rules. You can help. We can both be outlaws."

"Didn't you say that's a bad idea?"

"I did, but this isn't a normal time. I don't have any friends and you've got no home."

"You're offering to help me?" she said. "Is someone keeping score?"

"Now you're getting cynical," Thiago said.

CHAPTER 9

Troubled Seas

"That doesn't belong here," the jinn said.

He saw that the librarian looked about. They both stood on a raised, wooden platform at the rear of the little galley above its rowing benches and cargo hold. The crew went about their business, but waves hammered their vessel and the sailors shouted to one another over the noise.

Thiago pointed dead astern. "It's following us. The seas are rough—we're about to hit a storm—but you can see it there where it just surfaced."

They gripped the *Saint Boniface*'s wooden railing as the ship pitched downward into a trough between swells and then climbed the shoulder of the next mountainous wave, crested its summit and slid down the other side, only to repeat the process endlessly.

"Everything is gray, the water, the sky," Lubna said. "I'm seasick. What you saw, isn't it just waves—no, you're right, there's a flash of red. It's got black stripes. It's very big, as big as the ship. What is it? A dragon?"

"From my world," the jinn said. "Someone sent it from my world's oceans to here. It's everything bad you can imagine if you're in a small ship like ours. It doesn't breathe fire; it will simply crush the boat and eat us. They're always hungry."

"Is the *Saint Boniface* faster?" the librarian asked.

"Not at all."

The creature had a serpentine neck and a long spiny crest from snout to tail. Webbed, clawed feet alternately churned the water or folded themselves along its sides to streamline itself for efficient gliding. Despite its enormous size, it eased through the waves and spray nimbly, periodically sounding allowing them to see only a dim, shimmering, crimson shape tracking them beneath the gray-green water before it surfaced even nearer.

A sailor up in the rigging noticed the monster rapidly closing on them and called down to the captain and steersman handling the rudder. Uncertain what alarm the lookout yelled in the thunderous tumult, the captain and sailors crowded the ship's gunwales to look where Thiago pointed, back at the approaching creature. Then the captain bellowed orders, cupping his hands to project his voice. The rising wind ate many of his words, but desperate men understood enough to scramble onto the rowing benches below and run out oars and coordinate efforts to begin pulling the boat. However, the ship wasn't built for speed under perfect conditions and even oars pulled by panicked men hardly moved the boat through the heavy seas. Making matters worse, the jinn saw that the boat heeled over so far that, much of the time, one bank of oars or the other pulled at nothing but air. The ship's modest sails had been reefed as the winds picked up, and lowering them again to gain speed would risk dismasting the vessel.

The monster would overtake their clumsy tub and devour them all.

"You're magic," Lubna yelled over the tempest. "Can you fight it?"

"If only," the jinn shouted back. "I can't make it vanish. I can't distract it by turning to fire and harassing it. It's raining too hard. I'd be snuffed out like dunking a candle into a rain barrel. There are rules even with magic."

"Bend the rules."

"I'm supernatural, not superhuman," he said.

Thiago saw that she was both terrified at the monster's inexorable approach and disappointed at their powerlessness to escape.

The storm had turned into a cyclone, driving rain horizontally and chopping the tops off of waves to send the water smashing into the boat's wooden sides. The wind and waves tore aside canvas sheets battened into place to cover the lower deck and hold and shelter the crew and cargo from the weather. The jinn watched the sheets swirl away and vanish into the gray like windblown phantoms.

The scarlet monster surged forward untroubled by the tumultuous seas. It looked organic to the tempest and gained on them rapidly, now near enough so Thiago saw its green eyes staring into his.

"There is one thing I can try, don't know if it will work."

He heaved himself up onto the gunwale and dove over the side, but before hitting the waves, he transitioned into a whirlwind. In this form, his strength was determined by what surface he moved across. Over hot sands, he was a desert zephyr; over raging water, he evolved into a waterspout. Thiago felt the storm, cold insensate, mindless, exultant. He didn't challenge the cyclone; he became part of it, not really thinking or capable of complex thought, but aware and joyous. This was the most visceral of the forms he could take, more so than fire. His blood flowed as he rode through the sky, hell-for-leather; it was kill-ingly cold, but he was unstoppable.

He sensed that the storm stretched over the entire western portion of the Mediterranean from Africa's Berber Coast to Andalusia behind them to the land of the Franks in the north. Even becoming wild weather himself, a waterspout, a satellite to the bigger storm, Thiago couldn't alter by the smallest degree the cyclone's course. Instead, he could change the path of the little ship and push it out of the direct track of the storm's center to its periphery where the boat might—or might not—stand a chance of eventually making it to some safe harbor, assuming the monster didn't catch and consume the vessel first. It was part of the storm, too.

As a waterspout, the jinn nudged the *Saint Boniface* ever so gently forward and away from the beast and in a lateral direction to the cyclone's path. Finesse might just win the day. Detached, from a great height, he watched Lubna and the crew hang on for their lives as he pushed them in the direction he wanted. He was as much danger as savior since he generated rapid, violent sheering winds. He needed to be careful or he'd tear the boat to pieces.

He tired from the relentless effort, but he saw that the ship slewed away from the sea creature, eventually leaving it far behind and out of sight. He supposed it could stalk the ship and attack later, but even monsters became fatigued and it might give up.

Something had taken the effort to transport it from the Erythraean Sea, through a portal, and set it to pursuing them. That monumental effort could only have been conducted by the king. Maybe he'd decided not to bother letting Thiago find the treasure and instead gamble that Lila could somehow recover it.

In that case, Thiago was expendable and could be eaten by the beast.

He shifted back to human form and landed on the *Saint Boniface's* elevated stern deck in a gust of wind and rain. The exhausted crew didn't notice.

His first sensation was of smelling dirt mixed with brine. Shore wasn't so far off.

He sneezed.

"Better air ahead," a lookout shouted down at men draped over oars or sprawled on the deck. "Still rainy and very choppy, but we've outrun the worst of it and there's no monster to trouble us." He called aloud a prayer of thanks.

Sailors embraced one another and several kneeled on the deck thanking various saints. The captain walked unsteadily from his post at the *Saint Boniface's* stern where he'd helped the steersman wrestle with the rudder during the tempest. He grasped the lines leading up the main mast and wearily climbed up to where the lookout perched. Both men held on carefully to the sodden, slippery rope as the vessel pitched about. Together they stared around them. In the far distance, other vessels, storm-battered, began to move purposefully as they realized they were no longer in the cyclone's grip and they'd once again become masters of their courses.

"We're in the Ligurian Sea," the mariner called down to his crew. "Genoa ahead. We'll live. Make the ship right. She needed the help of her patron protector, Saint Boniface, today. We all felt shepherded on our course by a blessed wind driving us to safety. And the red monster is far behind us. Raise the main sail. The wind's dropped, so we won't lose the mast."

The captain wiped rain out of his face and continued to peer ahead at Genoa slowly coming into view through the haze. The lookout pointed something out to him and they conferred up in the rigging.

"I'll be damned," the captain said. "There's a longship ahead. And a dozen more further back. They're very far from home. Thank God we're not seeing that lot on the open water away from shore. They'd come after us like the fat duck that we are. I'll take my chances with a monster over Norsemen. One of their boats is headed into the port. I think it's trading, not raiding. That could change. They've got enough muscle in reserve if they want to sack the city."

Seamen, already beaten down by the cyclone and sights of a gigantic, otherworldly creature, crowded the ship's side to observe the Viking fleet on a parallel course ahead of them.

"Look sharp," the captain yelled at them. "They mean us no harm at the moment or we'd already be boarded and dead. Clean up the ship, and you can drink yourself senseless once we're ashore and tell your stories of this strange voyage to whatever women will listen to you in whatever taverns will serve a crew as pretty as you."

The sailors cheered weakly and resumed their nautical routines more aware than ever of their vocation's fragility.

Lubna dashed over to the railing to vomit over the side. None of the sailors laughed, and the most seasoned of them looked like they could also empty their stomachs into the sea at any moment.

Spent from his bruising effort to tear the boat away from the storm's grip, the jinn collapsed on a big coil of rope. It wasn't a conscious act; his legs simply gave out and the rope cushioned his fall to the deck. The hollow in the coil's center formed by the hawser's loops was the gentlest womb, secure from the still blowing wind, but not from introspection.

The cyclone was just the latest calamity. He'd brought this violent adventure on himself and, worse, he'd entangled family, friends, and innocents who knew nothing of the stakes at play. If stopping an invasion really had been his intention—and he had to think that it was one of his motivations—then stealing Sheba's Treasure might have been the only way to throw sand in the gears of his rapacious king's war machine. However, it would predictably goad the tyrant to level mountains and slaughter thousands to recover his riches.

He saw Jai's shade leaning against the railing next to the rope Thiago sat in. He knew the phantom wasn't there; his friend looked real enough, but sea spray periodically came over the gunwale and washed through him.

"This didn't turn out so well," Jai said.

He still wore the robe he'd died in, but, thankfully, it wasn't bloody. That would have made the sight of his friend unbearable. Thiago talked to a figment of his exhaustion, but he knew that Jai wouldn't go away unaddressed.

"I saved the ship."

"Congratulations," the shade said sardonically. "That wasn't what I meant."

"Yes, I stole for ignoble reasons," Thiago said. "Worse than that, they were stupid reasons, and my trust in Lila made it inevitable that we'd all be found out within hours of pillaging the treasure and I had no plan to deflect pursuit other than hiding the stuff under a pile of sand."

"Some strategist you are," Jai agreed. "And now you can't even find the pile of sand."

"Give me time," Thiago said.

"I could have done without an iron spear through my gut answering for your crime. I was the best friend that you ever had and strongest fighter in your troop. I felt invulnerable until I wasn't."

"You should have blamed me before the king."

"It wouldn't do to turn a mate in," Jai said. "It just wouldn't do. I couldn't have lived with myself."

They both laughed at the bad joke.

"He would have killed you anyway," the jinn said.

"That makes you feel better?" Jai asked.

"No."

"Good. It shouldn't."

Sailors moved about working to repair the ship. They gave Thiago a wide berth as he talked to himself sprawled in a coil of rope.

"What *will* make me feel better is wrecking his plans," Thiago said. "And spending his wealth, and running a sword through his chest on his own throne. Or incinerating him. That's fitting. I told him I was fire."

"What about the ifrit?" Jai asked.

"I haven't decided yet."

"Good luck with that. Just a thought: Iron was my end, but maybe it's your salvation."

"How?" Thiago asked. "How?"

But now, even he could see that he talked to no one.

CHAPTER 10

High Strategy and Low Company

"Why can't I awaken to good news?" asked the caliph, Abd-al-Rahman, may his name be much blessed. "Why wake me at all?"

His bed was expansive and full. He shared it with three women amid pillows and sheets heaped in disordered white waves about the four of them and spilling onto the marble floor. They'd played in an ocean of silk.

The caliph felt at once energized and spent from recent love-making and in no mood to be disturbed, but he'd long since learned that ruling his Caliphate of Córdoba in unsettled times was like breaking a stallion: Allow yourself to be distracted for a moment and you risked being thrown and trampled. So, he'd hear out his visitors.

The two officials stood awkwardly halfway between his bed and the room's entrance, caught between an urgent need for an official update and discreetly edging out of the room. They'd talked their way past the guard captain so it must be important. However, they were obviously uncomfortable in the presence of their ruler's recent intimacy.

As the most senior adviser present, the vizier stepped forward to speak. The caliph observed sardonically that he affected not to notice the three women in his bed. The man was a born diplomat and clever, but indecisive and a prude. Well, one worked with the tools at hand and tried to play to their strengths and exploit their faults, the caliph supposed.

"There's been a murder in the courtier's chambers," the vizier said.

A hot wind blew through tall windows lining two sides of his corner room. The gust came off distant and indistinct hills in the night and pushed aside sheer curtains, wafting them up to the high ceiling above the room's occupants before letting them flutter back down to flank the windows.

"I ordered the killing?" the caliph asked. He didn't think he'd needed anyone assassinated recently, but his memory wasn't what it had once been.

"Not to my knowledge, lord," the vizier responded.

"Do I know of the dead man?"

"I don't think so, lord. He performed a minor role in your court." The vizier conferred quietly with the second visitor, Salman. "It was Matias, lord. I believe he was a native-born Spaniard, Christian, ambitious, but not a great talent."

"The killer or killers?" the caliph asked.

"Have not been found—" the vizier began.

"They will be soon, lord," Salman jumped in. "Matias had been behaving strangely, so I visited his chamber earlier tonight to understand his circumstances. I discovered the body and promptly gathered available guards and searched the palace interior and surrounding grounds."

"Very resourceful," the caliph said. "Catch anyone? Ah, that's right. You haven't caught them yet, but you said you'd find them soon."

The vizier cut in, reasserting his preeminence over Salman. "There's more to this, lord, than a murder in your retinue."

"A murder in my retinue is more than enough. However, you're here to tell me that's not all?"

Abd-al-Rahman was angry already at the friction between his senior subordinates. It was all well and good that they competed for his attention—it made collusion against him less likely—but adjudicating intra-court disputes was a waste of his time and his mind drifted back to the three woman nestled against his body and one another.

"Your scribe and librarian, Lubna, has vanished," the vizier continued. "These issues may be connected, as both she and Matias apparently sought a mysterious map leading to riches beyond belief—Sheba's Treasure, no less."

Abd-al-Rahman sat upright in bed. This was important, after all. Regretfully, he gestured for the women to leave.

"We had fun, my dears," he said. "There will be other times."

One of the women ran a lingering finger over a scar from an old sword wound on his chest as she got off the caliph's bed. He liked how that felt.

"Save a little treasure for me," she said and then left with the other two.

The caliph eased himself out of bed and dressed unselfconsciously before his two visitors and waved away servants who materialized to help him clothe himself. He was short and well muscled despite his age. In his youth, he'd led troops into battle riding in the front ranks. The scars he bore were testament to a relentless drive in consolidating and expanding his domain.

"This business grows more worrisome by the moment," he addressed his vizier and minister. "I rather like Lubna. If she's gone missing, find her. And Sheba's Treasure, isn't it a legend?"

"Probably a legend," the vizier said.

"It may be real," Salman said.

"Well, which is it? Real or legend?" the caliph asked. "Who's got the map?"

Neither of his advisers volunteered anything. This was typical. They'd raise a burning issue to his attention and then not have any solutions, leaving him to sort through the mess and resolve the crisis. Amazing that he ruled almost all of Andalusia and was the dominant power in the western Mediterranean with this sort of dismal counsel. He planned to expand his reach into the Christian kingdoms in the north and perhaps establish a colony in Italy, but he would need more capable advisers to accomplish that.

He also needed more wealth than Córdoba had at hand. Wealth for ships to transport troops, wealth to hire mercenaries to supplement his own soldiers, wealth for weapons and supplies, and wealth to hire better advisers.

Endless wealth to fund endless ambition.

Sheba's Treasure, if it existed, might be the source of that wealth. He imagined himself as the scourge of the unbelievers entering Rome's walls at the head of a host. Well, why not?

However, tonight the task at hand was to see how much substance there was to the wild tale his vizier and Salman were plying him with. All roads led to this mysterious map.

"Lord, I'm not sure how to put this—" his vizier began.

"Put it plainly," Abd-al-Rahman snapped. "What's the worst that can happen? I could have you strangled."

The vizier's expression fell, but he carried on. "As recently as yesterday morning, we had both the librarian and the map in hand."

"But now . . ." the caliph coaxed, already guessing that there wouldn't be a happy ending to this story.

"But now," the vizier said, "the librarian has vanished from the dungeon—"

"Stop!" the caliph shouted. "Why was she in the dungeon? I didn't order her there."

"Lord, Matias placed her there."

"You just told me he's a minor player in my court of little talent. On whose authority did he act? Yours?"

The vizier looked shaken by his rage. "Actually, he forged your signature on a written order of imprisonment."

The caliph noted that Salman had subtly stepped back to let the vizier take the full brunt of the storm. Coward. He pounced on Salman.

"What about you? You've a senior adviser. So, advise me. You know better than the vizier? What happened?"

Visibly nerving himself to face an onslaught, Salman said, "I've talked to the dungeon guards and your executioner, the Sardinian—all a bit drunk, I should note. Matias convinced them that you wanted the librarian arrested for stealing something of great value."

"That would be this map?" Abd-al-Rahman demanded.

"That would be the map," Salman confirmed.

"You'll anticipate my next question," the caliph said. Did he have to wrest each morsel of information from the man?

"We don't know where the map is," Salman said. "Matias seized it from the librarian. He was seen with a scroll and a squad of guards. These guards didn't belong to any detachment authorized to patrol the palace."

"This keeps getting better," the caliph said. Irony drenched his words. What cretins he employed. "Matias, a minor functionary, searches for a map to a treasure beyond counting in my palace, imprisons my librarian, all the while leading his own private army of soldiers."

"Not an army, lord, just a detachment. He only led a dozen or so warriors. However, they were an odd-looking company, more demons than men."

Abd-al-Rahman shivered in mock fear. "I'll sleep with a sword under my pillow. Matias conducts his peculiar behavior unmolested by an entire palace full of my 'loyal' and 'fearless' minions. Have I got the basics right?"

His two advisers glanced at each other and nodded.

"There's more, I'm sure," the caliph said.

Salman likely wanted the caliph to shift focus back to the vizier, but seeing that the vizier was perfectly happy to keep the caliph's attention on him, he gamely plunged ahead. "Then Matias was murdered. His throat was ripped open. In fact, the wound was so severe that his head was separated from the rest of him."

"The killer took a commendably firm approach," the caliph said. "You'll guess my next question."

"There are many possible killers to choose from."

"Oh, good," the caliph said sarcastically. "Come, Salman, look me in the face as you tell this lurid story."

"The map was not on Matias's body," Salman said. "I checked."

If Salman expected approval from the caliph for his diligence, he didn't get it, so he continued.

"Another courtier, Ahmad, has also gone missing. Besides being a respected member of this court, he seems to have led a second life by cultivating connections to our Muslim and Christian rivals, perhaps including the pope."

"So, he's a spy?" the caliph asked.

"Not to put too fine a point on it, yes, he's a spy."

"And you did nothing?"

"We had him imprisoned," Salman said. "Until recently, none of this was apparent. The scramble for the map revealed a lot."

The caliph noted that now it was the vizier who looked anxious to duck blame by edging away from his colleague. Briefly, the caliph had a delightful vision of both of his senior advisers slowly roasting over hot coals on a spit. Well, that could be arranged.

"Vizier, you've been quiet recently," the caliph said. "You'll let your colleague take all the credit for this splendid display of governmental efficiency that would make the Caliphate of Córdoba the envy of our neighboring realms?"

"Lord, there is no disguising the missteps that led to this calamitous state of affairs. For that, all must accept blame."

"Including me?" Abd-al-Rahman asked gently.

"Assuredly not, lord, may your name be blessed endlessly."

"I'd gladly trade a few of those blessings for the map."

Unbidden, Salman resumed his account.

"Ahmad was known to associate with Matias, so it's possible Ahmad murdered his colleague and stole the map."

"This is the same Ahmad who you threw in my dungeon?" the caliph asked. "Just how did he murder Matias?"

"He seems to have escaped," Salman said. "The librarian is gone, too."

"Every time I think your story can't get more spectacularly idiotic, it does!" the caliph shouted. "Then what happened?"

"Two strangers have also been seen, one a tall man and the other a young woman in a gray cloak, so it's possible one or both of them killed Matias instead of Ahmad. I personally saw them fleeing from Matias's room and gave chase with palace guards. Probably Ahmad was with them, but I didn't get close enough to identify any of them. They used the sally port to leave the palace."

"The entrance that I keep demanding be better guarded or sealed up entirely?" the caliph asked. "The port whose sole purpose is to facilitate nighttime debauchery among my court officials?"

"Yes, that's the one." Salman appeared happy to confirm Abd-al-Rahman's insight.

Again, if he expected thanks, he was disappointed; the caliph was beyond rage at this point and simply motioned for Salman to proceed.

"The three made for Valencia and there separated, according to port officials, perhaps to confuse pursuit. Or they may have had a falling out. Both parties took separate ships to Genoa."

"I believe I know the answer already, but do we understand anything whatsoever about these two strangers who were able to evade walls, gates, and guards to make themselves at home in my palace?"

"Nothing, lord," Salman and the vizier answered in unison.

Abd-al-Rahman had a strong urge to chop both men into pieces with a saber. In his younger days, that was how he'd dealt with vexing problems, but he didn't have a sword handy in his bedroom.

"Another question: Just how did my librarian escape from the dungeon?" the caliph asked.

The vizier took this one. "The short answer is: She had help. She was scheduled for rapid execution on your supposed command—actually Matias's forged order—but the chalk markings on the cell door that identify who among your thousands of prisoners is to be executed at dawn were mysteriously wiped away. As this confusion was being straightened out, someone stole the keys to the cells—"

"Did mysterious strangers and drunken guards contribute to this?" snarled the caliph. "And chalk markings? Is that how life-or-death decisions are made in the dungeon?"

"Well," the vizier said. "Chalk markings have worked until now. If the wrong person was executed, so what? They were guilty of something even if not the crime they'd been accused of. And the mistake was usually soon discovered and the right person executed the next day."

"That's reasonable," the caliph said. "Though in this situation, it almost lost me my claim on Sheba's Treasure—and the services of a trusted librarian."

"Lord, there is one other aspect of this sorry mess which cannot be ignored: Whoever or whatever once possessed Sheba's Treasure may still be around and want to keep it for themselves. That owner may be supernatural, which explains the ease that their agents have had evading our best efforts."

"Oh, I don't think it takes demonic skill to explain the theft of my map. It sounds like most any collection of moderately smart children could have done it."

The caliph waved aside his advisers' protestations.

"If it exists at all, the treasure is mine by rights," he said. "The map belongs to me, so the treasure belongs to me. If there are competing claims, I'll crush them, natural or supernatural."

"Of course, lord," the vizier said.

"Spies, mystical beings, treasures, mysterious visitors, murders, and imperial dreams, this has the makings of an epic poem," Abd-al-Rahman said. "However, this is real and it speaks to incredible stupidity on the part of the people I depend on to help me rule the realm. I should have half the palace killed starting with you two. Maybe I still will, but I've learned over my long life that sometimes achieving the goal is worth more than executing the guilty. The goal is the map, my map. I'm sure that you both would have thought of this given time, but we don't have time, so I'll tell you what we'll do: Since the Sardinian or his lackeys succeeded in losing my map, we'll set him to recovering it. If he happens to stumble on my librarian, he should recover her, too. Any strangers, mysterious or otherwise, he can deal with summarily. He'll be motivated since I'll hold his family hostage. I could send a fleet of ships after the map, but I think a few men properly motivated may be speedier. The Sardinian can take along whoever he thinks will be helpful. They'll ride for the port of Valencia today and take ship to Genoa. They can commandeer whatever vessel is leaving soonest on my direct order. However, we won't rely completely on the Sardinian. We can't. There's too much at stake and nobody's loyalty is assured with so much gold at play, so we'll send other agents to Genoa and the coastal cities of Pisa, Amalfi, and the Papal States."

"That's brilliant plan, lord," the vizier said.

"Clever indeed," Salman echoed.

"Get out," the caliph said. "And send the women back in."

~

"Why send an executioner after a scroll?"

"I'm not a simple executioner. I'm a torturer, too." The Sardinian was clean shaven. The Genoese nobleman supposed that facial hair got in the way of his work.

"Handy if someone won't talk about the scroll," Tommaso, the nobleman said.

"You catch on fast," the Sardinian said. His voice was the deepest bass Tommaso had ever heard and sounded like it came out of a stone well.

Their second-floor room was little, bare, and out of the way, a place to meet and nothing more. Genoa was close-knit enough for people to notice, and the nobleman didn't want notice. Tommaso had enough greedy rivals from other families—and even within his own family.

There was no place to sit, so they both stood face to face. It was as much confrontation as negotiation. Whatever it was, the nobleman stood to make an enormous amount of silver if one of the several parties desperately interested in the scroll was willing to pay. Ahmad, the man he'd gotten the scroll from, seemed to have alerted all of Genoa that he had directions to Sheba's Treasure for the right price.

"We have business, then," Tommaso said. "About a poem and a map."

The Sardinian waved this aside. "I know what I'm looking for. I need to know how much you want for it. By rights, I should pay you nothing. The caliph, Abd-al-Rahman, long may he reign, had possession of it, or rather his librarian had possession of it, and I had possession of the librarian, but she escaped. Somehow."

This complex chain of custody baffled the nobleman.

"What's a librarian?"

"Someone who keeps scrolls."

"Ah, I see. A little like a scribe. It makes sense that a librarian would be entrusted with a poem and map. But somehow they lost it? Or you lost them? Somehow."

"You describe it badly," the Sardinian said.

The nobleman watched the executioner pull a silk scarf from his leather jerkin and begin twisting it. His hands and forearms were blunt and powerful. Except for his face, the man was as hairy as a gorilla, particularly his forearms, and had an apelike physique to match. Tommaso wished he'd brought along his retainers, but they were downstairs suspiciously facing off with the Sardinian's henchmen in a tense standoff while, upstairs, he and the executioner came to some agreement—or not. However, he wasn't helpless. He wore a sword and had a dagger for close-quarters work. He thought his reactions were good, too. It might come down to his speed against the Sardinian's animal strength. The room was too cramped to swing a sword, but his dagger would be appropriate. He hoped it didn't come to that.

"I meant no offense," the nobleman said. "We can both profit from this. I just wanted to understand what I've gotten into."

The executioner collected himself with effort and began again.

"I have not seen this scroll myself, but the caliph's librarian—" The Sardinian paused as if expecting more interrogation on this point, but the nobleman held his tongue. "The librarian had been brought down to the palace dungeon for me to exercise my persuasive skills on and understand the scroll's meaning."

The executioner wrapped the silk scarf around his fists and stretched it taut. The nobleman was amazed it didn't snap.

"A traitorous courtier named Matias," the Sardinian continued. "His name means nothing to us here today. He wrested the scroll from the librarian before she arrived in my dungeon, but he was murdered and the scroll disappeared from Córdoba. Somehow."

"I'm sorry, sir, but I must ask: That's the scroll which I hold here in Genoa? Whoever murdered this courtier fellow brought the scroll here to sell?"

"Who cares who murdered who? It's here and I'm going to get it," the Sardinian said quietly, ominously. "Somehow."

"You do know that what I've got is only a fragment? I'd say about half of it. And what I have is somewhat burned. Also, this fragment has attracted all manner of attention even in a backwater like Genoa. As to the man who brought the scroll, poem, map, whatever it is, to the city, he's dead, so there's no one left to torture. Ahmad was his name, in case you're interested."

"How did he die?" The nobleman thought the Sardinian looked genuinely unhappy at losing the opportunity to deploy his persuasive skills.

"I killed him. He *wasn't* stupid enough to treat with me alone, so he'd hired bodyguards to support his case. However, he *was* stupid enough not to vet them thoroughly; they were my men he hired. I run one of the biggest Genoese trading houses, so it's hard to avoid people that work for me. Anyway, his price was too high despite his wild stories about it being the key to finding Sheba's Treasure. And he only had half the map."

"You believe this treasure business?" the Sardinian asked.

"The only reason I dealt with him at all was that I'd heard independent rumors from my trading representative in Valencia corroborating that a fantastical treasure is indeed at play here."

"So, your price?"

"You'll need to outbid the pope. Oh, and there's a rather strange woman who's just arrived in Genoa from somewhere. She's interested, too. And a Norse longship is in the harbor. They're armed with every imaginable weapon, spears, axes, swords, and bows. The leaders of their war band also want to make an offer. They hint that they'll sack the city if they don't get the map. They brought just one ship into harbor so as not to give away their hand, but they've got a fleet offshore, or so the lighthouse keeper tells me. They promise to do worse than the Saracens did twenty years ago when they burned the city."

~

"All this work to track a half of a piece of burned scroll with a great many words and a pretty drawing at the bottom?" Orm Silvertooth asked.

"Not a drawing, a map," Halfdan said. "I've seen it."

The two men sat on a load of teak on the wharf off-loaded from their longship. The wood was wet from the recent storm, but both men rested comfortably on it. They'd already negotiated with several of Genoa's merchant houses who'd sent assessors by to value the lumber.

"Half a map, then," Orm said. "And a lot of words that may or may not connect to the map. So we are halfway to finding a treasure beyond counting, but really, halfway to nowhere. Half is as good as nothing at all. Becoming wood merchants hasn't made us a fortune and we sure as hell didn't sail a cold, open boat halfway around the world for no gain."

"Time to become warriors again," Halfdan said. "We have our swords and twelve boats full of true fighters, true to us, true to themselves, none of whom wants to return to Ribe with nothing to show for it but the meager earnings from selling lumber and furs. We'd be scorned."

"Stoutly said, my friend, but word is that sea monsters roam the sea around Genoa and demons stalk those who chase the map," Orm said.

Halfdan rubbed a pendant with a small iron jewelry piece depicting Thor's hammer. "There is always some word from someone about something. Usually, it's meaningless. No doubt sea monsters exist; our storytellers relate tales of our ancestors fleeing before them, but they live in far places where the sea and heaven meet. Have you ever seen one? They make good stories to amuse ourselves over drink and impress elder-folk and children back home. As for demons, our own Norse gods know a thing or two about demons. My hammer token has the blessings of the God of Thunder, so we have protection. You wear one, too, as does everyone on our crews. So let's set all this dark talk aside and you tell me what you know of this thing that we're after."

"It's writing or runes of some sort," Orm said. "Someone put learning on this paper. I can't read it—I can't read at all—but the seller says it speaks of a mountain of riches from ancient times."

"Ancient times." Halfdan shook himself theatrically making his mail armor and sword scabbard creak. "Well, it must be true, then. Men only lie in modern times."

"Brother, you know what I mean," Orm said. "Put the mockery away. If you don't believe me, believe half the town—who are also after the scrap of a scroll. At least, let us set eyes on it. A Genoese noble currently holds it. I met him. He killed the previous owner."

"Ah, a serious fellow, my kind of man," Halfdan said. "You showed him your ax?"

Orm nodded.

"Then he knows we're serious, too. Well, let us meet him with a few more of our company and see how persuasive we can be with silver coins or steel blades. It's his choice, really."

Halfdan scratched his beard. "I do wonder, who has the other half of the map? And if we secure both halves, is it in any language we would understand?"

"Besides Norsemen, we have warriors in our crews from half the world. A few read. Someone will be able to decipher this thing."

CHAPTER 11

The Leopard's Spots

The jinn was in Genoa. The ifrit sensed him, so she came, too. If he was here, his poem and map would be here since he pursued them with the same determination that she did, but the ifrit wouldn't share. She would kill him and take the map. If the librarian still accompanied the jinn, she'd kill her, too.

She could have seized the map from Córdoba's library if she hadn't been called off the hunt by the king's demand to convene his tribes for a trial to indict the jinn for banditry. This was pure theater on the monarch's part to awe his restive subjects with his acumen at discovering the culprit so quickly and his ruthlessness in punishing the perpetrator. If revolt in the demon kingdom simmered, then shocking his subjects with the king's justice on full display at a trial might be a cheap way to stave off civil war. However, everyone already knew that Thiago had orchestrated the theft, so the ifrit saw no point in this tactic.

Then the king had further impeded her search by deploying his own agents to retrieve the scroll. They'd only gotten underfoot. Arrogantly pairing a court official from Córdoba's palace with a dozen of the king's ifrit warriors was a recipe for disaster and it was predictable that the band of ifrit would be completely unfamiliar with the human world's customs and lose patience with Matias and try to murder him, but they hadn't recovered the map. A human had beaten them to it and murdered Matias himself.

Operating alone, she was better than an army of demons at finding the map. However, the jinn had been hard to follow since his trial before the king's dais. She'd eventually tracked him to Córdoba and discovered that he was gone, but the entire palace had mobilized to find the map lured by visions of endless wealth. In fact, the caliph's henchmen might already be in Genoa along with other parties interested in the map.

The ifrit had puzzled over the jinn's destination after he'd fled Córdoba and thought she'd lost him crossing the sea, but then, by good fortune, he'd exerted himself mightily. He could be strong when he wanted. She couldn't discern the details of what had motivated this titanic effort, but it didn't matter. She prided herself on being gifted and intuitive when it came to detecting the activities of other demons, even at a distance. The greater the effort, the more likely she was to notice. And the jinn had expended such copious amounts of energy that he stood out like a bonfire on a nighttime beach.

So, here she was in Genoa—the ifrit couldn't call it a true city—it was a forsaken backwater of stone walls enclosing muddy roads surrounded by mountains that hovered close enough to almost push it into the sea. The whole affair would be less than a sewer in her world. However, she did have to admire the vitality the natives displayed as they purposefully went about their activities. They looked hungry, so simple survival drove them to keep busy. Men and women from the surrounding farmlands carried meager produce by hand or in primitive carts to stalls by the wharves to sell to sailors and townspeople.

She looked about. Seawater, muddy from a recent effort to dredge a deeper channel into Genoa's harbor, lapped against the pilings supporting the wharf. Offshore, a dozen ships bobbed in the choppy water from a recent storm waiting for an open berth to off-load their cargos. And the bad weather wasn't over. Lowering skies promised another storm pushing in from the Ligurian Sea, and a cool, damp breeze off the water was the leading element. The swells toyed with a body amid the pilings, sending it bumping into the barnacle-encrusted wood. Nobody paid it much mind. As always with humans, savagery was the order of the day. In that regard, her world and this one were identical.

Low warehouses fronted the wharves, and a little further back, she saw bigger houses, some stone, some wood, with drifting smoke pushed sideways by the breeze. The ifrit suspected that whatever passed for Genoese aristocracy lived in them. However, excepting the Santa Stefano church ringed by wooden construction scaffolding and a few stone watchtowers studding the city walls, three stories was as high as buildings got in Genoa. Her family's elegant manor house had towers twenty times higher than anything she could see around here. Her ancestral home had been built with architectural ambition beyond these locals' wildest imaginings.

Given the protection offered to Genoa by mountains on its landward side, the greatest threats to the city would come from the sea, and signs of a past attack by Arab Fatimid raiders still remained on Genoa's smoke-blackened city walls and burned-out warehouses, half repaired, scattered about. However, the town had used the intervening years to rebuild itself and she smelled salt, tar, sweat, fish, and the innumerable other odors of a hardworking port. She heard cordage creaking and shouts in a dozen different languages as sailors shifted lumber, linen, and raw silk from the city's wharves into ships' holds while off-loading spices, incense, and herbs from Byzantine and Islamic empires shipping out of Alexandria, Tripoli, and Tunis. Between sacking and pillaging rival kingdoms and city-states, humans traded relentlessly with one another.

Enemies weren't permanent, but greed was.

In the harbor, a heterogeneous collection of shipping including galleys, sailing ships, and a Norse longship nestled against the wharves and one another. Several of the longship's warriors lounged about on pilings, surveying the dockside activity. They weren't overtly threatening, but they'd stacked spears against piles of lumber on the wharf. Other ships and crews stayed well away from the longship and it sat at the most remote berth, sleek and dangerous, a dragon-headed greyhound amid fat rabbits.

The jinn, may any god that listened blast his soul, reveled in such rude life and vibrant activity. In contrast, coming from the world of demons, violent, decadent, and debauched, but refined, Lila's senses wanted more sophisticated stimuli. Here she felt overwhelmed by the crudity and chaos around her from this all-too-human setting. She consciously focused on shutting this out to concentrate on the task at hand: finding the jinn. She doubted that he would repeat his recent volcanic expenditure of energy if for no other reason than to avoid crushing exhaustion, so she'd have to deploy ingenuity to locate him. It wasn't that big a town. He would stand out.

She'd carefully considered what she'd do with Sheba's Treasure when she located it—certainly not hand it over to the king so that he could finance baubles for his endless concubines and embark on a self-aggrandizing effort to conquer the human world. On his side of the portal, the king's self-absorbed taxation sucked the energy out of innovative activities. How many exquisite, delicate palaces and parks filled with the most beautifully improbable creatures did the demon realm need? How many masques and festivities where all beings wise, beautiful, or appalling vied with one another to impress the rest of the host and the king, the final adjudicator of their worth, did it take to keep the court entertained? It was all an unsustainable idyll that required fountains of riches to exist. The economic underpinnings of her world were as illusory as a demon's dream. It had taken generations to come to this circumstance, but it was now obvious to all. So the king's strategy was to use their collective patrimony—Sheba's Treasure—for expansion through the portal. She'd been privy to his plans during their pillow talk—one advantage to sleeping with the king.

It was time to replace the king with a queen, the Queen of Sheba's Treasure to pay for a new queen. The ifrit saw herself as a more than fitting heir to the throne in the realm of demons. Her ifrit tribe would support her especially if handsomely compensated with the biggest portions of the treasure. And a queen could lead an attack on the human world as well or better than a narcissistic king, so she wouldn't derail plans of conquest. Instead, she'd pursue them with more vigor.

On the human side of the portal, everything was primitive and half finished. Still, there was no denying the mercantile industry that surrounded her. Plundering this world would sustain her world of demons.

Until now, the touchpoints between the human and demon worlds had been incidental or accidental, a shadow where none should be spotted out of the corner of a human's eye, a sudden unexplained sickness that killed the sheep in a shepherd's flock, a man standing where an animal had just been, a half-remembered legend told around a desert campfire of strange doings in abandoned ruins. This was fodder to inflame credulous humans' superstitions and seed their nightmares. Individual jinn and ifrit might wander through the portal from time to time to amuse themselves by tormenting humans, but there had never been a systematic campaign on the part of demons to attack the human world if for no other reason than lack of organization and a disinterest and contempt for anything beyond their own realm. That would all change if Sheba's Treasure was recovered. For this, she needed the map. She also needed the king out of the way. There was a lot to do. It would be useful to find help.

~

"Why send an executioner after a scroll?" the ifrit asked.

"I keep answering that question," the Sardinian said. "I'm not a simple executioner. I'm a torturer, too."

"That's wonderful," the ifrit said. "Can you be an assassin?"

"I've done that before," the Sardinian said. "Who hasn't? But my true calling is in the caliph's dungeon. If the job's assassination, they always try to escape unless you take them by surprise. It's tiring to catch them."

They sat across from each other at a table near the back of the tavern's main room. Both the ifrit and the Sardinian kept themselves away from the entrance. She thought their table, the room, the whole establishment was filthy. Even the tavern's few windows were just irregular openings punched through the wall and covered with thin cloth to keep weather out. Currently the cloth was pushed aside, allowing dim light from outside to penetrate the gloom. She tried to have as little contact with any surface as possible though that meant sitting uncomfortably on the very edge of a bench. Two mugs of ale sat before them, untouched.

It was midday and sailors, dockhands, and stall keepers half filled the tavern. Mostly, she'd drawn little attention from this crowd until a trio of men detached themselves and approached their table.

"What's your name?" one of them called to her.

In one motion, the Sardinian stood up, sending his bench bouncing to the side. With two blows, he sent two of the trio to the straw floor.

"I could do more," the executioner addressed the man still standing. "Do you want me to?"

Deftly he pulled a silk scarf from his tunic and looped it around the neck of one of the fallen men struggling to regain his feet.

"I don't need a knife," the Sardinian said. "This small bit of cloth is enough to finish all three of you." He suddenly tightened the silk and the man whose neck he'd encircled went limp with his head lolling to one side.

"He'll come to in a moment," the Sardinian said. "Unless you want to see what else I can do, get him and yourselves out of here."

Silently, two of the men dragged their unconscious companion toward the entrance. The crowd made a path for them, then resumed their drinking. They ostentatiously paid less attention to the ifrit and the executioner than before.

"I've clearly chosen the right person for an assassination," she said.

"You have a name?" The executioner righted his bench and sat down. He carefully folded the silk and replaced it within his tunic.

She debated for a second telling him that she didn't want a name and that it was insulting and patronizing to think she needed one, but decided that this would be confusing.

"You can call me Lila."

She was in the human world and needed to play by its rules to avoid needless friction until she could take over and enforce her own rules.

"No need to use it unless absolutely necessary."

"I understand," the Sardinian said. "You have your secrets. We all do."

He pulled a dagger out of his boot and carved a small hole in the center of their table. Then he extracted a human finger bone from a pocket. Yellowed skin and tendons covered the mummified digit. Here and there, bone was visible. He jammed the finger into the hole and tamped wood shavings around it to hold in upright on the table.

"A little quirk of mine," he said. "I'm leaving my mark on the place, if you will. Pay it no mind."

The ifrit thought it was an odd gesture, but perhaps human assassins advertised their prowess this way.

A serving woman on the way over saw the severed finger and swerved away to cater to other tables.

"I can pay you," the ifrit told the Sardinian.

"No offense," he said. "But I'm not hiring myself out for a few silver dirhams, especially as this is outside of the remit from my emir, Abd-al-Rahman, may he have many male heirs. I'll consider this job only if it doesn't interfere with the task he set for me."

"This task complements your lord's orders. If you kill the individual that I intend for you, you'll be a step closer to securing the treasure for your caliph."

The ifrit pulled an emerald from her black cloak and tossed it to the executioner. It was Thiago's gift to her and she'd wondered what she could use it for. She hadn't planned to keep it for any sentimental purpose, so this greedy killer was the perfect recipient.

He caught it midair and examined it.

"It's worth more than I can make in fifty lifetimes," he said. "This kind of payment means whoever you want dead must be uncommonly well protected, hard to reach, and on the lookout for threats."

"Right on all counts," the ifrit said. "You need to know what you're in for so I'm going to tell you a little story. It's about two worlds, yours and mine, and a pile of ancient riches beyond counting and a king who once owned all those riches, but lost it through hubris to an outlaw jinn. The king, of course, is willing to burn empires to get it back—"

"The treasure I keep hearing about," the executioner interrupted.

"The treasure you keep hearing about," the ifrit confirmed. "This is no bedtime story. It's real enough and I want it. Then we can give it to your lord."

The ifrit had no intention of sharing Sheba's Treasure with anyone in this world or any other, but recruiting the executioner needed a few lies to grease the skids.

"This king stands in the way and you want him dead," the Sardinian said.

"Yes."

"It's a gripping tale? Tell me."

The ifrit kept her voice down, looking about at other people in the tavern as she related the story of her chase after Sheba's Treasure, the jinn's nefarious actions to stymie her, and the king's malevolent role in ruling one world and planning to conquer another. The ifrit described herself as a disinterested and benevolent individual who would be satisfied with a very small share of the treasure and the satisfaction of knowing she'd prevented war between cultures and widespread destruction. Lila downplayed her supernatural capabilities. She had no idea how much of the story the Sardinian believed, but he stayed attentive.

"Why me?" he said when she'd finished. "If this story is even partly true, you're more than able to kill the king yourself especially if you share a bed. A bit of hemlock in the wine during foreplay would bring things to a quick conclusion, or a knife in the throat at the right moment would make a memorable climax."

"That's just why I can't do it," the ifrit said. "Everyone would suspect it was me. I'd like to rule as queen, but that's harder if the dead king's loyalists think I had a hand in his death."

"Sounds like Córdoba's palace politics," the Sardinian said. "Being the caliph's torturer gives me a rare window into the mind's devious workings."

Human politics didn't interest the ifrit.

"You don't come from my world so no one knows you exist and I'll be far away when you kill him," she said.

"The king of a demon tribe could be a tough sort to kill. Is he vulnerable?"

"I won't tell you how to do your job," the ifrit said. "Be creative. An exotic poison might work if he drank enough."

"And how do I get to him?" the executioner asked. "Go through one of these portal contraptions?"

"No need. I'll bring him to you when he comes to take possession of the treasure in Arabia. He also wants to personally kill the outlaw who stole his treasure and caused this fuss."

"And what of this jinn fellow?" the Sardinian asked. "I've heard there is such a fellow and his woman—probably Córdoba's court librarian—recently arrived in Genoa asking after the map. He seems as worthy as your king for a slit throat."

"I'd be the last one to stop you if your paths cross, but he's elusive and I plan to kill him myself."

"You?"

The ifrit became angry at his skepticism. "Do you doubt I could do it?"

"You're an extremely pretty, well-dressed woman very capable of poisoning a lover or slipping a thin blade between ribs into a rival's heart."

For a moment, the ifrit teetered on the edge of becoming fire and incinerating the Sardinian, the tavern, and all its foul patrons. She held herself in check just barely. Who was she trying to impress, a mindless thug who she planned to use as a tool to remove a royal rival without incurring suspicion? She had to keep her goals in mind: secure Sheba's Treasure and use that to become what she deserved to be.

"I can do poison and knives between the ribs," she finally said. "I can do other things, too. I'll show you one day, but meantime, if you want more than just that emerald I gave you, get on a boat to Alexandria. Members of my tribe will meet you at Pompey's Pillar three weeks from today at noon."

The executioner plainly didn't sense the fury he'd aroused. "If you do succeed in usurping the throne for a world of demons—"

"Not if," the ifrit corrected. "When I succeed in taking the throne."

"Fine. When you succeed, will your court need an executioner? And a torturer, too?"

"Good executioners and torturers are hard to come by, but doesn't your current lord, this Abd-al-Rahman, hold your family hostage until you deliver the map to him?"

"What's family to me, just mouths to feed. Now killing a king and seizing a treasure, that's a worthy endeavor."

"We have a deal," the ifrit said. "I'll leave you to it. I have other business to get to."

"Careful when you walk about Genoa as a woman unaccompanied," the Sardinian advised. "These streets are not as well patrolled as Córdoba's or whatever exotic locale you come from. No one dares lay a hand on any of the caliphate's citizens in its capital, women included. Here, in this pigpen, you take your life in your hands even in daylight. And the city guard is as bad as the criminal element."

The ifrit wasn't entirely sure what this warning meant. In the land of jinn and ifrit, she was no more or less at risk as a woman. Whatever her sex, anyone crossing her did so at their own peril.

"I'll be watchful," she said.

~

"What's your name?"

While Lila had been lost in thought, three men approached her, sailors or dockhands; they looked to be the same individuals who'd approached her in the tavern.

Now she was alone.

Based on the Sardinian's warning, their intentions were clear.

She'd loitered inconspicuously near a cluster of vendors at the end of a wharf suspecting that in a city this small, the jinn and the librarian would eventually show themselves. Until now, none of the sailors, warehouse laborers, merchants manning their stalls, or servants buying goods for family tables had paid her any attention. She'd blended in, discarding her elegant but foreign-appearing gray robe in favor of a simply cut, linen tunic belted around the waist and a head covering tied under her chin. She'd taken the trouble to smear dirt over her garments. However, though she'd dressed as a servant or famer's wife on an errand to sell produce from her family's plot of ground, her otherworldly beauty had drawn unwanted attention.

"My name is Lila." The ifrit spoke in the local Genoese Italian dialect. Though she had nothing but contempt for the innumerable human tongues, she could speak several of them when needed. She remembered the jinn taunting her with the name Lila in front of the king and the entire palace court including her own tribe. Remembering this made the ifrit even angrier than the approaching trio. The name tasted like ashes and she used it sparingly even here on the human side of the portal. However, these three men were about to die anyway, so that was compensation of a sort.

She slipped into an alley, shadowed even in daylight, between warehouses fronting the wharf. The men followed.

The ifrit knew that turning to fire would bring attention, but she hadn't tried an animal form recently and thought that reimagining herself as a leopard would suit this occasion.

She didn't need to manufacture her explosive fury. In her world, violence was extraordinarily common, but never casual; instead it was planned. She expected to be attacked with murderous intent for understandable reasons, feuds within her tribe, vendettas with other ifrit tribes, hostilities with jinn, angering the king. In this world, she would be attacked simply because she looked weak.

She didn't think of herself as weak.

As a leopard, she was herself but detached from herself, an animal of pure, uncurbed hunger and incendiary rage.

Within seconds, the muddy lane was covered with blood mixing with standing pools of rainwater, and blood and viscera splattered far up the warehouse walls like crimson dye applied by a mad painter. Her attackers screamed, but the ifrit cut this off immediately with ripping claw swipes across their throats. No need to draw attention.

The slaughter ended quickly and the ifrit transitioned back to her human form. Reason replaced unthinking action. She resisted a residual feline predatory urge to toy with her dead victims' entrails. Amused, she noted that leopard spots lingered on her skin before fading. Now she was again a modestly clothed citizen of Genoa's surrounding farms. Avoiding the three eviscerated corpses, she walked out of the alley back onto the main street. She was better motivated than ever to subjugate this human world.

Rain began again. She looked behind her. The rain diluted the pooled blood and washed splattered guts off the alley walls. She guessed it would all be clean tomorrow. Except for the corpses. Those wouldn't wash away.

CHAPTER 12

The Jinn, the Librarian, and the Vikings

"You wear iron," the jinn said.

"I wear a pendant with a hammer representing Thor, our god of war and storms," Halfdan said. "As does Orm Silvertooth. And the rest of our band of warriors. They're made of iron. What's it to you? Surely you bear some token reminding you of your own gods?"

"That's complicated," Thiago said. "I'm not fond of tokens. Or gods, for that matter."

"How did you know we wore them?" Orm asked. "They're under our tunics next to our skin, not visible unless we show them."

The jinn didn't want to expose his susceptibility to iron, not when negotiations about the map were about to begin and could become fraught. That would signify weakness to the Norsemen.

"Just a guess," he said. "Men from your part of the world sometimes wear them."

Taking this for interest, Orm pulled out his hammer and proudly displayed it to Thiago and Lubna. "I'm Christian, as is Halfdan, recent converts to satisfy the priests and earls in our home country." The jinn saw a small smile indicating ambivalence. "But we keep to the old ways, too. In dangerous waters, one can never have too much support from on high, and Thor is a power to have in your corner."

Now with the hammer on full display, the jinn acutely felt its toxicity. Fortunately, the token was small. Also, fortunately, he'd developed some tolerance for iron exposure that would have laid any other demon low. Nevertheless, as unobtrusively as he could, Thiago edged his bench away from the tavern's common table he shared with the Vikings.

Thiago saw that Lubna noticed his discomfort and leaned across the table, appearing to inspect Orm's hammer while also shielding the jinn from it.

"Enough about what we wear and why we wear it," Halfdan said. "Why deal with you at all?"

"Because we each have half the map," Thiago said. "And we each share an enemy."

"I have only friends," Halfdan said. "Any enemies for you, Silvertooth?"

"None that are still walking around to trouble me," Orm said.

The jinn, Lubna, and the two Vikings sat around a scarred and gouged wooden table covered with the accretions contributed by generations of visitors. Thiago suspected that whatever covered the tabletop included rotting food, dried ale, and blood. Some previous drinker had embedded a finger bone into the wood. Dried ligaments still held the digits together. It pointed accusingly at him. The crud on the table looked almost as poisonous as iron. Cleaning the tavern's main room wasn't of high importance to the women servers who brought endless rounds of execrable ale to the patrons and dodged their drunken advances.

Thiago tried to minimize contact with the surface as he sipped from an earthen tankard. The mug looked only slightly cleaner than the table and the ale tasted like water with a bit of ground barley haphazardly added. Drink was infinitely better on the other side of the portal.

No one else touched their mugs. Lubna had given the stuff one sniff and turned green while Orm had upended his mug onto the straw floor, prompting a round of laughter from a neighboring table. Halfdan ignored his tankard. It was simply an excuse to be here out of the rain so they could discuss business where they didn't stand out too much among sailors from the world's four corners and where the talk was so loud that no one could easily overhear. If anyone tried, they'd have to decipher the mixture of Norse and Latin the four spoke.

Even in the tavern's rough crowd, no one sat very near the Norsemen. They both wore mail shirts over woolen tunics and carried swords along with daggers. Thiago estimated that he was taller than either man, but they were thicker and most of it looked like muscle, good company to have at one's side in a tight spot.

Thiago asked, "Would one of those men who won't trouble you further happen to be a wealthy Genoese noble who until recently owned half of a map?"

"Quite possibly," Orm acknowledged.

"Just from curiosity, where is this noble?" Thiago asked.

"They fought better than expected, but we had shields and chain mail," Halfdan said. "We left him—what was left of him—with a dozen of his retainers—what was left of them—in an alley not far from here. There were already three bodies there, so the locals are accustomed to this sort of thing."

"Three dead men?" Thiago asked.

"Bodies in bad shape," confirmed Orm Silvertooth. "Not the usual battle wounds."

"We need to leave Genoa right now," Lubna said. "Three bodies of men of no reputation that you stumbled on may or may not arouse worry; this city has probably seen worse. However, a dozen corpses including a prominent Genoese aristocrat will be noticed. This place is more rustic than Córdoba, but they'll be up in arms over an alley full of bodies."

"Besides a few other rival noble trading houses with armed men in their service, you're the only group in Genoa capable of killing on this scale," Thiago said. "They'll be after you shortly."

"Well, that means we get right to the point," Halfdan said.

"It means we leave here and walk to your ship," Thiago said. "We'll talk along the way. How quickly can you get under way?"

"Fast if we have to," Orm said.

"We have to," the jinn said. He heard horses' hooves in the mud outside the tavern. Someone in command shouted questions at men lounging by the entrance. "That's the city watch. They'll mobilize whatever militia they have once they find you."

"A few dotards in tin helmets and some bar toughs looking for a fight," Halfdan said. "We should burn the city. We'll call in our other ships. We have more than enough men to sack the place."

Thiago yelled above the tavern's growing hubbub, "And you'd have the glory of slaughtering some ancients and a few youths, and you'd gain nothing except more lumber and dry goods from the warehouses, maybe some spices and incense if you're lucky. Quite a haul. Is that what you came down from northern fjords to find?"

They had bulled their way toward the entrance through the tavern crowd quickly emptying into the street and curious about the commotion and what the watch was shouting about.

Outside, rain fell and it was nighttime. Attention hadn't coalesced around the four of them, but that was about to change.

Thiago saw a mounted captain of the watch in a slapdash collection of leather and quilted armor dripping with moisture stand tall in his stirrups and survey the crowd before spotting them among the milling pack of taverngoers still holding tankards. He yelled for his men, some on horses, some on foot, to make for the Norsemen.

Orm and Halfdan drew swords. Dozens more Vikings by their longship observed their leaders in trouble and ran down the dockside bearing whatever weapons were handy. An arrow arced over the crowd and just missed the guard captain.

"To your right," Lubna yelled at Thiago, pushing him violently in that direction. An arrow zipped past where his head had just been to embed itself in the tavern's wall. Men around them dropped to the mud.

"Who's fighting with whom?" someone shouted.

"Hold your men," Thiago shouted at Orm Silvertooth. He shoved his way through the crowd toward the guard captain and his mounted officers. As he drew close, the horses heaved and bucked before turning tail and galloping away from the jinn despite their riders' curses. Seeing his effect on the animals, the taverngoers backed away, too, packing against one another and crowding against walls.

"The guard spoke of scores of bodies mutilated beyond recognition," a man yelled. "They did it. These are sorcerers!"

"Not sorcerers, Norsemen," another voice shouted. "Worse than sorcerers. The devil's own. They'll eat our hearts. And a witch stalks our streets, too, clawing the life out of good seamen. Surely we are cursed as sinners."

A few torches had been lit, but these guttered in the drenching rain to leave everyone in confused darkness.

"Go," Thiago yelled. "To your ship."

He grabbed Lubna's hand and sprinted in the direction he remembered the longship to be, barging through the crowd half seen in the gloom.

"You spooked the horses to frighten the city guard?" Lubna shouted.

"Yes, but more to impress the Norsemen so they wouldn't just kill us out of hand and seize the other half of the map. If they were happy to slaughter a Genoese noble and a dozen of his armed men, they'll figure they could make short work of the two of us. I'll show them a bit more of who I am before the night is out. Meantime, Genoa has seen enough of us. Also the ifrit is somewhere nearby. The three bodies with strange wounds are her doing. I'd rather deal with Norsemen."

~

"So again, why treat with you at all?" Halfdan asked, once onboard their ship. "We have half the map. You have half the map. We take your half. Then we'll have the whole thing. It's a simple issue to resolve to our satisfaction if not yours."

The jinn thought that the Norseman was measured like he was trying to settle with a buyer on the going rate for a ship's hold full of lumber or a pouch of amber from Denmark's North Sea coast. However, he had his sword unsheathed across his lap.

"Interesting trick with the horses back in Genoa," Orm said. "I suppose that makes you a magician or seer worth our respect. We have such individuals living alone among the pine trees and snow where we come from. A wise person doesn't anger them, but I've seen men do similar things to horses with a bit of hot pepper tossed in their nostrils—and they're not magicians."

They were under way with Genoa fading rapidly behind them amid flickering lightning. The Norsemen had been as good as their word, and after loosing the lines securing them to the wharf, Halfdan and Orm's sleek longship had speedily been rowed backward away from the dock by warriors manning the oars, then pivoted to face forward and raced out of the port. Eleven other longships closed formation around them and they headed south in driving rain.

The wind was strong, but they'd raised their mainsails, keeping them close reefed to fill with the storm's wild air. Carved dragon heads capped the vessels' curved prows, and the thin ships knifed through the rough seas at an incredible clip, as if the vessels had transformed themselves into real dragons that reveled in speeding through the black water. This was a night for monsters and demons.

Pursuit would be far behind. However, the jinn doubted whether anyone, in wretched weather, would dare trail a fleet of the long, lethal boats packed with grim men intent on making their reputation through plunder and rapine. This was a far cry from the fat, peaceful merchantman he'd arrived in. Genoa wouldn't welcome him back soon.

Thiago sat on a rowing bench. He couldn't find a comfortable perch no matter how he shifted, and he reflected that this was a functional boat fit for war and not much else. No concessions had been made for the crew's comfort. He heard lashing rain rattle the canvas overhead that was their only shelter, but it was open on the sides so waves coming across the boat soaked him. The Vikings didn't mind, but he was frozen and Lubna looked just as miserable. The drenching salt water plastered the librarian's black hair to her head like a skullcap.

The warrior crew starred impassively ahead, taking what shelter they could from the canvas but unmoved by the tumult. Periodically sheets of lightning washed them with pallid light. At the rear of the vessel, a massive Viking grasped the rudder, keeping them on an unswerving path across the Tyrrhenian Sea.

The Norsemen were as elemental as demons. However, if it came to it, the jinn felt that he was more than a match for the crew. He could become more destructive. However, he wanted to husband his energy if he could. Was there a middle path between him transforming into a supremely damaging elemental or them slaughtering him and Lubna? He needed a fleet full of violent men to help contend with the king and his demon warriors, if he could somehow recruit them. However, if he couldn't convince the Norsemen that they'd be more effective as a team than working at cross-purposes, or defeat them, then he and Lubna would be tossed overboard. Even if Mediterranean sharks weren't as hideous as the monsters that populated his world, they'd nonetheless make a meal of the two of them.

"I haven't impressed you," he said to Halfdan and Orm.

"You haven't," Orm confirmed. "So this could go badly for you. And the woman."

"Let's hope it doesn't," Thiago said. "I think I can impress you." Halfdan and Orm looked skeptical. "But before I try, let's look at the map together."

Lubna subtly nodded, guessing what he intended.

The jinn pulled out his half of the map trying to protect it from the storm. Halfdan did the same while Orm held up a shield to shelter the scroll's pieces. They flattened the fragments and aligned them as best they could on a rower's bench.

"Well, make sense of it," Thiago challenged.

Both Viking leaders leaned forward to examine the intact document. Periodically, lightning illuminated it.

"A map obviously and what appear to be verses, but it makes no more sense as a whole than it did as a fragment," Halfdan admitted. "We'd thought we could decipher it when we had the whole thing. However, maybe not. I've traveled far and wide and know some of these southern shores, so the map may point to a location that is south of us in the deserts—or it may be on the moon."

"Not the moon, but almost as far," the jinn said. "I can lead us there. We're already going generally in the right direction, south toward Arabia."

"Why would you know any better than us?" Orm asked.

"Because I wrote the poem and drew the map."

The Vikings looked impressed despite themselves.

"So you're saying that we shouldn't just pitch you two overboard?" Halfdan said.

"That's what he's saying," Lubna said. "That's *absolutely* what he's saying."

Halfdan held the pieces in front of his face. "The map is all we need. Let's tear away the rest and throw it into the sea. It's nothing but scrap."

"No!" Thiago and Lubna shouted at once over the storm.

"Why not?" Orm asked.

"The words are a code to understand the map," the jinn said. "Everything works together."

"And the words make a beautiful poem," Lubna said.

The jinn glared at her. This wasn't the time to discuss meter, rhyme, and failed love with barbarians.

"Read us a bit," Halfdan said.

The jinn didn't think the Norsemen would have much interest in his poem. However, he'd challenged them to interpret the map and they'd failed. Now Halfdan was reciprocating with a challenge of his own to Thiago.

"It's a long voyage on a rough sea," the Norseman said. "We grew up on verses told around fires when the weather howled outside. What's the harm in sharing a bit with us? At worst, we grow bored and tell you to stop."

Thiago felt his face turning red and hoped no one could see his features in the darkness, rain, and pitching sea.

"Come on," Lubna said. "It's good work, too good to keep private."

The jinn motioned for Halfdan to hand him the scroll. He paused to collect his thoughts, trying to imagine what had gotten him to such strange circumstances, reading sonnets to a pack of savages. He'd need to translate into Norse as he read, no mean feat if he wanted to keep the original work's cadences and subtleties.

He began to read. After a few stanzas, he fell into the work's rhythm, timing its beats to the longship's sliding motion through the rolling waves. The tempest added drama to his words. It really was good poetry describing heartfelt emotions, but he wondered how verses about an otherworldly ifrit fundamentally unknowable even to her fellow demons would be understood by Viking warriors, but they hadn't told him to stop. He'd heard that Norse mythology was packed with strange, malign entities, so perhaps his poem would be somehow familiar. Nearby men sitting on their benches leaned closer to hear over the storm.

~

In the clouds above, the ifrit listened too with preternaturally acute hearing. She'd become a whirlwind and integrated herself with the storm. It was perfect cover to shadow the dozen long-ships since they'd left Genoa. She'd been tempted to plunge down at them, smashing everything in her path to somehow seize the map, but why? It might be lost in the struggle as had happened above the Empty Quarter when she'd dodged iron-tipped arrows. Further, the jinn and the Norsemen were doing her work for her. Thiago must have convinced these raiders that there was gold and jewels in it for them if they helped him unearth Sheba's Treasure by heading south. Let them try. Despite all odds, if they made it, she and her tribe of ifrit would be waiting and she would ally herself with the king and his forces. Together they would form a crushing army that would easily defeat whatever help the jinn planned to cobble together, perhaps a combined force of Norsemen and the Fire Horde. She'd step on them easily. Then she'd look for an opportunity to seize the treasure entirely for herself. Assassinating the king would be a good start.

The treasure would finance her efforts to fend off the inevitable other pretenders for the throne and gather together an army loyal to her, with her tribe as its core. Then she'd decide between two appealing options: remain on the supernatural side of the portal and preside as queen over the enchanted world of demons or pick up where the king had left off and move to plunder the human world. However, why choose? She could do both.

She played in the clouds. However, as exhilarating as it was to tumble about in the sky feeling the frozen rain and touching the lightning bolts as they tore the sky, she grew exhausted and risked plummeting into the water below. Why not discreetly join them by dropping onto the deck of one of the longships? Amusingly, she'd be a stowaway. One of the twelve boats would suit her, as it was sparsely manned and carried spare weapons and supplies. A slender demon materializing on a remote bench far from the steering oar in the pitch black amid a storm would be easy to miss. When daylight arrived, she would need to be more careful, but she was elusive and there were enough crawl spaces, spare packs, and cordage to hide her from the skeleton crew manning the boat. If they somehow discovered her, she'd simply slaughter them and take to the air again.

Meantime, she dipped lower over the ship where the jinn held court reading his poem to the crew. It translated surprisingly well into Norse. She'd heard it before, but she'd hear it again. It was flattering to be described in flowing verses. Whatever his faults, the jinn did verses well.

~

Thiago finished the poem and braced himself for a torrent of mockery about his lovesick longing for Lila. None came. Halfdan nodded to him and the huge Norseman handling the steering oar told another Viking to take over and came forward to embrace the jinn.

"A good rhyme," he said. "Better than most. My ax is yours if you ever need it." He walked back to his oar.

"There is a piece to this story that I didn't put in the poem," Thiago said. "The woman I desired was a literal demon, fundamentally evil."

Orm slapped him on the back. "Who doesn't feel their mate is an evil demon from time to time? That describes all of my former lovers. Halfdan, that's true for you, too?"

"Oh, yes," Halfdan said. "I don't honor them with pretty verses as you've done. Instead, I curse them. They curse me in return. Love never ends well. You're better off just calling it lust.

A meaty topic, let's break out some ale—better than that Genoa shit—and discuss this further."

The conversation wasn't going where Thiago wanted it to. "I'm more optimistic about love. But what I meant was she really is a demon. I wasn't being symbolic. She's the common enemy I spoke of earlier that we share."

"What? Magical?" Orm said. "In your poem, she sounded too beautiful to be deadly."

"Yes, magical and deadly," Thiago said. "Like some of your Norse goddesses."

"Like Hel," Lubna said.

Thiago noted that Halfdan and Orm became suddenly paler, but that might have been the lightning.

"I've read of your demon goddesses in scrolls from my library," Lubna said.

"It's a foul night to speak of such beings," Halfdan finally said.

"You saw bodies in the alley near Genoa's docks, unnaturally handled," Thiago said.

"Guts torn out, throats ripped away," Orm admitted. "They were already there when we dumped our own load of corpses next to them. We left that place quick. We give our enemies a clean death with stabs to the body or an ax chop through the skull."

"Is that distinction important to the dead?" the jinn asked dryly. "The three bodies you saw were Lila's handiwork."

"Lila. A soft name," Halfdan said.

"A hard woman," Thiago said.

"Just how is it you could ever have loved such a creature?" Halfdan asked. "You were smitten with her."

Thiago felt himself reddening again from anger and embarrassment. "There's not enough ale on your ship for that story," he said. "She'll come for the map just as I did. She's followed me."

"Well, we're safe on our ships unless she can swim like a serpent," Halfdan said. "We're moving fast."

"She can turn to wind and fly, but she'll tire. Then she'll have to go about as humans do, by boat, on foot or horse."

"Can she track our ships?" Lubna asked.

The jinn nodded. "If we draw attention to ourselves. She can sense me at some distance. She's gifted in that way. That's how she's been able to follow me. I'm not as good. I might sense her if she were very near, but maybe not."

"You know a great deal about this creature," Halfdan said. "You're not altogether natural yourself, are you?" The Norseman fingered his sword's edge. "That thing with the horses back in Genoa wasn't just throwing pepper in their noses."

Thiago sighed. "It wasn't spices. Time for more about me. I come from Lila's world. I'm a jinn."

"Jinn are different than demons," Lubna said helpfully. "He has a soul, or so he says."

Thiago tried to guess what reaction this would get from the two Norsemen.

"I'm unhappy doing tricks to amuse humans because it brings unwanted attention," he said. "But under the circumstances—"

Thiago stood up, clambered awkwardly over the side of the longship, and dove off it. Before hitting the waves, he morphed into a whirlwind that rose to meet the black clouds, madly spinning waves and rainwater in all directions. A timely lightning bolt lit the nighttime sky around the longships and the waterspout he'd become. The entire crew looked upward to gesture and swear. As quickly as he'd changed, Thiago shifted back to his human form. He'd made his point and he had no inclination to face the exhaustion a sustained show of strength would have needed. Also, the more energy he expended, the more likely he was to be noticed by Lila.

His robe was already soaked from the storm, so he was none the worse for wear as he dropped back onto the bench he'd occupied. He huddled further under the overhanging canvas trying to avoid the driving rain, and sneezed.

Halfdan reached out and touched his arm. "You're solid enough now. How do you do that?"

"I don't know. It happens when I want it to. In this world, if they knew of it, learned men would study the transformation process and try to understand it so they could exploit it. In my world, nobody questions how it happens. It just does. However, there is some logic to which form I selected tonight. Fire wouldn't have worked in this downpour, and your boat is too cramped to change into a large wild animal, so wind was my choice. I think you'll agree, I'm a good partner to have."

Both Vikings nodded emphatically. "You needn't fear this demon who chases us," Halfdan said. "Hell, you just scared my crew of warriors half to death and they've seen bloody fighting."

"She can do everything I showed you and more," Thiago said.

"Do you have other help besides us?" Orm asked.

Thiago nodded. "On our trip south, I'll try to recruit a group of jinn bandits that helped me steal Sheba's Treasure. We didn't part on the best of terms, so I'll have to be persuasive."

"They'll want a cut, but I won't divide my share of the treasure," Orm stated flatly. "You should know that whatever you give them comes from your portion."

"And you?" Halfdan asked Lubna. Perhaps he was trying to cover the awkwardness of haggling over dividing the spoils.

Perhaps he was genuinely curious. "What part do you play in this?"

"I'm no demon," she said. "I can't turn into the wind or fire. I come from a library." Seeing their bemused looks, she elaborated. "A place to keep and study scrolls and books."

"Who reads besides monks and poets?" Orm asked.

"You should," Lubna said. "It might help all of us find this supposedly fabulous treasure. Thiago's map tells us where to look, but not how to get there. Your longships won't sail over sand. You need a water passage to the Red Sea. As near as I can tell from Thiago's poem and the map, this treasure is several days' camel ride from the Red Sea's Arabian shore. You need to minimize your trek across the desert by sailing from the Mediterranean to the Red Sea. Otherwise you'll all die of thirst without seeing any gold."

"You've read of this?" Orm asked.

"Yes. Arab explorers describe some of the path we need to take including a so-called Pharaoh's Channel linking the Mediterranean Sea and the Red Sea using the Nile River."

"I've heard of the Nile, but not this channel," Halfdan said.

"You should read more," Lubna said.

CHAPTER 13

A Mediterranean Meditation

Lubna stood far forward on the longship. Beside her, the wooden dragon head at the vessel's prow leered at the sea ahead, tongue lolling obscenely out of its mouth between bared fangs, daring other boats to show themselves and risk plunder. Today, no one dared and they had the narrow passage through the Strait of Messina to themselves aside from a few local fishing craft unworthy of attack. Even these hugged the shore and kept their distance from the ominous raiders.

The Viking fleet transited between the Tyrrhenian Sea out into the Ionian Sea. Lubna knew from inspecting Arabic explorers' texts and cartographers' maps that this was all part of the greater Mediterranean. Having observed the longships' marvelous speed, she did a mental calculation. From here, in less than a week, they would make their way south and eastward toward Egypt, presently barely under the control of the Abbasid Caliphate, and then, God willing, to Arabia and a treasure beyond counting.

She had to laugh at this last part. The notion of mythical wealth passed down from the ancients to be fought over by present-day natural and unnatural beings challenged her credulity. Still, the jinn and his otherworldly powers were real, as was the growing pile of bodies who'd died seeking the treasure.

Lubna set aside thoughts of gold and murder to look at what lay ahead. It was a cloudless day and she could see forever. On her left, the hills of Calabria held by the Byzantine Empire crowded down to the shore and, on the right, the coast of the Emirate of Sicily stretched in a rocky perimeter around the island's northern tip. Recent storms had turned the landscape on both sides of the strait bright green with vegetation and crops. Cows looked like brown dots against the hills they passed.

Greeks, Phoenicians, Romans, and others from long-extinct empires had sent ships through this strait and described its splendor, but also its unpredictable navigational hazards. However, though boulders and rocky beaches funneled the Viking ships into an ever narrower channel, the waters ahead looked calm.

Since their encounter with the enormous, crimson sea creature offshore from Genoa, Lubna watched the waters she sailed through closely. However, today, nothing malign materialized. Perhaps the longships intimidated any supernatural sea creatures. Instead, porpoises played in their bow wake.

The gap between the two land masses formed a natural choke point before entering the Mediterranean Sea, allowing customs boats from both the Byzantines and Sicily to sally forth and accost passing vessels for fees to allow passage. However, today they stayed in port, letting the sinister Viking fleet pass untaxed. Word of the Danes' raids had reached even this far afield from the despoiled northern European coastal towns and monasteries that comprised the Viking's usual hunting grounds. Lubna guessed that any locals watching the fleet prayed that they would pass by en route to other victims.

After the storm that chased them out of Genoa finally dissipated, the sunshine and warmth felt exhilarating. Lubna tasted salt on her lips. The longship's surging passage through the waves sent spray at her and she sensed a desire to wander that she'd never recognized in herself. She tossed back her robe's cowl to let her black hair blow free in the wind and her face take in the sun. No one reminded her of modesty; the Norsemen didn't care.

Looking about at the pretty natural landscape and man's patchwork of competing empires and kingdoms, she saw the geography that they traversed and realized how artificial her readings had been. They gave her only the vaguest of notion of what she now saw. Of anyone on the longship, Lubna had the best understanding of this world, but her perceptions were still artificial. Standing beside a dragon's head on a pitching sliver of oak showed her reality. Rather than reading about these exotic locations and resigning herself to the inevitable biases and inaccuracies of their authors, she could now write her own texts and draw her own maps. She'd petition Orm or Halfdan for scraps of spare sail to record her descriptions of what she saw and use tar in lieu of ink. It would be a mess, but it would suffice. She would transcribe her crude calligraphy and drawings onto fine vellum once she returned to Córdoba—if she survived to return to Córdoba. It would be her contribution to the palace's library.

Her reverie stopped as the longship abruptly slewed sideways. They weren't traveling in a straight line any longer and, from her vantage point, Lubna noted the fleet being pushed toward the rocks on the Byzantine shore not far off. Cordage and wood strained to absorb the sudden stresses. Above, the ship's mainsail flapped violently as the wind fought with the current for control of their course while behind her the huge warrior manning the steering oar struggled with the current and worked to straighten the vessel out. He was bare-chested and the muscles stood out on his shoulders and arms. He called over another big Viking to help, and together they wrestled to set a true course. The oar looked thick, but Lubna wondered if it would splinter under the stress. These waters had a mind of their own and disregarded human intention.

Orm and Halfdan stood by the oar calling frantically to other ships in their fleet to head away from the rocks, but two of their longships were sailing toward ruin. Vikings lined the railings watching their friends' circumstances deteriorate. Everyone had been as sanguine as she was about an untroubled passage through the strait on a warm, sunny day. Excepting her and the jinn, they were all experienced sailors, but unfamiliar with these waters. The huge fellow manning the steering oar looked about for the closest free man and yelled for Thiago to replace him at the oar while he ran forward the length of the ship to where Lubna stood at the prow.

"I'm Njal. You understand Norse, the language of the gods?" the warrior said.

Lubna nodded. "A little."

"Let's hope it's enough," he said. "This stretch is treacherous as hell and I don't understand these waters. I know the currents from Denmark to Andalusia, but this mad expedition is taking us all away any from seas I've seen. Maybe we'll all pitch into oceans of fire soon."

"No, that won't happen," Lubna said. "When we clear the straits, the currents should lessen until we make Africa's shores. It will get warmer as we go."

He seemed doubtful that her readings would tell him anything useful, but, since he was desperate, he would at least entertain the idea that she could help.

"Halfdan says you've got a wide body of knowledge. How much further does this passage go before we're in open water?"

Lubna didn't remember precisely and the charts she'd seen back in Córdoba's library were wild distortions of the reality they sailed through. Further, almost nothing had been depicted to scale. She'd have to be honest with the oarsman, but give him the best information she could.

"You can see already where the strait widens," she said. "Look there, where I'm pointing. From what charts I've seen, I think that's the end, but I can't see far enough to be sure."

"You've learned this?"

"Yes, from my reading. It's not totally accurate."

"We'll use our eyes to prove it," the huge man said. "This current will break us all against the sharp stones off that shore, but we may just clear them if we use enough muscle on my oar."

He glanced back. "Your fellow knows how to steer *Trana*. Our vessel's path has become a bit more true. Perhaps he's sailed before?"

"He's done many things," Lubna said.

The big Viking shrugged. "I'll use what help I can get. Two of our boats may not be so lucky. They're too close. They're stupid. Halfdan and Orm should have placed better mariners to captain them. Too late for that now. They need to run out their rowing oars and pull for their lives. Their sails aren't enough. The current is not your friend in this channel. One of them is only supplies and few men are in peril, but the other is filled with true fighters, men I grew up with from my village."

Njal called back to a red-bearded Viking sitting on a rowing bench to come forward.

"Birger, stay here with—"

"Lubna."

"Yes, Lubna. Odd name. Let's hope you know what you say you know."

A tall, bearded warrior joined them at the prow. "I'm the apprentice oarsman," he said to the librarian. "Njal, I'll do whatever I can. What is it you need?"

"I'm looking ahead of us from my position on the oar at the back of our longship, of course, but you two have the best vantage point on the vessel. You're my eyes. Look sharp. If things change, call it out to me and the rest of us—Orm Silvertooth, Halfdan, all of us. But mostly make sure I hear. I'm steering this thing." He pounded a huge fist possessively on the ship's wooden railing. "Birger has a loud voice; you have good vision, Lubna, and you know better than the rest of us what we should be seeing, so you'll make a good pair. We can't help our friends in those two boats, so we must save ourselves and the rest of the fleet and maybe pick up whatever survivors haven't drowned or been bashed to pieces on the stones."

Njal sprinted back to his steering oar, leaping from bench to bench.

Lubna said a quiet prayer. She watched the approaching rocks. The cows on the green hills just behind the rocky beach were almost close enough to touch and stared at the Norsemen without interest.

"Will we make it?" she asked.

"Maybe," Birger said. "If the gods are agreeable and don't want to invite us to dine with them in Valhalla tonight, we'll get through. Good boat-handling will help, too, and Njal is the best. We'll lose those, though." The Viking gestured to the two boats closest to shore.

Heavy surf pounded the rocks and Lubna didn't have to use much imagination to picture Norsemen dashed into the huge stones as their ships splintered around them with the spars crushing anyone. They'd finally run out their oars and Lubna heard them clatter against rocks. Several oars snapped with loud cracks as they were squeezed between the longship and the rocks. She heard the Norsemen frantically shouting at each one another.

Both Lubna and Birger twisted around to see a tornado of tightly wound ocean water soaring away from *Trana* toward the two hapless longships. To Lubna it sounded like a hundred carts all rolled downhill on a stone-paved road. The waterspout periodically touched the waves, sending up geysers of water as it bounced along the ocean's surface and then interposed itself between the longships and the rocks, violently shaking the ships and sending shields and packs into the surf. The violent wind gusts snapped the yards and severed ropes, but also pushed the two vessels back into the strait's central channel away from destruction.

"It's working," she yelled.

The jinn was a sheep dog nudging straying members of a flock to safety. And then the waterspout collapsed in on itself, the tearing winds died away, and the remnants of the tornado arced back toward the *Trana*. Thiago materialized out of the tornado's midst at the vessel's stern.

He sneezed loudly.

"Your companion?" Birger asked.

"He's done this before," she said.

"A good fellow to have along." However, the Norseman appeared ambivalent about the jinn's presence even after witnessing him save his fellows. The rest of the crew had also watched the rescue intently, but no one cheered its success. Instead, Njal nodded thanks to Thiago, and Orm and Halfdan slapped him on the back. A few of the crew waved at him, acknowledging his effort, but kept their distance.

"I want a share of whatever you sell the lumber for on that supply ship I just helped," Lubna heard Thiago call to Halfdan and Orm.

The rest of the fleet gathered around the two damaged boats like wolves helping injured pack mates. Warriors threw ropes over to them to tow the battered craft through the rest of the strait.

As far as Lubna could tell, they'd passed beyond the powerful currents and were now close to what she believed was the strait's terminus.

"What is he?" Birger asked.

Lubna explained what she knew of the jinn from her observations and from reading arcane Arab and Persian texts that described them mainly as malevolent beings that toyed with humans for fun.

"You don't seem terrified," she concluded.

"We Norse walk among spirits, trolls, and giants. They are part of our landscape even if Christian priests suggest we not talk of them. Some are harmful, some not. Your companion fits in the latter category. I just saw him save many of my friends and kin. Our myths say there are nine overlapping worlds around a giant tree. These jinn may come from one of those places."

"Have you ever seen a spirit or troll?" Lubna asked.

"No, but my cousin did at twilight when he cleared forest by his farm last year. However, he was drunk at the time and prone to making up stories even when he's not drunk."

"We need our stories," she said. "Things are strange and we need to understand our experiences. Stories help. Nonetheless, I prefer science to explain things to me."

"What's science?"

"Taking what you observe about the world to understand what you don't know and then testing it to see if your new knowledge is true," she said.

"I believe what my senses show me," he said.

"Your senses are the starting point, but suppose you could learn about things beyond what they show you?"

"Magic?"

"The opposite of magic," Lubna said.

"Your—" Birger paused, evidently choosing the right word to describe Lubna and Thiago's relationship. "Your companion uses magic?"

"Call him my friend," the librarian said. "And yes, he is magical." Why hide it when the crew had seen Thiago transform into a massive waterspout leaving Genoa and, just now, save two longships? They'd seen something unnatural and, excepting Orm Silvertooth, Halfdan, and perhaps Njal, they stayed a respectful, fearful, distance from it.

"So why is science superior to magic?" the Norseman asked.

"Because you don't have to be supernatural to harness science. You and I can use it."

Njal walked forward to the prow. This time he didn't hurry.

"Too close," he said. He looked behind them to where the crew was attaching the supply vessel to *Trana*. Their ship had been selected to tow the wounded boat into open water beyond the strait.

"But we all lived to tell the tale. No small thanks to your companion back there." He nodded at Thiago. "And thanks to your knowledge of the waters and lands hereabouts. Who knew such knowledge existed?"

"I did."

"Yes, you did. We're not through this damned passage yet, but my gut tells me we won't be further troubled by rogue currents. We'll see."

Lubna smiled to herself. In essence, she was the Norsemen's guide, if not their navigator, though until the last few weeks, she'd never set foot on a ship and had been violently seasick as she and Thiago had journeyed to Genoa. The seasickness had passed to be replaced by a familiarity with their longship's rhythms and how it reacted to the oceans they sailed over and the ever-changing currents and weather.

She'd found her sea legs.

"Can I show you a skill Arab mariners use to understand their position in open water?" the librarian asked Njal and Birger.

"I don't trust tricks that my father didn't teach me about finding a path through troubled waters to a distant shore," Njal said. "But I'll listen over ale tonight."

The big Viking turned and strode back to resume his post at the steering oar.

Birger said, "Njal and the rest of us don't tempt fate by learning too much. The gods despise human arrogance."

Lubna frowned. "No gods I know of tell us not to learn. Only people speaking on their behalf."

She looked toward the stern and saw Thiago conferring with Orm and Halfdan.

"Tell him thanks," she said. "He won't bite."

Birger nodded and walked aft to help secure the fleet's supply ship to the *Trana*. She saw him stop by the jinn. He kept his distance, but they talked for a while. Lubna couldn't hear what they said, but the conversation looked animated and friendly. Good enough.

She leaned against the wooden railing and looked up at the *Trana*'s dragon head.

Had it just winked at her?

Maybe it knew her life had been a strange voyage. She'd come from a village in the County of Castile before her family sold her to the Caliph's court. There she'd risen through sheer talent and hard work to a respected role as the chief intellectual and librarian, and now she'd joined a mad expedition with an outlaw jinn amid a fleet of Norsemen after a mythical treasure. Despite troubled waters, she'd flourished—so far.

"I'm never sure whether to hide as I transform," Thiago said. He'd joined her at the prow. "By now, they all know what I am, so there's no point. You convinced Birger to approach me?"

Lubna nodded. "That waterspout thing saved the day again. Very impressive."

"If Lila is anywhere near, she'll have sensed my 'waterspout thing.' Actually, she is near. I can feel her. I don't know where exactly, but she is."

"If we keep going at this speed, she'll never catch us," Lubna said. "You said she can't just fly forever without resting."

"It doesn't matter. She knows more or less where we're going even without my pyrotechnics to mark the way. She'll guess we now have the map and are en route to the exact place I buried the treasure. No need to intervene; she'll just follow along. Demons find a way. And she won't come after us alone. She'll mobilize her tribe and combine with the king's forces. She'll hire humans from this world to help, too. Hopefully, we can recover the treasure before they come."

"Is that likely?"

"No. It's my wishful thinking," he said. "We'll have a fight."

Together they looked at the path ahead of the longship. They were done with the Strait of Messina and sailing into the Mediterranean's open water. She shaded her eyes to peer back at where they'd been. The cows were out of sight.

"If we survive this, how will you go back to Córdoba's library?" he asked.

"You mean *can* I go back or *will* I go back?" She stalled for time. She had no ready answer and had been mulling it over since fleeing the palace weeks ago. Everyone was defined by what they did. What role would she have outside the library?

"Will you go back if you can go back?" he asked.

"The *can* question is easier than the *will* part. I believe I can return to the palace because the caliph, may he be much blessed, respects me though he doesn't necessarily like me, so I've got a place. He can hardly blame me for fleeing for my life after Matias had me imprisoned and almost executed."

"Rulers assign blame in the most amazing ways," Thiago said. "My father is wasting in a cell for something he had nothing to do with and would have actively advised against if he'd known what I planned. Will your caliph quibble that you didn't inform him immediately of the scroll when you realized what it was? Matias couldn't have confiscated it if you'd already transferred it to Abd-al-Rahman."

"The caliph is unpredictable," she acknowledged. "I'll spin some tale about needing to understand its significance before passing it off to him. He'll believe me—or I'll lose my head."

"You meant to keep the map."

"I'll confess to you that I meant to keep it, not because I wanted the treasure. Until I met you, I didn't understand where the map led. Even when I found out the story behind it, I thought it was a fantasy until the corpses piled up. I would have kept it because I thought the poem was original and very clever and only I and a select few would appreciate it properly."

"I won't share that with anyone," the jinn said.

Lubna shuddered. "God forbid."

"So that leaves the *will* you go back to Córdoba question," he said.

"I harvest scrolls and books from the whole world. It's an unrivaled collection," she said knowing that pride came through in her voice. "Things I select for the library have a chance to survive for coming generations."

"You're the mistress of memories," he said.

"I like that," the librarian said.

"It's apt," the jinn said. "Things you don't deign to acquire will turn to dust. Chances are, no one will ever read them. I'd like to think my poem and any future verses I create have a spot there. However, important as your role was, it's all a bit dry, don't you think? You rarely left the confines of the palace to see Córdoba let alone the rest of Spain. It was your home and place of study, but also a prison."

"Prison?"

"A very comfortable prison," the jinn said. "But you couldn't just leave to travel about on your own."

"No, I couldn't leave," she admitted. "But now that I have left, however involuntarily, I don't know if I want to go back. Why can't I be the one exploring new lands and seas and writing about them instead of reading someone else's adventure?"

She'd said this with more honesty than she'd intended. She preferred to keep self-doubt to herself. Córdoba's court was neither interested in nor forgiving of that sort of reflection. However, the jinn had no expectations of her other than that she might help him with his own mad plans. And be his friend. Couldn't friends also be confidants?

"We could travel the world looking for lost treasure," he said. They both laughed, appreciating the joke, but also admiring the audacity of the idea.

"Become your partner in crime?" she asked. "I'll consider that question after we've recovered your almighty treasure. I've assembled a collection of written work surpassing all others including Baghdad. Even the lost library of Alexandria may not have been as extensive. Who would continue my work if I didn't go back? I'd betray the caliph, visiting scholars, and myself if I didn't carry on. Still, I'm nothing except a pampered servant. Oh, I'm a learned servant they take care to indulge for the prestige of the caliphate, but a servant nonetheless. I'm an exotic animal from a menagerie. Out here on the water, I'm free. Do I want to be a servant again?"

"You know your heart better than me," Thiago said.

"What would you do?" Lubna asked the lascivious dragon's head next to her.

Had it winked again?

She patted it for luck.

"Your turn to answer awkward questions, Thiago. Will you go back?"

"To where? I'm an outlaw in a land of demons. Sounds wild and romantic, but really it just means savage killers are doing their damnedest to tear me to shreds and blast my soul. Every time I feel a cold breeze on my back, I wonder if the game's up. And if I did somehow go back in disguise, what would I be returning to? The place I come from is crumbling. Without intending it, I'm the nudge that may send the whole brilliant, awful edifice tumbling down in a cloud of sparkling dust."

Above them, the longship's garishly colored mainsail boomed and strained in the prevailing wind as they raced south. Occasionally, they saw small triangular or square sails on the horizon as other ships got close enough for their captains to recognize the longships as unfamiliar and dangerous intruders into Mediterranean waters and react by sharply changing course to run away. Despite everything confronting them, Lubna felt unstoppable. She'd never had this sensation before and wanted to yell out a challenge across the waves to whatever came their way. The librarian wondered if the jinn had this feeling of utter power. He could become fire or a tornado at will and, in human form, he was strong beyond reckoning.

He stared ahead with her and seemed to read her thoughts.

"It's easy for now," he said. "Look at the plump geese we're chasing out of the way. We're a terror to them. But as we get closer to recovering the treasure, everything we meet will be hellish and vicious beyond what you can conceive. Enjoy the moment."

"I was," she said. "Couldn't you have let me do that a little longer? So, you won't go back?"

"How?" he asked. "Either the king will recover the treasure and use it to prop up his world and conquer this one, or I beat him, in which case that world—my world—loses the wealth it needs to sustain the pomp and glory. If I win, I'm not sure whether to feel happy or sorry."

"What will you do with Sheba's Treasure if you get it?" Lubna asked.

"When I first decided to steal it, my thinking hadn't gotten beyond making myself fabulously rich, having a great time, and sticking a sharp stick in the eye of a ruler I hated. I'll give myself credit for wanting to stop the king from seizing this world, but if I'm honest, my greed had just as much to do with it, maybe more."

"And Lila," the librarian said. "She was inspiration for the theft, too?"

"She was," Thiago acknowledged. "That motive wasn't so noble."

"But now . . ." Lubna prompted.

"But now, I believe there are parts of my world worth saving. My world isn't just more debauched than yours, it's also more advanced in some ways. I could use Sheba's Treasure to preserve its gaudy palaces, parks containing the most amazing creatures, paintings, sculpture, architecture, that no artist here can touch. No one has to worry about the grubby part of living that plagues your world. I sound like my father. I can't abide his views, but he has a point that there are things worth appreciating in my world. I'd just like to change the bad aspects."

"Don't patronize my world," she said. "Remember Córdoba. That's something."

"That *is* something," he acknowledged. "Especially your library. The two worlds are like fractured mirrors of each other. I suppose shuttling back and forth makes the contrasts and similarities more obvious. What would be ordinary criminality here doesn't exist there. Bad things happen all the time, but there's a motive behind them."

"That makes it better?"

"No, just more explainable," he said.

"So what about stealing Sheba's Treasure?"

"That was transgressive, but then I'm an outlaw, so rules don't apply. And, yes, I'm being arrogant."

The jinn turned around to look back at the longship and the dwindling European landmasses. Much of the crew including

Orm and Halfdan slept curled against rowers' benches or the wooden sides of the longship, exhausted by their struggle with the current. Njal remained alert and held the steering oar, immobile as a rock except to periodically look to the sails or at the position of the supply ship they towed to see that it wasn't too close to the *Trana*.

"You've become a philosopher in just a few weeks without reading a single book or scroll in my library."

"I'll take the compliment, but I think of myself as an outlaw by vocation and a poet by calling."

He regarded Lubna for several moments.

"What?" she said. "Why the look?"

"There *is* something I've got to do before further confrontations with the king, Lila, and a whole host of ravening demons. I need your help if you're willing."

"Your father?"

"Excellent guess. Yes, my father. Win, lose, or draw in whatever fight is coming up, if I can't get him out before then, the king will kill him out of spite. I can't put my family through more. There's no love lost between me and them, but they're already scattered in the wind thanks to me. Sheba's Treasure is worth less to me than an old jinn's life. I didn't think that a few months ago, but I do now."

"I don't know what I'm in for, but I'll help if I can." Lubna amazed herself by volunteering. It must be the sea air. And being away from the familiar library.

"How can I help, though? I'm a librarian. Or I used to be. Now I carry your dagger at all times out of habit. I even sleep with it, but that doesn't make me dangerous to anyone except myself. So what about our new best friends?" She nodded at the Norsemen. "They're better at stabbing people than me."

"A crude weapon," Thiago said. "Surprise is the only way. It would be endlessly complicated getting a large Viking raiding party through the portal without everyone and their mother finding out. We'll have a better chance of success with a small group, maybe just the two of us—or a few more to help out."

"You have your jinn fellow outlaws, the Fire Horde, or some such quaint name. They come from your world. They'd know what to expect."

"We're not on speaking terms at the moment. I lost their treasure. They don't care about my father one way or the other. And if I somehow patch things up with them and enlisted their help, they'd be worse than the Vikings. A few of them can be subtle, but mostly they're good at wreaking havoc on a grand scale, not sneaking into a prison. With the whole crew along, I wouldn't get anywhere near my father without the king's personal guard—not to mention the jailers—realizing we'd arrived and what I planned. They'd kill my father. And us, too."

He regarded her again. "I won't lie and say this will likely work; it probably won't work, so you'd be clever to opt out."

"Well, I like to think that I am clever," she said. "A clever person would want to know why they'd be helpful."

"You're good with iron," he said. "He's in an iron cage. I can't get close. I can nudge a ship out of harm's way, but this is another kind of problem altogether."

"You got me out of a cell," Lubna said. "Can you do that here?"

"Your cell door was mostly wood. All I had to do was manage the iron keys and the lock. I'm better than any other jinn with iron, so I did it, but it hurt. I stood on an iron chariot—for about three heartbeats, but a cage is too much. It's built to keep demons in and ward off other demons trying to break them out."

"Besides iron, are there other challenges to releasing your father?" she wondered aloud.

"I was getting to that. High walls, endless guards—some of them human on the inside of the dungeon because iron doesn't bother them—and creatures bigger than the one that chased us outside of Genoa primed for blood."

"And what do we have going for us?" She knew her voice sounded unhappy.

Thiago shrugged. "We'll go unnoticed as long as we can. I'm bribing the guards, too—I kept some gold before I hid the rest of Sheba's Treasure. My father was well liked and had many friends even beyond our tribe. Some of them are in the king's guard. We'll also need a distraction."

"Tell me about your plan."

And he did. Lubna didn't feel better about their chances after hearing it.

"That's it?" she asked incredulously.

"That's it," he said. "We'll do this the jinn way: low cunning, bad magic, unexpected allies, and fast work with a blade."

"How can we lose?" She tried to keep the dry-as-dust irony out of her voice and failed. She was torn between the adventure of it and the likelihood of a sticky end in some far-off land.

"Portals sound dangerous," she said after she'd pondered awhile.

"Most passages are easy," he said. "You start here and you wind up there. My cousin didn't make it, but I think he wanted to die and the portal was a convenient place to do it."

"In your world, do we have a place to hide if we need to?"

"My family's home. It's a palace." She heard ambivalence in his tone.

"It's got memories," he said. "But it will do. The king's watching it, but we'll get in. I've not been all that welcome these last few years, so I'm not as familiar with the place as I once was, but there are ways. We'll need somewhere to conceal ourselves until the right group of guards is on duty at the dungeon."

"The bribable ones?"

"Yes."

"What's the capital city called?" she asked.

"Bethinia. If they're feeling formal, its residents call it Purple Bethinia since the palaces appear that color at dusk. You'll see them for yourself when we go."

"Your world is unimaginable."

"It's as real as here. But first, we need more help than we have."

CHAPTER 14

Petitioning the Fire Horde

"W e're not mercenaries," Ajmal said. "You can't hire us to clean up the shit you've stepped in."

He addressed Thiago, but spoke to the assembled Fire Horde sitting or lounging in Palmyra's long-abandoned Roman amphitheater. Empires had come and gone and it was half covered in drifting sand, but enough exposed stonework poked through to accommodate the warriors. Thiago couldn't call them "his" warriors any longer; who led the Horde would be negotiated tonight.

The jinn had draped themselves on benches or leaned against columns. Several sat far up on the cornices and roofs of the thousand-year-old structure. Thiago reflected that jinn instinctively gravitated to ruins on this side of the portal perhaps because they connoted age and mystery, while superstitious humans steered clear of them. There were no ruins in the demon world; anything that decayed was simply ripped apart and rebuilt grander than ever. Until recently, cost was no limitation.

Some of the assembled jinn looked like men, several like predatory animals, others like spheres of flame in various colors, and a few were whirlwinds. Looking about him, Thiago admired their vivid appearance, but their casual, contemptuous attitude angered him; they projected arrogant nonchalance.

More than ever, they'd devolved into an anarchic gang, free and untamed—and maybe ultimately untamable. However, he needed them to follow his lead. They'd convened grudgingly at his request, but the Horde made no secret that their support for him was conditional and, for many, nonexistent.

Ajmal wanted to be the outlaws' leader and made no secret of it. Thiago knew that, after Jai, the bearded jinn was the most popular member of the group. Many deferred to him who would never defer to Thiago. They might consider Thiago brave, but the loss of Sheba's Treasure had destroyed whatever credibility he'd once had. Now he simply looked reckless. Besides, even in his human form, Ajmal looked more like a "real" jinn than Thiago, complete with fierce, misformed features adorned with clawed feet as if he'd planned to morph into a raptor but then stopped the transformation part way through. His color was oddly pale like he'd tried for alabaster but gotten pallid white instead. Thiago thought his form was disquietingly fluid and insubstantial. In contrast, the Horde believed Thiago pandered to a human sense of aesthetics by appearing as a handsome man.

Thiago stood dead center on the ancient stage. Tonight, he could either turn this into a powerful position or make himself an easier target for disrespect. It might get him killed.

"Despite all appearances to the contrary, you're not mercenary?" Thiago scornfully addressed Ajmal's challenge.

Come at them strong, he thought.

"You all wanted to steal Sheba's Treasure," he said. "That's the biggest pile of booty on either side of the portal. Sounds mercenary to me."

"We'll take on anyone either side of the portal," Charun interceded. "You know that. But this time we're not ambushing a caravan. The king has armies. It's a hopeless fight. It's presumptuous to take our loyalty for granted. Besides, you lost all of it, the treasure. You've got nothing to offer us."

"*Presumptuous.* I like that word," Ajmal said. "I don't know words that big. However, the lad does make a point: You presume a lot, Thiago."

"You're not making friends," Aaliyah said quietly to Thiago so the rest couldn't hear. She sat atop a broken stone pillar near him on the stage. "Charun's right, you can't take their loyalty for granted. They follow success. At the moment, you don't look so successful with half of this world and all of ours after your head. Flatter them a bit. You used to know how to do that. I chased after Sheba's Treasure because I chased after you. You can charm if you want to."

"She's right." Lubna stood inconspicuously behind him. "You're the supplicant here. Hide your arrogance—if you can."

Thiago looked about him. He *was* losing this audience fast. They didn't suffer weakness. They would drift off into the night or attack him outright amid the ruins unless he could convince them that the cause he proposed wasn't simply self-interest. Thiago felt a cold night breeze rearranging the sand among the ruins. The wind also probed for chinks in his emotional armor, looking for a way past his youthful certainty.

Persuade them to my cause, he thought. *It would be ironic if my band of fighters slaughters me before Lila or the king's agents find me. Is there any sympathy in this crowd?*

"I saved some of you," he said. "You were planned for execution because we thought you'd alert the king about who stole Sheba's Treasure. That didn't happen. Instead, you're now part of the group."

"And what has that gotten us?" a voice shouted back. "We can't go home. We have no wealth. We just have your words. Small consolation."

So, no sympathy in this crowd.

"I'm nothing but words?" Thiago asked. He projected his voice out to the far reaches of the amphitheater where the real skeptics sat reserving judgment. If he could move them, he could move the rest.

"How about these words: I'm giving you another chance to take the treasure," he said. "You got a taste of it, quite a taste."

"We spent that," Ajmal shouted, playing to the crowd.

"Long gone," said a jinn in the form of blue fire. Thiago vaguely recalled that his name was Kaveh. He should have exerted himself to know them better. Kaveh's voice emanated from the center of the flames. "It was a real celebration."

"Wish you'd invited me," Thiago said.

"We only invite our friends," Kaveh said.

The outlaws laughed.

The blue flame shot from the back benches and arced downward toward the stage to circle where Thiago stood. Kaveh passed so close that Thiago flinched from the flame. He smelled something charred. It might have been his robe or his hair. So would they attack him immediately without hearing him out?

"You burn hot, my friend," Thiago said. "Is it just heat or is there some light there?"

Kaveh ignored the challenge and floated above him for a moment before settling on the side of the stage near Charun and Aaliyah.

This was high entertainment, and he saw those jinn currently in their human form passing jugs of wine among themselves. Thiago rarely saw jinn drunk, but then again, their normal behavior was so volatile that he might not notice the effect of liquor. Nonetheless, it didn't bode well that they were drinking tonight.

"You made us all fugitives," Kaveh said. His blue flame ramped up, emphasizing his statements.

"At least fugitives have a home, a fire to sit around. We're refugees," Ajmal said. "It's a sorry state, it is. I don't dare cross the portal, and even on this side the king has infiltrated demons who threaten us all." He pointed at Thiago. "You have your family's palace to return to."

"*Had* a palace," Thiago corrected. "The king seized it when he imprisoned my father."

"I ain't been in a palace," Ajmal said. "They ain't fond of folks like me."

"You're not missing anything," Thiago said. "And I can't go back. My trial showed you that. The king will be much more creative in designing my execution than he was with Jai. I'm a refugee like you all."

Mentioning Jai was a gamble. Reminding the Horde of his popular friend could cut both ways: The jinn warriors might recall Jai stoutly defending Thiago from the king's fury and blame him for his friend's murder. Or the outlaws might assign fault to the tyrant and decide that vengeance against him was long overdue. Thiago hoped to persuade them to the latter course of action.

"Where's the rest of the treasure?" Charun said. If Thiago had allies in the amphitheater, Charun was one of them, but even he looked skeptical.

"You were clever where you hid it," Ajmal said. "He's a clever fellow, our Thiago is. Too clever. And too careless about losing the only way to find our gold to that bitch, Lila, his lover."

Ajmal caressed his crotch to the crowd's huge amusement. "Was she good to you? As good as she was to the king?"

"*Former* lover," Thiago said flatly. Just what he needed, his infatuation with Lila paraded before a half-drunk pack of supernatural outlaws more intent on mocking him—goaded by Ajmal—than listening. Steer the argument back to the treasure.

"The king's agents can't find it and you can't, either," Kaveh said. "Not even Lila with the map has recovered it."

Here was an opening. Thiago jumped on it.

"She lost the map, too," Thiago said loudly. "Yes, I'm too clever for my own good as everyone keeps reminding me, and, yes, my choice of romantic partners leaves much to be desired, and, yes, I've got nothing to offer—except this."

With as much drama as he could muster, he pulled the scroll out of his tunic.

"Let's have my friend, Kaveh, with the brightly burning flame, illuminate what I've got. Come on over, Kaveh. Highlight it for the crowd. No time to be shy. I don't suppose you read?"

Kaveh morphed into a rotund human with a broad sash encircling his tummy and ambled across the stage to examine the scroll.

"It's your damned poem," he said. Thiago sensed the rest of the warriors clustering closer to the stage. They loved a good confrontation.

"Yes, my damned poem. A bit tattered, but readable. It was torn in two, but she was able to repair it." He pointed at Lubna.

"Who's she?" Charun asked.

"A librarian."

"What's a library?"

"A place to keep scrolls and books," Lubna said. "It's where all the world's knowledge is kept."

"Then it must be a small place," Ajmal said.

The assembled warriors, two hundred of the Fire Horde, roared with laughter. Thiago hoped that they weren't too deep in their cups yet, though he noted that at least two fights had broken out. He supposed it was good that they attacked one another and not him except that he needed them to coalesce if they were to take on the world, a mad king, and Lila.

"This library can't be any smaller than your brain," Aaliyah shouted at Ajmal. Her natural combativeness came out.

"It's just words," Ajmal said. He looked ready for a clash, too.

"It's important words and a map," Thiago said. "Now I can find—no, now *we* can find—Sheba's Treasure." He saw Aaliyah discreetly nod her approval at being inclusive.

Thiago jumped up on a stone block in the middle of the stage.

"Am I rash? Absolutely. However, you followed me once. You trained with me, too."

"You trained us too hard," a voice from near the back snarled.

"It worked," Thiago yelled back. "Better jinn than you have criticized me. We seized the caravan. And I never asked you to perform a task or take a risk that I wouldn't take myself."

This elicited a sullen silence. He wasn't getting credit for shared suffering.

"Are we jinn or just demons?" Thiago shouted. "Ambition lets us try things that no one in our world or this one could even imagine."

"This is as charming as you can get?" Aaliyah whispered.

"At least they're listening," Thiago whispered back.

Thiago jumped down from the block and strolled over to stroke a lion's mane. The creature was enormous, bigger than any actual lion. One of the warriors had chosen this form for the assembly. He looked ready to claw Thiago's face off.

"We split Sheba's Treasure evenly among us," Thiago said. "When this all started, I wanted the biggest cut. I conceived the plan, after all. The king would come after me first. The biggest risk gets the biggest cut. Selfish me. No more. You all risked more than you knew. You all deserve more than I meant to give you. Instead, we all get an equal share. Buy your own damned palaces. You'll find them cold and unfriendly like I did, but it's your choice. They do look pretty and they have great views."

The outlaws collectively leaned toward him. The background rumble of disinterested hostility died away, replaced by silence except for the desert gusts twisting through the Roman columns. He had their attention now. Cynically he understood that appealing to their greed rather than their ideals was his path forward. Those who had morphed into their fire form burned brighter. Those who were animals leaped forward to climb onto the stage beside the lion. Soon a menagerie prowled about, occasionally sniffing at him hungrily. Those who were wind joined the desert air in encircling the amphitheater. Those who were men crowded forward, raising their swords and spears toward the night sky.

"Decide," Aaliyah shouted to the assembled group, her voice carrying to the back tiers. "Decide one way or the other. No middle ground. Follow Thiago or cut him to pieces."

"We can always cut him to pieces if we don't find the treasure," Charun added.

"Let's not go that far," Thiago said.

All the Horde surged onto the stage yelling their readiness for a brawl.

"This is your second chance," Aaliyah whispered to him. "Make it count."

"Thanks," he said. "I'm as dead as the rest of you if this doesn't work."

"Cold comfort," Aaliyah said.

"I want the poem when this is all over," Lubna said. "It goes in my library."

"Will anyone see it?"

"Everyone who visits. I'll display it. Scholars from centers of learning the world over visit."

"Then it's yours," Thiago said. "I'll write others that are better."

"Is it us against the world?" Charun asked.

"We have help," Thiago said. "They're from the north and they ride ships with dragon's prows."

"Sailors?" Aaliyah asked. "Doesn't sound like much help."

"Raiders," Thiago said. "They're human—sort of. They wear small iron hammers around their necks for good luck, I guess. It's a token of respect for one of their gods, Thor."

"Just what we need, more gods," Aaliyah said sarcastically.

"It wasn't their original purpose, but the iron tokens will also be some protection in a fight with hostile jinn and ifrit."

"Whoever these sailors are and whatever they wear, they'll want a cut of the treasure," Ajmal said. "That comes from your share, not mine."

Greed, the great motivator for my lukewarm supporters, Thiago thought.

CHAPTER 15

The Canal of the Pharaohs

"I'm bitten," Njal said.

Thiago saw the huge oarsman brush a dark snake off his calf onto the longship's deck. He tried to stamp on it, but the serpent avoided his boot and reared back, spreading its hood ready for another strike. It looked like a coil of greasy black rope.

Aaliyah jumped past the others at the ship's stern to grab the snake. It promptly bit her hand and made to strike again, but she tossed it over the side into the Nile. There was a soft splash.

"It feels like nothing," Njal said. "Just pricks."

"It'll feel worse soon," Thiago said. "Then you stop breathing."

"Birger, take the oar," Njal said. "Watch our course and mind the shallows ahead to the left."

"Let me see to your bite," Thiago said.

"I'd like to keep breathing," Njal said.

"What about her?" Lubna said, urgently pointing to Aaliyah.

"We have worse where I come from," Aaliyah said. "It left one of its fangs in my hand, but I'm not hurt." She pulled the tooth out of her palm. "Thiago should care for this man. He's best at steering the river."

Thiago kneeled and yanked the oarsman's pants out of his boot and jammed them up his calf to expose the wound, two barely visible red dots on the Dane's leg.

"Lubna, your knife please," he said. Then to Njal, "Sit down with your back against the side. I'm going to cut you over the bite right now. It will hurt."

Thiago made two deft slices, drawing a flow of blood from the Norseman's calf. Then he sucked at the blood and spat it onto the deck, repeating this several times. The oarsman looked on, bemused.

Most of the crew, Norsemen and jinn alike, clustered at the *Trana*'s stern. Some called out suggestions, but most watched quietly and intently.

"What are you doing?" Njal asked. "This isn't sexual?"

"Nothing of the sort," Thiago said.

"Oh, for sure it's sexual," Ajmal shouted. Both jinn and Norsemen laughed.

"He's trying to extract the venom," Lubna said. "A Jewish court doctor from Baghdad describes exactly this process for snake bites in a Persian text."

"I've heard such stories, too," Halfdan said. "Never placed any belief in them. He may die."

"Not on my watch," Thiago said.

"If you're immune, why didn't you kill the snake?" Birger asked Aaliyah.

"It was a cobra," she said. "They were sacred to the pharaohs. We're in their land now. Unlike Thiago, I don't offend gods, even human gods. Besides, cobras eat rats. I hate rats."

"I don't feel good, faint," Njal said.

"I got some of the poison out, but not enough," Thiago said. "What I'll do next will hurt more than the knife, but we need to do it." Again, he didn't wait for the oarsman's acknowledgment. Murmuring a verse, he put his hand over the bleeding bite. For an instant, orange-yellow flame passed from his forefinger into the wound. The odor of burned flesh permeated the air.

Njal kicked his leg away from the jinn, cursing.

"I'll take the serpent's poison over being scorched."

"You'll recover," Thiago said. "Wash it with drinking water, wine would be better if there's any onboard. Don't use river water to clean it or you'll rot your leg off. After flushing the wound, find the cleanest rag you've got and bandage it."

"I'll see to the wine and a cloth," Orm told his oarsman. "Not so different from a sword cut. We need you to navigate the Nile, so whatever Halfdan says, don't die just yet." He slapped Njal's shoulder.

The crowd of Vikings and jinn dispersed back along the length of the longship to sit on benches chatting among themselves about Njal's chances of recovery. They stuck to their own, though the confined space among their weapons and packs prevented wide separation. Still, Thiago didn't see overt animosity between the two groups. Good. If they were to survive, let alone prevail over the king and the ifrit's forces, they needed to cooperate. He also needed to train them to work as a unit. He'd talk to the Viking chieftains and the loudest voices among the jinn—Ajmal, Charun, and Aaliyah—about that tomorrow. Maybe members of the two groups could start by sharing benches and rowing together. Predictably, no one would be happy. However, visions of riches would motivate them.

Thiago nodded thanks to Aaliyah. "Fast work."

The jinn warrior made a show of nursing her hand where the cobra had bitten it, then doubled over laughing.

"Want to suck my hand?" she asked.

"That would be sexual," Njal said.

"You sailors need to be tougher," Aaliyah said.

"They aren't bothered by iron," Thiago said. "That's something."

"Where did you learn how to treat reptile bites?" Lubna asked.

Thiago dropped down, sitting on the deck to lean against the longship's side. He felt fatigued from the spell he'd used to heal the oarsman.

"I read a lot when I was in the desert by myself, books and scrolls I'd picked up from sellers like Yonah, Sarah, and Lior. I wasn't selective about what I looked at and I came across texts on medicine. Of course, most of it has nothing to do with jinn. It was like studying some peculiar, exotic species prone to the most amazing variety of illness. We don't get sick like you do, but it passed the time. As did composing poetry."

"None of the texts mentioned using a fire spell to cauterize a cobra bite," she said.

"I improvised that part."

"Not a typical jinn," Lubna said.

"I'll take that as a compliment. I'm not a typical anything—for all the good it's done me."

~

Tyrants and empires came and went, but the farmers remained.

They worked the earth along the Nile's banks and watched as the longships moved single file down the middle of the channel, but then they returned to their animals and plows.

Who knew what they thought.

And then Thiago did know what they thought. They wanted to be left alone to care about the river's seasonal floods and the soil's fertility. They wanted to be left out of imperial dreams.

Thiago, at the *Trana's* prow, looked back. The line of Viking warships stretched behind him as far as he could see, bisecting the river, a black line with red sails in the blue-brownish water. Even in a land of tombs, the boats stuffed with demons and Norsemen looked baleful and otherworldly.

Maybe that's why we haven't been challenged by somebody's warships. He'd seen cavalry parallel their course along hills overlooking the Nile, but they'd veered off. The number of warriors and shields on the longships dissuaded curiosity.

He knew that human realms now contended for Egypt as they had for four thousand years. Currently, it was the Byzantines and various Arab caliphates as well as raiders from the city-state of Venice, and things were fluid without any power controlling the Nile's traffic.

The Norse vessels traveled slowly, feeling their way along the unfamiliar waterways. This wasn't the North Sea. *Trana* led the fleet still towing the supply ship, where repairs were ongoing. In places silt narrowed the river's course. However, the longships didn't draw much water, so Thiago felt confident they could get through if they slowed to a crawl at night.

The prevailing current was against them as the river's water pushed unstoppably from African headwaters far upstream out to the Mediterranean, but they'd trimmed their sails to make steady progress against it as they headed south. When the wind failed, oars came out. Thiago had expected swamp-like conditions, but it was only warm and humid rather than an inferno. Nonetheless, when they rowed, Viking and jinn alike stripped to their waists to pull, sweaty demons on an unholy mission.

On some stretches, tilled land pushed close to the riverbank; on others, sand came right down to the water's edge and nothing could be cultivated. White ibises stalked through grasses, and Thiago saw red lotus flowers. Far above, an eagle tracked their progress.

At night, he felt Egypt's age. Black, indistinct structures that might have been tombs or temples drifted past in the Stygian darkness, and it was quiet enough so he imagined he heard a pharaoh's subjects, goaded by an overseer's shouts, dragging enormous stone blocks to be dressed and then erected into edifices to honor gods and men who thought they were gods.

"Is the leg better?" Thiago asked.

"Strong as ever now," Njal said. "However, your cure may be worse than the wound."

"You survived," the jinn said dryly.

The huge oarsman and the librarian had joined Thiago at the prow next to the ever-vigilant dragon's head.

"This is the Nile?" Njal said.

"This is the Nile delta," Lubna replied.

"Big river—we've been on it for days—but I like the open ocean better. Where is this Canal of the Pharaohs?"

The librarian peered ahead. "Soon, I think. I know this area less than the Strait of Messina. I have a very good memory, but I've seen too many maps pass through my library to perfectly remember them all. Besides, this delta has been sailed since forever and there are maps ancient and recent, but none of them were meant to be navigational charts."

"I've complained about this to Orm and Halfdan," Njal said frankly. "We're staking everything on your memory."

"That got us through the Strait of Messina," Thiago said. "It's all we've got to get the longships into the Red Sea. Still, let's do a little reconnaissance. If the Canal of the Pharaohs exists, it may be easy to miss."

"Put in to shore and send out scouts?" the oarsman asked.

"I'm afraid he's thinking of something else," Lubna said.

~

"It's an old stream bed," Njal said. "Some parts are more mud than water. The chieftain that designed this was a lazy bastard. Nobody's kept it clear."

They looked down at the small stream that veered off the Nile's main course. Thiago believed they would have missed it entirely if they hadn't flown. Though partially obscured by foliage, the passage appeared man-made with artificially straight banks extending eastward toward the Red Sea. Farmers' huts nestled up against the channel.

The librarian and the oarsman hadn't complained about their airborne surveillance. However, the wooden board they sat on wasn't big and the ground was far, far below. Both of them clenched the board and sat rigid. The eagle that had followed their progress since reaching the Nile now flew at their same height. Maybe it was skeptical at this intrusion into its realm.

"Two centuries ago they tried to starve a revolt into submission by letting the channel overgrow," Lubna said. She looked down briefly, then closed her eyes. "I'd read that they'd dredged it since then."

"So much for reading," Njal said.

"So much for carrying," Ajmal shouted. "We're putting them down. They can inspect the bloody canal from the ground."

The four jinn descended with the plank carrying the oarsman and Lubna. It had been Thiago's idea to do the search from the air, so he'd tried to do most of the lifting, but Charun, Aaliyah, and the ever-complaining Ajmal had done their share holding the board's other three corners. Between them, they had just enough lift to carry Njal and Lubna. The librarian was light, but the oarsman weighed as much as two men.

They landed haphazardly in the mud near the water's edge. Thiago was so tired he wondered how they'd make it back to the *Trana*. After all his time on water, even finding his footing on the muddy shore was tricky. The others floundered about too as they alighted, but both Njal and Lubna appeared thrilled to return to terra firma.

"What's the *Trana*'s draft?" Thiago asked Njal.

"Loaded or unloaded?"

"Both."

"Very little," the big man said proudly. He extended his arm. "Unloaded, from my shoulder to my fingertips. Loaded, another arm-length maybe."

"Not much at all?" Thiago asked, incredulous. Though he'd been on a longship for weeks, he hadn't realized how high they sat in the water.

"How do you think we raided Europe's shores from end to end? We went far up rivers in the lands of Saxons, Franks, and Rus, farther than they expected that we could."

Thiago waded out into the muddy stream to gauge how deep the water was.

"It will be close," he said. "The longships may push through with their oars and a favorable wind—or not."

"Leave the ships and the Norsemen here," Ajmal said emphatically. "Jinn can travel just fine on our own to get the treasure."

"If I had my ax, I'd slice you in two," Njal said.

So much for cooperation, Thiago thought. *I've done a fine job of bonding everyone together.*

He stepped between the two. "We'll need all of us together to have a hope of taking on the king's warriors. Go your separate ways after we've got the riches. You'll all have more wealth than you can carry. No point in fighting now."

Aaliyah, Charun, and Lubna also stepped between the jinn and the Viking. Thiago didn't worry that the jinn would be hurt if Ajmal and Njal decided to go at it, but it was bold of the librarian to get between them.

"You're standing in only hip-deep water, Thiago. So, how do we get the boats to the Red Sea?" Charun asked.

"Hide the boats here and go on foot?" the oarsman asked.

"He's thinking of something else," Lubna said.

"We keep the boats," Thiago said. "We'll need them on the Red Sea. And I like the *Trana*. So—"

"So?" Charun asked.

"If the ships are loaded and we hit impassable water, the jinn lighten the boats by carrying weapons and packs and flying them ahead while the Norsemen pull the boats forward. There's plenty of rope aboard for that, but it will be a lot of effort."

Thiago saw that this had the desired effect. Now Ajmal and Njal had something they agreed on: hatred of Thiago.

～

"A sea of sand," Halfdan said. "How can you live here?"

"How can you live at sea?" Ajmal countered. "Nothing but water."

"Jinn don't live in deserts necessarily," Thiago interrupted to forestall further animosity among his motley band of hot-heads. "The city I live in on the other side of the portal has parks greener than anything here."

Over the last week, he'd labored to train them to fight together. Battles were won by preparation before the fight as much as by prowess during it. Luck helped, too.

They sat on a Red Sea beach a few days' sailing south of where they'd finally reached open water after a hard effort to traverse the Channel of the Pharaohs. It had come close to mutiny along the way, but they were here. Being surrounded by sand as far as they could see on both the eastern and western shores of the sea disconcerted the Norsemen, but at least the water was navigable and they made excellent time relying on Lubna's knowledge of geography.

Thiago took off his boots and walked down to the breakers to feel the salt water on his feet, not caring if his robe got wet. The librarian followed his example while several of the Vikings tossed aside clothing and ran into the water to swim.

Both the jinn and the Vikings had begun to show signs of tension at the coming fight to recover the treasure. No one was frightened—both groups had seen enough battles and raids to manage their feelings ahead of combat—but Thiago saw that the warriors had become more vigilant about their surroundings. He felt that way, too.

"A strange body of water, the Red Sea," Halfdan observed. "It's warm. If you fall into the North Sea, you'll freeze in no time." He stooped to dip his fingers in the water.

"It's as salty as the North Sea. Some things are common to all ocean water."

Halfdan had joined them at the water's edge. Unlike his men, he kept his clothes on. Thiago guessed this was because the

Viking chieftain didn't think disrobing becoming for a leader's dignity. It might also be because this area was wholly unfamiliar to him with unknown threats; he kept his sword at this side and wore a mail shirt despite the heat. He'd posted clusters of guards inland. Thiago noted that the steel links in the shirt were beginning to rust. Normally, the Vikings used animal grease or oil to stave this off, but the last several weeks had been hectic.

The rust on the Viking's armor was modest; the steel had been well forged. Nonetheless, Thiago felt its effect and stayed further from Halfdan than he would have otherwise. Given more time, the salt air would rust the armor if it wasn't properly cared for.

"They'll outnumber us," Halfdan said.

"Certainly," Thiago said. "So we need an edge beyond what we have. Your little iron hammers will protect your warriors somewhat, but not as well as we need."

He remembered Jai's suggestion as they approached Genoa that he look to iron to save himself and pulled out his dagger.

"A fine blade," Halfdan remarked. "No trace of rust, unlike my own which requires frequent care."

The Dane examined his weapons. "No rust, but that's because I've kept them clean."

Lubna peered down at the blades.

"From all your reading, what would make them behave differently?" Thiago asked her.

"Charcoal and iron," she said. "That's what's in Halfdan's knife. It's common knowledge for any capable smith about how to toughen iron with a bit of charcoal. Scrolls in the library describe how much charcoal should be combined with the iron and at what temperature to get a particular strength of steel. For your blade, Thiago, I don't know—there are Persian texts that point to an unknown element being helpful in defeating rust if added to steel. No one has mastered it in this world. How are weapons made in yours?"

"In forges from the mountains north of my home city," Thiago said. "It's a strange, magical alchemy that I never bothered to understand."

"I see where you're going," she said. "For the coming fight, having inferior, rusted weapons is a good thing."

"Another edge for us," Thiago said. "Halfdan, my warriors need to borrow Viking weapons if you have any to spare. Your supply ship is loaded with extras. Everyone needs to expose their blades, arrowheads, spear tips, whatever, to sea water. Don't protect them with oil. They'll rust, of course."

"We'd have to be careful we don't poison ourselves," Charun said. He and Aaliyah had strolled over to join them.

"Too much iron and we can't wield the weapons," Aaliyah said. "Not enough rust and they won't work against the king's demons."

"A fine balance," Thiago admitted. "We'll also use leather sheaths and scabbards to shield us. That worked months ago when I fought Lila for my map over the Empty Quarter. It should work now, too."

"You know," Halfdan said. "This is all quite mystical. It would be nice to test this wild notion of yours first before full-scale battle."

"We could stage a mock combat among ourselves," Aaliyah said. "However, with the mutual suspicion, it might turn into real combat. We'd slaughter ourselves before we got to the king's forces."

"He's thinking of something else," Lubna said.

CHAPTER 16

Towers Touching the Sky,
Dungeons by the Sea

"One of the spires is lost in the clouds," Lubna said. She looked straight up. "How did they build that with stone? Has anyone been to the top?"

"No one except me," Thiago said. "The rest of the family was never curious, but I liked the views. On a clear day, the vistas are endless."

"Lots of stairs," she said.

"I wouldn't know. I flew."

He looked about at the pastel towers and parapets. Evening came on and purple began to dominate other colors in Bethinia's skyline. It looked beautiful, but also washed out as if the vast city had experienced too much dissolute life and this had leached away its vitality.

"I remember from playing here as a child, none of the upper floors have stairs. Jinn don't need them."

"The other spires are almost as high," she said. "How many towers does your palace have?"

"I never counted," Thiago said. "We can do that now if you want."

His family's palace had been this way for as long as he remembered. Until she'd mentioned it, Thiago had observed his family's edifice without reflecting on it—except to think that it was a beautiful building, but not much of a home.

They stood on a balcony so far up on one of the towers he could barely see the marble boulevards below stretching off to the capital city's center and the king's alabaster palace or out to the Erythraean Sea. He'd once played on the beach with other jinn children where the boulevard met the sea. As always, huge, improbable creatures sported in the waters, visible at this distance because of their vivid coloration.

"Those are the things that chased us," Thiago remarked to Lubna.

Her gaze followed his outstretched arm, but after a glance at the scarlet monsters she looked away.

"I still have nightmares," she said. "But the rest is pretty—no, it's extraordinary, like nothing I could imagine or that I've read about from any earthly explorer however far they've traveled. To the left, does the water below us in that brook run uphill?"

Thiago looked where she pointed. "Yes, I think some ancestor or another wanted it that way. It made the grounds look better."

"But that's not possible."

"It is here."

"How?" she asked.

"Rules are different. We can go down to see it, run our hands in the water. It will feel real."

Surrounding the brook, the parklike grounds below contained flowers of many shades. Thiago liked the ones where one flower had different-colored petals. He'd never seen that on the human side of the portal. The grounds separated his family's palace from neighboring structures, giving each its own setting and providing privacy.

He wondered what the scenery, pretty but ordinary to him, must look like to her.

"The horses?" she said pointing to a herd grazing by the brook.

"What about them?"

"They're flying. Unless I'm seeing things."

"They fly," he agreed. "It's tiring for us to have to fly ourselves around all the time, so we bred horses to carry us, one of my family's many talents. On this side of the portal, they can go further, faster than a jinn or ifrit. I'd like to see if they can do that in your world. We'll take some back with us and find out."

Thiago looked about and compared it with the caliph's sprawling complex in Córdoba and other big structures on the human side of the portal. Frankly, there was no comparison. Those were rude and crude. Though human rulers and their architects were ambitious and visionary and built impressive cities and populated them with remarkable edifices, they were like children assembling toys in contrast to what generations of demon aristocrats had accomplished on this side of the portal.

True, vision and aesthetic achievement in his world had gone hand in hand with savage persecution as periodic revolts had shaken the realm and been crushed. And now the dry rot of flagging economic power coupled with a sclerotic bureaucracy would accomplish what violent insurrection hadn't. Thiago knew that irreversible senescence had set in. The death throes of this empire would rattle his world and human realms as the king of the demons and his elites grasped onto waning power like drowning mariners gripping anything that floated on a sinking ship.

"The city has no walls," she said.

"There aren't external enemies," Thiago replied. "The threats come from within."

"And before you ask"—he gestured downward—"the dots below on top of the streetlamps are heads. The king has more enemies than ever these days, so there are more heads than ever, though there have always been some down there. I remember seeing them as a child. They're among my first memories."

"Let's go inside," she said. "Fabulous parks and palaces as far as the eye can see and severed heads right below us make me happy I'm living on my side of the portal. Very bad things happen there, too—I was almost strangled in Córdoba's dungeon—but the contrast isn't as sharp between what should be and what shouldn't."

They moved into a marble hall with teak furniture and satin pillows. It was pristine and perfect except for a layer of dust and dying plants situated around the room. Under the king's threat, Thiago's family and their servants had deserted the immense structure, leaving it to be commandeered by the court. Now only memories and ghosts enjoyed the countless rooms and dozens of spires with balconies. However, it wouldn't sit empty forever and some court sycophant would even now be sizing it up for their occupation.

Thiago and Lubna had been forced to sneak past ifrit guards from the king's personal retinue to get in. He didn't know whether the king expected his surreptitious return, but the guards were clearly prepared to ward off more than curious citizens anxious to inspect the consequences of sedition and the fall of the realm's most prominent jinn family. However, every sizable, self-respecting manor would have a half dozen hidden tunnels into the palace. There were informers everywhere including among his family's own servants, so some of the secret access points were known to the king's warriors, but not all, and

Thiago and Lubna had discreetly entered via a passage into the stables many floors below. They now had the grand structure to themselves. The guards were all outside.

"What are those?" Lubna asked, pointing to frescos. They faced infinite brightly colored murals in the long hall. The hues had faded in the distant artwork, but still depicted vibrant, affecting scenes. The furniture had been positioned to allow viewers to sit in contemplation.

"We're in the hall of memories. These images are hard for me to look at, but I'll tell you about them anyway," Thiago said, trying to think about how to describe his family. This rubbed raw wounds—

When they appeared as humans, they were cool and beautiful; when they were fire, they were beautiful fire. If they chose an animal form, it was the sleekest, most elegant form of that creature they could conceive. In any form, warmth wasn't an important part of who they were. And when they died after long lives well lived, they were simply not there one day and a new fresco went up depicting the salient events and happiest moments in that individual's existence. They never really left until the last living soul stopped remembering them. Respecting that tradition, Thiago's family paid "rememberers" to visit this room periodically and think about the individual depicted in a given fresco to stave off the cruel day when a deceased family member was forgotten completely.

"So, it's not their deaths that bother me," he concluded. "It's that any sentiment about them is artificial. My family is good at that sort of sleight of hand."

He looked down the hall. "Of course, I'm not blameless. I'm the cause of my family's recent travails." Only half joking he added, "So it's not good for me to stay too long or I might throw myself off a balcony and stay in human form till I hit the marble below in a bloody mess."

"My parents sold me to the caliph's court," she said. "You don't have the only disturbed family."

"Speaking of family, it's time to spring my father," he said. "Let's see if my bribes will get us into the dungeon's courtyard. However, bribes won't get us back out, so we'll need to come up with a distraction. And use your immunity to iron."

"Can we get the guards drunk on wine?" Lubna asked. "That helped you release me from the caliph's dungeon."

"I like how you think, but these guards don't drink or they'd be fed to the sea creatures. However, let's fortify ourselves with wine from the palace cellar before we go. My reactions will be slower, but my nerves will be calmer. And there is one other thing—"

"I'm afraid to ask what."

"Nothing dangerous. We'll set the horses free. They've fended for themselves on the grounds since my family's been gone, but they'll starve eventually, so we'll let them out. They could fly out, but there's no one else to take care of them. I think they remember me. We'll take them with us on tonight's expedition. If and when we free Father, we'll need to move away from the dungeon fast before they can organize a chase."

"I've never ridden a horse," Lubna said.

"It's not that hard."

"That's what you say about everything."

~

Soldiers in leather and metal armor prodded the haggard jinn forward with spears. The spears were tipped with iron. They moved the prisoner inexorably to the cliff edge and a long drop to sharp stones, surf, and carnivorous creatures. A few of the guards held torches aloft to light their way in the nighttime darkness, but there was little obvious organization to this execution and the whole affair was both casual and part of the routine order of things.

The torches wavered in the wind coming off the Erythraean Sea and their light splashed the guards and the prisoner with yellow illumination. Across the water, celebrations of festive life lit Bethinia's purple palaces and the royal courtroom. If Thiago listened hard, he could hear merriment.

The captive jinn wore iron shackles around his wrists and ankles and it was all he could do to half stand, half crawl, thanks to the metal's toxic effect. The prisoner made a weak, despairing effort to transform into fire. Blue flame blurred his extremities, but the iron restraints stifled transformation and the fire died and he looked like a tired, old man again resigned to his demise.

Thiago watched horror stricken. He couldn't see the jinn's face in the poor light, but everything about the way he carried himself suggested agony and a being in extremis.

It could be his father.

Whoever the prisoner was, he wasn't that important since more-elaborate killings were prepared for those deemed true threats to the realm. The king believed in execution as spectacle. However, tonight, being pitched over a cliff was fine for minor lawbreakers, someone who'd protested too strenuously about royal edicts or spoken too frankly to other demons against conditions in the realm. When the group got to the cliff's edge, there was no ceremony; the captive simply had no more room to stand and pitched over the edge. There was a pause as the body fell. From his hiding place, Thiago heard the sounds of a melon dropped down a flight of steps and then snarls and bones crunching as sea creatures fought over the corpse in the surf and rocks, altogether a tawdry demise for the unfortunate soul being dismembered.

The guards milled about commenting about their latest killing. One of them tossed his torch over the edge so they could watch the macabre events below, careful not to get too close and fall over themselves. They were all human and unaffected by the iron in their weaponry and the constraints and bars confining their demon prisoners. Detachments of jinn and ifrit warriors guarded the outer approaches to the king's open-air dungeon, whereas men were the species of choice within the prison's confines. Humans inside, demons outside was the security strategy the king employed to capitalize on the strengths and weaknesses of his forces controlling the prison.

Thiago barely kept himself from lurching forward into the prison's central courtyard to see whether his father had been killed, but held himself back by force of will. Getting impaled on an iron-tipped spear wouldn't help anyone.

The structure was built in the shape of an immense amphitheater with one side open to the cliff's edge, a convenient killing ground visible to every cell in case anyone wondered what the king's justice looked like. A few captives cursed the guards. Their turn would come soon enough, and protesting loudly while they lived showed to their fellow prisoners, the guards, and themselves that they still could argue against their fate. Whether they liked the recently executed jinn wasn't the point. However, most captives in their cells paid no attention to another execution.

"For shame, for shame." Thiago heard a thin voice cut through the others.

"That's him. He's alive," Thiago whispered.

He and Lubna watched from an unused ground-level cell. Though only the door was iron and the rest was hewn stone, the jinn felt nauseous and faint every time he got close enough to see through the bars out to the central courtyard where his father's cage was.

"This armor smells," Lubna said. "It's also way too big."

"It's your disguise," Thiago said. "It got us in. Dump it when we leave."

"If we leave," she said.

"When we leave," he said. "It's now or never. Maybe this is their night for executions."

"Just give me a moment," she said. In the cell's dim light, Thiago watched Lubna nerve herself for the next part. Even in the near-total darkness, he saw her features teeter between abject fear and resolve. Eventually, resolve won.

"Spear," he said. "Remember your spear. Look the part. No one else here is paid off. Just the crew at the outer gates who let us in. It helped that they were from my tribe. It helped even more that I gave them everything I kept from when we first uncovered the treasure, but the next bit depends on us being convincing."

The librarian yanked the iron-barred door open, grabbed the spear propped against the cell wall, and motioned him out of the cell with its point. She got into her role, swaggering as she creaked along in the armor. He almost fainted passing through the narrow iron cell door, but that was good; he didn't have to fake his staggering gait as she prodded him forward.

"Careful," he hissed. "Not so close with the tip."

The cage holding his father was a distance off across the courtyard. The two of them walked toward it. The librarian was a slender woman of medium height, so he was thankful for the oversized armor that added bulk and heft to her appearance in keeping with the other soldiers' hulking size. The general gloom of the place also helped. Still, anything other than a casual look would identify them as frauds.

Resisting the urge to bolt toward the cage, Thiago shuffled along and twice fell to his knees. Lubna took the cue to jab at him with her spear. Thiago's arms and legs were bound with wooden shackles mimicking the iron the rest of the prisoners wore when guards moved them around the dungeon. Within earshot of several soldiers dispersing from the recent execution, he plaintively swore as if their very touch against his skin was agony that drained his strength.

When he'd been here before in daylight to visit his father, this open-air dungeon had seemed smaller. Now, in the darkness, he looked upward at the endless rows of cells above him. Pinpoints of light marked the passage of guards making the rounds while holding torches to inspect the cell's occupants. Occasionally, a jinn or ifrit prisoner would blaze into flame inside their cells, perhaps goaded by a guard or railing against their doom. When not confined by iron, they were massively potent beings; here, they were helpless. Their pointless theatrics illuminated the surrounding stone with orange or blue light. Under different circumstances, Thiago would have thought this looked pretty.

A breeze off the Erythraean cut through the prison stench. He heard sea creatures roaring and shrieking in the nearby waters. Tonight, their appetites had been whetted and they wanted more.

"Keys?" he asked quietly.

Lubna responded by jangling her set. They were iron albeit heavily rusted. If one of them snapped in the cage's lock, they'd never rescue his father.

They arrived at the cage. "Here we go," he said.

There was no official reason for them to be in this part of the dungeon's yard, but he hoped that with thousands of prisoners guarded by hundreds of soldiers, no one on duty tonight would pay them much attention, giving Lubna time to unlock the cage and pull his frail father out of it. Getting the keys had cost Thiago an emerald, a lifetime's fortune and more for the guard sergeant who'd sold them. However, there had been no way to test whether any of the dozen keys on the ring actually opened the cage door. If the sergeant had provided the wrong keys out of malice or fear of retribution or simply by mistake, Thiago, Lubna, and his father would be cut to pieces. This jailbreak was based on faith as much as planning—fleetingly, he recalled that this had also been how he'd engineered the theft of Sheba's Treasure.

He didn't rely only on faith. If and when things went wrong, he had a backup tactic. Whether it would work was another matter.

Lubna sauntered over to the cage and with some difficulty inserted a key into the lock. He saw his father rouse himself from the cage's dirt floor and look at them with terror. No doubt he thought he was next for execution. He remained silent standing in the middle of the cage in dirty rags.

Meantime, Thiago with as much nonchalance as he could muster let his robe slip to the ground.

Underneath the cloak, he wore the same kind of armor as the librarian. She was right, it did stink, and it creaked as he moved and was heavy, but his arms were unencumbered. The leather breast and back plates were studded with steel; if it had been iron, he couldn't have worn this disguise. Greaves protected his shins and bracers protected his forearms. At least his set fit him, though he'd replaced the original owner's iron short sword with his steel dagger.

While he'd disentangled himself from the robe and fiddled with the leather harness, a guard approached him.

"You're him," the soldier said. He thrust a burning torch into Thiago's face.

The jinn looked up, startled and angry at being caught unawares. He'd have to bluff this one out.

"I don't know you," he said.

He felt the torch's heat on his face. The soldier meant to be crudely intimidating.

"You admitted stealing Sheba's Treasure before the king's court. Arrogant as all hell, just dance right up to the throne and explain that you and your partners took it. That's your father in the cage held hostage for the return of the treasure. I was right at the king's side, good view of proceedings. Just coincidence that you're here at the old jinn's cage, I'm sure. There's a family resemblance. You're the rebel."

"And you're full of shit," Thiago said.

As he looked closely at the soldier in the bad light, he recognized the man who'd shoved a spear into Jai. He turned away to mask his rage. Friends should be avenged whatever the cost, though Jai would rest no easier.

"I'd have happily shoved a spear through the rebel—which is you, just so you don't think there's any doubt here—if the king had just said one word, one little word, but we had a near riot on our hands when this cocky jinn started tossing gems into the crowd and his friends showed up. Even without your little performance in the throne room, I'd know you. I've seen you about the city flying here and there with a pretty crowd. About that crowd, the ifrit, the one you call Lila, was part of that set, but things didn't go so well with her. You wouldn't know me, of course. You live in a palace and I don't. They'll burn your palace."

The man looked at Lubna's efforts to unlock the cage. "Here, let's have a gander at what your friend is up to."

The soldier grabbed Thiago's shoulder. "You come along, too. You ain't getting out of my sight."

The jinn shook the man's hand off.

"What's the matter? Can't get too close to an iron cage?" He leveled his spear at the jinn.

Thiago drew and threw his dagger in one fluid motion. It caught the soldier in his neck, which wasn't covered with armor. The man pitched over backward at the impact. It had been a rushed throw, but true nonetheless.

"Fast work with a blade," he said to himself.

"What now?" Lubna called over to him softly.

Thiago scanned the yard and surrounding cells. "Keep working the key," he said urgently. "He's dead. If someone sees us, we're dead; if not, this helps."

"How?"

"We have another set of armor," Thiago said. "Thanks to this bastard."

Clusters of guards lounged about the yard, but none of them was close. However, very soon someone would notice the fallen man and two soldiers near the cage who had no reason to be there.

Thiago kicked the dead soldier's spear well out of the way and worked to loosen the man's armor as quickly as he could. If he could get it on his father, it would be three soldiers moving toward the gate rather than two guards escorting a jinn out of prison. Bribes or not, this was always going to have been the trickiest part of his plan.

"Can you move?" Thiago whispered to his father who sat beside moldy bread and rancid oil. These probably hadn't been refreshed since he'd last visited weeks ago.

"Maybe," his father responded weakly.

"I can't get any of these keys to work," Lubna said. "I've tried them all. They sold you the wrong set."

"Always a risk. Do any of them fit?"

"One, but it won't turn far and I'm afraid to break it."

"The oil," he said quietly.

"What?" she asked.

"In the cell, in the bowl. It might lubricate the lock mechanism, keep the key from breaking. Father, you'll have to help. The keyring is iron. Lubna will throw it into the cage. Put it in the oil. Don't think, just do it. Then throw the keys back through the bars to her. Don't feel, just do it. We just saw what will happen if we don't get you out now, tonight."

The librarian gently flipped the keys into the cage on its dirt floor accurately enough to land next to the bowl of oil. His father nodded understanding of what had to be done, but clearly not sure he could survive touching the key. He squeezed his eyes shut and grabbed the keyring and dropped it into the oil. With an agonized grunt, the old jinn then grabbed the wooden bowl and threw it and the keys at bars. The bowl rattled against the˚ bars, but the ring landed near Lubna.

By now, Thiago had the chest and back plates of dead soldier's armor off. There were other pieces, but there wasn't time, so these would have to pass muster if they could get them on his father.

If the key could somehow be made to work.

Lubna rammed the ancient key back into the lock and twisted.

"It's not moving," she hissed over to Thiago.

He pushed toward her. At first, momentum carried him forward, then each step felt like he waded through mud as nausea and weakness ramped up sharply. As painful as approaching the iron chariot had been months before, this cage was composed of much more of the poisonous metal. Every body part ached including his eyes, which felt like they floated in a sea of fire that no tears could extinguish. He wanted to retch, but all he could muster was intense nausea. He should have practiced more with iron.

"Some help," he said as he got within grasping distance of the librarian. She left the lock and grabbed his arm and pulled him to the lock. He envied her ease of movement. He now saw the iron bars as vertical bands of fire. The cage was the most secure confinement in the dungeon with bars thick enough to hold a sea monster. Touching them would scorch his flesh.

They both gripped the key together and wrenched. In his mind, Thiago saw rusted tumblers forcing themselves into alignment. He willed the oil-soaked key to stay intact and not break under the twisting stress. With a grating thunk, the lock opened and the cage gate swung outward. Thiago vaulted backward away from the cage and collapsed beside the dead guard. For several moments, he simply focused on moving his lungs to inhale air and recover his senses.

Now, if Lubna could drag his father out of the cell on her own . . .

And if all of this could be done without being noticed . . .

A guard shouted down at them from an upper tier. Other soldiers at the courtyard's perimeter noticed what he pointed at and began converging on them. Even in the darkness, they'd seen unauthorized activity by the cage. Thiago guessed there were three dozen of them and more called down from the upper stories. He heard boots on stone stairs. He'd disturbed an ant hill and they would face an army momentarily.

"Away from the cage," an officer screamed at them.

More torches blazed, illuminating the prison yard's entire expanse. All about them, prisoners awoke realizing that something was up and began yelling questions between cells.

"You had unexpected allies?" Lubna asked. "Where are they?"

"The second part of the plan," he said. "Even riskier than the first, but no need for disguises and hiding anymore."

Thiago transformed into fire and rose to the level of the highest tier of cells. He couldn't fly far up into the night sky; an iron mesh covering the prison yard prevented this. However, he just needed to fly high enough to be visible outside the prison yard. Nearing the mesh, he felt an enormous weight blunting his strength and he tumbled back to the yard as his flame extinguished itself and he reverted to his human form. The armor made him heavy and he wasn't used to how this affected his balance. He tumbled clumsily to the ground with his breath knocked out of him.

"What was the point?" Lubna shouted.

"That was the bad magic part," he wheezed. "It was a signal."

"To who?"

"To them, unexpected allies."

The sound of metal on metal erupted from the main gate into the yard. There was a sheering crash as the iron and timber door burst inward under Njal's ax strokes. His weapon was tempered steel and made short work of the rusty iron and rotten wood. The barrier was designed to lock demons in, not keep Danes out. Behind him surged Halfdan, Orm, and Birger kicking the remnants of the gate aside and then chopping at the shocked prison soldiers. And behind the Vikings, Charun, Aaliyah and Ajmal burst into the yard, stepping well clear of the remaining iron bolts and fittings from the destroyed gate.

"What shitty place is this?" Ajmal shouted over at Thiago. "I have half my strength." Ajmal began to transform into fire, but quickly reverted to human form.

"Stay human," Aaliyah called to him. She lunged forward at a group of guards, swinging right and left with her sword. An iron-tipped spear zipped past her head and buried itself in the dirt.

"Do I do this all myself?" she yelled.

Birger picked up the spear and hurled it back at the advancing guards, impaling two at once, then followed up by charging into the group with his shield and sword.

"A man after my own heart," Aaliyah said, rushing after him. Finished with the gate, Njal swung his battle ax in massive cuts, mowing down soldiers with each swing. Their leather armor offered no more protection than paper from his blade. Meantime, Halfdan, Orm, Charun, and Ajmal fanned out to form a perimeter protecting Lubna and Thiago's father and engaging the guards. They were only seven, but they pushed forward using shock and surprise on the disorganized mass of prison soldiery who weren't fighting with any sort of unit cohesion. Thiago expected the battle would teeter in the balance before their enemies' mass overwhelmed them. They needed to move quickly.

"Lubna, pull Father out. I'm no help. We won't dress him in armor. Now, we just run."

"I've got him," she yelled.

"Back out through the gate," Thiago yelled. He stumbled to his feet, still weak from wrenching the cage lock open with

Lubna. "Njal, chop some of the cell locks to bits. It may even the numbers."

"Add a verse or two for me in your next poem," the big man shouted.

"Done," Thiago shouted.

Guards from the upper stories joined the original detachments in the yard, but this created more confusion in the face of the Norsemen and jinn's utter savagery. Thiago saw one of their officers down, transfixed with Birger's spear, and Ajmal ripped the head off another to hurl it into the midst of the guards. Charun shot arrows with precision into the mass of soldiers. The prison hadn't been breached in living memory, and herding hapless captives off a cliff and taunting cell-bound prisoners was different from fighting heavily armed raiders with surprise on their side.

"We should come back and plunder," Halfdan shouted over the tumult to Orm. "The city outside is rich and ripe for the taking."

As their little group beat a fighting retreat toward the shattered gate out of the yard, Njal swung his ax at cell doors they passed, shattering them into pieces. Amazed jinn and ifrit prisoners seized the chance to dash out into the yard and toward the destroyed main entrance. There were hundreds of them.

"Come on," Thiago screamed at them. "Out the gate or you'll be tossed over the cliff."

Any guards in the way got trampled.

"Stay together," Thiago shouted at his Viking and jinn chieftains as he was pushed along by the mob. "Back to the portal."

He grabbed his father's arm. Lubna had the old jinn's other side and they pushed out of the yard trying to shelter him from the fleeing press.

"I've never transited the portal before," his father said. He was frail from weeks of privation and exposure to iron and disoriented, but he staggered along gamely.

Outside the main edifice, the ten of them headed toward the nearest boulevard into the city. Their flight was covered by the disordered movements of hundreds of recently freed jinn and ifrit bursting out of the dungeon and soaring or running in all directions haphazardly chased by groups of soldiers.

"Back to my palace?" the old jinn said.

Thiago shook his head. "It's not ours any longer. Time to see the other side of the portal."

They were clear of the dungeon and its outer barracks and moving into Bethinia's neighborhoods.

"We have horses," Thiago said. He'd left them untethered by a manor house, confident that the equines would stay out of loyalty to him. They snorted in recognition as he approached.

"We'll escape in style," Aaliyah yelled back.

"I'll fly under my own power," Ajmal said.

"That's work," Aaliyah said. "These are fine beasts. Let them carry me."

With varying levels of confidence, the ten of them pulled themselves onto the horses. He guided Lubna to the tamest mare and helped her climb on.

"She'll do the work," he told the librarian. "Sorry, no saddle. Just hang on and don't let her stop to graze. Oh, and keep her on the ground; she'll want to fly if you let her. That could be a bit of a mess."

"How do I keep her from doing that?"

"Talk to her. She likes humans, at least, I think she does."

The Vikings rode surprisingly well. He guessed that went with being opportunistic raiders who adapted to whatever they encountered when they made landfall. Thiago lifted his still weak father onto a horse.

"I'll manage to ride," the old jinn said. "They're mine. They know me, so they'll be easy on me. Let's go."

Thiago looked behind. Pursuit was erratic and uncoordinated. However, eventually, the guards would organize themselves to fan out after escapees, but for now, they hadn't determined which direction to begin their pursuit.

The contrast was immediate between the dungeon's chaos and the broad, nighttime boulevards and parks that they rode through. The palaces and manor houses were grand here and became more so as they went further into the city.

Bethinia slept except for a few late-night soirees. Thiago heard laughter and music from ballrooms far above. Periodically, young jinn, perhaps lovers, would soar off a balcony in streaks of flame, flitting between spires, continuing their dance in the sky as twined blazes of fire to the applause from their less energetic or more drunk fellow partiers who'd stayed on the balconies.

Thiago saw Charun, Aaliyah, and Ajmal looking upward with contempt and envy. They were familiar with the spectacle, but had never attended such parties as their families weren't from wealth. Becoming outlaws was their chance to change that. Thiago remembered that he'd once hosted these affairs before deciding that they were boring. Becoming an outlaw had been his chance to change that.

Thiago saw the Vikings gape about them, unaware of demon society's class nuances. He suspected they simply saw an effete civilization beyond anything Europe had to offer ready to be looted.

His father looked about at the nighttime city observing familiar sights that he'd thought he'd never see again. Maybe he remembered his youth in a more placid time when he'd danced across the sky with the city's prettiest young woman and they'd made love till dawn.

On the city's far side, a neighborhood burned, a smudge of orange sending up smoke that was barely distinguishable from the night sky.

"Yes, I see it," his father told Thiago. "No need to point it out. Thankfully, it's not near where we live."

Thiago thought that it must be occurring to his father that times were changing to a less refined, more brutal period in which Bethinia's future was uncertain.

"The king's taken our home?" his father said. "I don't like trespassers."

"You may get it back soon." Thiago sketched out his plan to recover Sheba's Treasure and defeat the king.

"Seems hopeless. He'll outnumber you and your little band."

"My crew fights well and we'll use the jinn way, low cunning, bad magic, fast work with a blade, and unexpected allies."

"Well, you've always been good at the low cunning and bad magic bits," his father said.

"We'll see if I can get the other parts right."

"The family?"

"They've scattered themselves among our tribe, in other neighborhoods and in other cities, being discreet," Thiago said. "Safe for now, I think."

Abstractly, the old jinn let this sink in.

"Good news, I guess," he said. "You came for me as you said you would. I wouldn't have lived much longer. And thank you, dear girl, for freeing me from that cage. Your name?"

"Lubna of Córdoba."

"The librarian, I presume."

"You presume correctly. Come and visit me if you want. We'll pass you off as a foreign scholar."

"It won't be hard to convince your world that I'm foreign. I'm not sure anyone would take me for a scholar."

"This is the portal," Thiago said. The ten of them confronted an indistinct bluish-black irregularly shaped area set in a park amid the trees. Beyond a low wooden fence surrounding the portal, no special care had been taken to prevent anyone from simply walking through it. He could almost hear his father question why would anyone bother, and most of the demon world would agree.

"Back to the human side," Thiago said.

"The king will go after the family when he learns I've escaped and you were behind it," his father said.

"No. His priority will be recapturing Sheba's Treasure. He's close, but we're closer. If he beats us, then he'll settle scores. The whole realm is restive and he needs the treasure to shore up his control. Rounding up our family is the least of his worries."

"The horses?" Charun shouted.

"Ride them on into the portal," Thiago said. "Don't give them time to think about it."

"Why?" Lubna asked.

"I can use them in the coming fight."

The rest rode through, leaving only Thiago, his father, and Lubna looking about at the purple city. It wasn't home anymore; he wasn't sure where home was.

"What's next?" his father asked.

"Get the treasure. After that, build something better either on this side of the portal or the human side. I'll use it more wisely now than I would have when I first stole it."

"You've learned a bit." His father said. "You can hardly do worse than what we have."

"Coming through?" Thiago asked.

"To join your brigands? What good would an old jinn do? You'd have to spend time minding me, not staying alive and just possibly prevailing—your chances don't seem good to me, but you're set on doing it. So I'm staying here. The king caught me once, but that won't happen again. I know our realm better than he does. You got into our home without being noticed and so can I. I'll hide there. And I knew many of the prisoners, the ones you set free. They've no reason to love the king. He was going to have them pushed off a cliff. If I can find them, I'll invite them to join me. What we'll do, I don't know yet."

His father leaned across his horse and embraced him.

"Something's coming and I don't know what," he said. His expression hardened and he cantered off toward the family palace, a lone figure on a broad, marble boulevard with magical beings dancing overhead. He brought his mount to a gallop and they took to the air.

"I hope he stays safe," Thiago said. "He's less capable than he thinks."

"Maybe he'll help you next time," Lubna said.

"I won't hold my breath," Thiago said. "I'm proud that we freed him tonight."

"Unexpected allies helped," she said.

"The jinn way," he agreed.

CHAPTER 17

Demons and Demon Kings
or Dangerous Banter

"**N**one of my predecessors died a natural death," the king remarked. "They came to bad ends."

And that's what's in store for you, Lila thought.

However, what she said was, "Sire, your subjects respect you. The ifrit tribes most of all, but the jinn too and other assorted demons as well as your human subjects."

"Never trust someone you share a bed with," he said.

Banter with the king is potentially lethal, she thought.

"It's truth, highness. If the realm is restive, restoring prosperity with Sheba's Treasure will quiet them."

The monarch looked at her. "I'm not inclined to take your flattery."

The ifrit reflected that this ruler of demons was endlessly fearful of treachery, the reason he'd survived as long as he had. He also concealed his capabilities. In a land of magic and monsters, what kind of monster was he? She knew many of his capabilities, but not all, so she'd have to plot carefully with the Sardinian to evade his defenses. The executioner had finally arrived in Bethinia a bit battered from his portal crossing having been smuggled into the city by her tribesmen. He'd have no time to marvel at Bethinia's sights since she'd take him with her into the coming battle. Now she had her tools in place and, despite the king's suspicions, she would find a way to kill him, but first she needed his warriors. Every time she turned around, Thiago had more followers motivated by visions of ancient riches.

She and the king strolled together by the throne room's windows overlooking the Erythraean Sea. As soon as she'd returned to Bethinia's royal palace from the world of humans, she'd discarded her crude clothing—costume would be a better description—and incinerated it for good measure in an inferno of demonic rage. Now she was civilized and wore a sleeveless silk dress that wafted about her in the ocean air. The light material and breeze caressed her.

Sea salt mixed with incense fumes from braziers suspended from the remote ceiling. Smoke spiraled upward around the silver chains holding the braziers. The fragrances were heady, but she didn't feel soothed, not by the silk touching her skin or by the king's probing for hints of sedition. The immense room was empty except for fifty servants and guards. The ifrit couldn't shake the impression that they all stared at her.

"If I'm so esteemed, why are so many heads on the street-lamps?" the king asked.

"Because you put them there, sire."

"For good reason. Every one of them had a trial as fair or better than the one your favorite jinn got before an audience of their peers."

"It was a performance without a concluding act," the ifrit said. "You accused him. He admitted guilt. You should have executed him."

"He lived because he had a better chance of recovering Sheba's Treasure than you. He's somehow drawn to the map because he created it. I need that treasure to continue buying the respect you assure me that I have. I put my faith in bought loyalty instead of earned respect."

She let anger wash over her. "I almost had the map before you called me back for the damned trial."

"I want to believe you're working in my interests, but why should I? You're the very incarnation of deceitful ambition. Look what you did to your poor, young jinn lover after he'd gone to the trouble of stealing Sheba's Treasure to impress you. You tried to take it for yourself."

"I tried to steal it back for you," the ifrit corrected.

"But that didn't work," the king said. "Worse, they freed his father just last night. There goes my leverage. And not just his father burst out. Several hundred other treasonous bastards are loose in our capital."

"His father doesn't matter," the ifrit said. "The rest of them don't matter. The prize is the treasure and I know where your treasure is because I know where Thiago is. However, he's mobilized a detachment of jinn and humans to help him recover and defend it. You already know about the jinn—that's the so-called Fire Horde that wrecked his trial—and a collection of humans called Norsemen."

"From the north of their world, I take it?"

"Yes, sire. They're fierce and they coordinate well with the Horde based on the rescue last night of the jinn's father. He's trained them together, so it was a joint effort. Also, they wear iron trinkets that may protect them somewhat from us."

"Protect them from some of us, but not all of us." The king drew an iron knife from his cloak. The ifrit backed away quickly, feeling its poisonous aura.

"I'm not going to use it on you. Not now, anyway. I'm just making the point that not all of us are fragile about iron."

The monarch kissed the blade and cast it down the length of the room at his throne. It was a very long throw, but the blade hit the stone chair with enough force to shatter the weapon and startle a peacock strolling past.

"I knew you were immune to iron," she said. "No need for a demonstration."

"You know, but almost no one else does including Thiago and his ragtag band. That may be helpful in the coming fight."

"You intend to fight with me?" This surprised the ifrit. The king had never passed through a portal. She estimated that he feared leaving his power center in Bethinia unguarded against usurpers, and that he was uncertain of the passage's safety. So, she'd assumed that she would lead forces mobilized to defeat the jinn and recover the treasure. She knew Thiago and she understood the human side better than anyone else in the demon world and she'd seen the general location of Sheba's Treasure. All good reasons to let her get on with it, but she'd underestimated the depth of his mistrust for her. He probably planned to kill her once he'd recovered it.

"My king, we don't know whether the portal can stand the passage of an army. Why risk yourself? So far, the treasure caravan has been the biggest assembly making the passage and that happened safely only because they split themselves into smaller groups and allowed time between the groups passing through. Maybe the portal needs to recover from heavy usage. It took forever for them to transit, which made ambushing them easy."

"Point taken," he said. "We need a way to assess the portal before moving wholesale through it. I have just the group to test that."

"Who?"

"You'll see. One would almost think you didn't want me along, but I intend to lead the tribes in an overwhelming combination of forces. Just as he recovers my treasure, we'll move in. After I have it and the jinn and his comrades are dead, I'll tour this strange world on the portal's far side. It will be mine shortly."

"It would be an honor to serve under your direct leadership, sire," she said with all the eagerness she could feign.

"A fine toss, your highness." The unctuous compliment came from an ifrit who'd arrived in the throne room along with nine other demon tribal leaders. Lila knew them all and didn't like any of them. It was amazing that the king had been able to corral them into the same space, given their mutual hatred exacerbated by the king's efforts to pit them against one another to foster his strength with disunity.

"I couldn't have held that poisonous blade or cast it with such accuracy," the ifrit tribal leader said.

The other nine tribal leaders added their praise at the king's fine throw in a chorus of flattery.

The king nodded acknowledgment. "To the council room," he said. "No need to tell the whole palace what we're planning."

They'll know soon anyway, Lila thought. *Nothing stays secret here.*

He led them into a chamber off the throne room, gesturing for guards and courtiers to leave. The leaders slowly assembled around an ebony table with the king at the head, trying to decide whether it was more advantageous to be near their monarch or opt for discretion and take a more distant spot.

It doesn't matter, Lila thought. *The room is too small to hide.*

Under different circumstances, it would have been intimate, but today it confined them like a menagerie with too many predators packed into a single exhibit.

As always, the king sat, they stood.

When I assume the throne, I'll keep that practice. I can learn from my predecessors. Keep your subordinates uncomfortable and off-balance.

There was an almost equal division of jinn and ifrit, five jinn and six ifrit, and, by chance, Lila stood flanked by two jinn, hereditary enemies of the ifrit. She shrank away from close contact with them. The tribal leaders would happily have assassinated one another given half a chance. However, fear of the king overcame mutual contempt and they selected spots at the table, shuffling uneasily.

Contrasting with the tension, stained-glass windows with serene, abstract images stretched from the floor up to the ceiling. Light transfused them and splashed the black, ebony tabletop with graceful patterns. The light also touched the demon lords surrounding the table. Here, crimson colored a tall, martial ifrit. Next to him, cobalt blue shaded a slender jinn. Because of where Lila stood, she was submerged in a rainbow of hues.

This is a pretty snake pit, she thought. *Everything in the palace is too beautiful, too pleasing; past rulers weren't constrained by cost. What a difference from Thiago's austere poem that could only have been composed in a desert's solitude.*

"So, a council of war," the king said. Already his tone was harsh and demanding. "My lords, nothing less than the fate of our fair realm is at stake. Recovering an uncountable treasure goes a long way toward fixing things, but it's just the start. To some of you, this is remote and theoretical, a problem for someone else in this room, but you've all petitioned me individually to provide support for whatever tribe you lead in whatever region you govern."

Lila saw the lords tense. The king normally forbade all reference to the rising tide of revolt.

"Within your own tribes, armed dissension is more common than ever and fine homes are torched daily. Between tribes, pitched battles are now the norm, fighting over once endless resources that are now limited."

"Sire, this may apply to some of your kingdom, but I've weathered these difficult times unscathed," the tall ifrit said. The crimson from the stained-glass window made it look like he'd been dipped in blood.

"You can't be talking about my lands," the jinn standing next to him said. Her blue shading amplified the cool certainty in her tone.

The king slammed his fist on the tabletop, cracking the wood along a boundary between colors from the window.

"You both have scorched parks and manor houses. I've smelled the smoke and seen the blackened patches when I visited. Bodies dangle from gallows with iron wire nooses around necks. I don't have enough soldiers in my own guard or enough gold in my treasury to help all of you extinguish rebellions or broker truces for your endless feuds. And I don't have enough streetlamps for all the heads of criminals. Besides your provincial citadels, all of you have fair palaces in Bethinia. If you want to keep them, we need to be farsighted and act collectively."

He traced his finger along the crack he'd just made in the ebony table.

"I've never used the portal," he remarked. "It was just a gate to nowhere. I didn't need to visit until now. In fact, the other side was so out of the way, it made a perfect place to hide Sheba's Treasure with things becoming unsettled here."

"Beyond getting your treasure back, how can we support you?" a jinn asked.

"Eventually we'll exhaust even Sheba's Treasure," the king said. "We need more. Plundering the kingdoms of humans gets us that."

At least I'm included in their council today, Lila thought. *I'm rarely invited into this inner sanctum. I'm here because he trusts them less than he trusts me. And he needs my followers, skilled warriors all, to recapture the treasure and invade the human realm.*

Lila raised her hand tentatively.

Deference is the order of the day.

The king nodded impatiently.

I'm here on sufferance.

"Ground rules," she said. "In the realm of humans, we need names."

Lila had never heard silence as bemused as the tomb-like quiet that followed her remark.

"I'm Lila. You all know I hate that name. It's not me. The thieving jinn who stole our treasure used it to goad me at his trial. He thought he was being defiant. We all know that human names are a mockery of our realm's sophistication with our ability to simply recognize each other. On this side, we sense who we interact with. It's a feeling. However, on the human side, that doesn't work. I'm barely able to track Thiago and he has only the vaguest notion that I'm nearby, so spoken names are essential."

"For us, too?" the king asked. "When we're on their side?"

"For us, too," the ifrit confirmed. "And if we want to make their side our side, we'll all need names."

Someone finally said, "How crude."

Someone else said, "How do we choose a suitable name?"

"I can help with that," Lila said. "I've picked some culture-appropriate names from regions we'll visit after squashing Thiago: Ayaz, Eren, Kerem, Beste, Ece, Elif, Miray, Avriel, Fleur, Grant. Take your pick."

No one rushed to select a name.

"Then I'll assign them," Lila said and she went around the table giving everyone a name.

"From my visits, I know that gender plays an immense role in human affairs, more so than here. That includes their names. There are men's names and women's names."

"Odd," Ayaz said. "I have to assume that Ayaz is a man's name, since that's the one you gave me?"

"A strong individual," Lila said.

Anything to get them to accept their new sobriquets, she thought.

"And Fleur is a woman?" Fleur said.

"A fierce, pretty, brilliant woman," Lila confirmed.

Fleur is fierce and pretty, but not so brilliant or she'd see the predictable storm coming and have shifted blame for last night's dungeon disaster to someone else. She's an ifrit, but I'm not going to help her.

"Whatever else we accomplish here, we'll practice using names," the king said. "I'm not risking losing the treasure because we were too proud to use them. But what about my name?"

"Adalric," Lila said.

"I'll consider it," the king said. "Your name, any meaning?"

"Thiago once told me that Lila meant dark beauty. So poetic, just like Thiago. He also said it meant someone who weakens others."

Careful, I'm being revealing, she thought. *I need to get them fighting among one another, not suspecting me any more than they already do.*

However, none of the tribal leaders or the king noted her lapse.

"Anything else we should know about the human side of the portal?" the king asked.

"They die a lot," Lila said.

"We die here," Fleur said.

"Here, it's through violence or, for the lucky few, old age," Lila said. "There, it's from sickness more than anything else."

"What's sickness?" Ayaz asked.

"Truthfully, I don't know," Lila said. "Their bodies simply fall to bits or rot away."

More silence settled over the council table. Plainly the concept was wholly foreign to her audience.

"Another striking thing is that women rule few countries and they aren't warriors. In fact, I was thought to be helpless because of my sex. Three humans attacked me."

"What happened to them?" Ayaz asked. He seemed genuinely puzzled that anyone would try to assault her.

"They're somewhat the worse for wear," Lila said. "It felt good, but it was a waste of time and it may have alerted Thiago that I was near him."

"A strange, weak place and ready to be sacked," Fleur said.

"Indeed, their heads would make fine decoration for streetlights," the king said. "Fleur—I'll never get used to calling you that, but rules are rules—your ifrit tribe is accountable for my dungeons, yet there was an escape last night."

The sudden pivot, Lila thought. *Things usually go badly from here.*

"And not just anyone escaped. Thiago's father was being held as leverage for him to lead me to Sheba's Treasure, but the father is gone, vanished from my most secure dungeon. Any number of other prisoners destined to be pushed over the cliff are gone, too. And any number of my guards wound up gored with spears or chopped in two with axes and swords. Thiago plays for keeps. It's a splinter in my eye."

"Sire, I was going to tell you—"

"Obviously, no need for that now since I'm already aware of the circumstances. No, don't worry, I'm not going to chop you head off with a rusty iron ax."

Everyone watched him pull a dagger from his robe. He scratched "Adalric" into the ebony tabletop. The wood was hard, but he was very strong.

"I'm sure you'll be honored to lead our foray into the world of men. There's some question about whether the portal will withstand passage of an army. It would be good to settle that before storming their world."

~

"Ah, well, good thing we checked," the king said as the war council reconvened sans Fleur.

"The portal gets indigestion when too many of us try to cross over at once," Ayaz said. "It was a sticky end for Fleur and her crew."

"Did any of you hear noises as they entered it?" Kerem asked.

"Screams," the king said.

Lila had always thought Fleur was a fool and led her tribe badly, but sacrificing thousands of warriors to make a point was stupid, too.

"We'll need to split ourselves into smaller groups to make the passage," Miray said. Lila looked at the short ifrit female. She led the smallest of the ifrit tribes and often was ignored for that reason. She also had a gift for stating the obvious like it was a revelation.

"Which means Thiago can ambush us just as we pass through the portal and defeat us in small groups," Lila said. "Those are the tactics he used to get Sheba's Treasure."

"Or we'll need to select the very best from each tribe and attack Thiago with a picked force," the king concluded.

"We'll still outnumber him, but that makes the numbers more even," Ayaz said. "I like overwhelming numbers."

"You think we can't take them?" the king asked.

The council room quieted suddenly. Would the monarch construe Ayaz's comment as defeatist?

"Spare me." The monarch held up his hands forestalling Ayaz's barrage of apologies.

"Anyway, you're right," he said. "We need an unfair advantage: a monster or two. I've sent one through already to see if it could be done. They're not too big for the portal, right at the size limit based on what happened to Fleur and her tribe."

"You have unexpected capabilities, highness," Miray said. "Did you prime it to track him?"

Ah, brilliant, Lila thought. *And what if the beast had eaten Thiago? Then no one could have found the map, let alone the treasure.*

What she said was, "We'll need to find beasts that tolerate heat and no water."

"So practical, just why I invited you today," the king said.

The more information I give them, the more expendable I become, Lila thought. *I have to keep some knowledge back.*

"But we have such creatures in your region, Miray?" the king said.

"We do, sire. It's dry in the west where they live, so they've adapted to heat and drought. They live on land and they're big, fierce and fleet. Do you want one captured and brought here?"

"We've no time. I'll transport it myself."

"Let's try fitting two through, one right after the other," Miray said.

"I like your spirit," the king said. "Iron isn't poisonous to them?"

"Right you are, sire," Miray said. "But Thiago's forces won't know that. They can attack them with iron weapons to no effect."

"And you're not poisoned by iron, either," Ayaz said.

"They won't know that, either," the king said.

"Those are advantages, but we need a strategy," Grant said. He'd been quiet until now, though he led the largest jinn tribe excepting the one Thiago's father headed. Lila knew that they were cousins, though if Grant harbored anger at the incarceration of his relative, he hid it well. They presided over relatively tranquil domains despite the unrest shaking the rest of the demon world.

Grant continued, "Besides warriors, we'll have monsters on our side as well. Seems unbeatable."

The jinn's voice reminded Lila of Thiago's baritone if he were older and had seen more of life. Perhaps it was his tone, or his bearing, but the other leaders paid attention and acknowledged the validity of his comments. Lila noticed that charcoal gray from the stained glass colored him.

"There's a *but* in there somewhere," the king said. "You're about to raise some risk to my plan, our plan, the council's plan, to retake the treasure and plunder this other world."

"Well, that's just my point," Grant said. "Highness, this isn't a plan, it's several plans bundled together. Let's focus first on getting the treasure back, then determine how best to take on human empires and kingdoms. I've never visited them, never seen any point to it. They may have surprising strengths. Lila, of all of us, you *have* been to this strange collection of oddities that constitutes the lands beyond the portal. What do you say?"

He'd asked a good question and she would answer it, though Lila saw Grant's disapproval of her. Was the animus because she was an ambitious ifrit, or because of her casual exploitation and summary dismissal of his relative? She sensed moral judgment and didn't want it. Jinn liked to think they weren't demons because they had souls, but she wondered what good souls were. They would only make her regret things she liked to do.

She said, "My experience with them has been that their kingdoms are primitive compared to us. What we can do with magic, they can only attempt with crude technology. But they are dynamic and seasoned in war. They fight incessantly among themselves, making them battle-hardened, and they are every bit as—"

"Enough," the king said. "We don't need a history lesson about barbarians."

"In Lila's opinion, they're tougher than we'd like," Grant said. "So being rash won't defeat him or recover your treasure."

Lila held her breath. This sounded like open skepticism, but she sensed that others around the table agreed.

Things hung in the balance. At one point or another, he'd enraged all of them. The king could defeat any one of them or even several banded together, but if the majority united against him, he would struggle to prevail.

"Well, of course we plan carefully," the monarch said reasonably. "We don't have a full army to squash Thiago, but still we can get enough of us through the portal in one go to outnumber him three to one, and we have Miray's monsters. Let's get Lila to diagram the area we'll be going into."

He reached into his robe. Lila thought he was going to produce yet another knife, but instead he tossed her a stick of chalk.

"Draw," he told her. "Yes, on the tabletop. We won't know the exact location of where Thiago buried it until he digs it up, but with my ifrit's help, we'll know the surrounding area. That's going to be our battlefield."

Lila leaned over the table and sketched out the landmarks as she remembered them. The white chalk contrasted with the ebony while the colors from the stained glass soaked her chalk marks in variegated hues.

The jinn and ifrit tribal leaders watched her impassively. No one asked the kind of questions they should be asking if they were vested in this raid—how to arrange their warriors, where Thiago's followers would likely be positioned, how to deploy Miray's creatures without them turning on their own soldiers, how to time their attack with regard to when Thiago excavated the riches.

"We let him do the work for us," she said. "Then we move in."

Ambivalence permeated the room.

She was ambivalent herself. If she helped the king and his lords eradicate Thiago and recover the treasure, what were her chances of getting it for herself? The king's success could be her failure and likely death.

And she wasn't fool enough to think that nights of passion with him meant anything in the morning.

She wasn't as naïve as Thiago.

However, for the moment, she needed to play along and wait for her chance.

"There are opportunities for us here." She pointed to her diagram. "On the high ground along this ridge, these are ruins, a good place to hide until we move on them. The timing will have to be perfect. I'd propose putting our warriors here, and here, and here."

The king nodded, acknowledging her handiwork. Then he said, "And—one important point as we consider this expedition—we split Sheba's Treasure evenly among us."

I'm not hearing him right, Lila thought. *He must sense doubt. It's all over our faces. He's buying our support.*

"For centuries, I thought it was my treasure," the king said. "For two thousand years before that, my ancestors thought it was theirs. However, it really belongs to our realm and you all deserve it as much as me. So, we all get an equal share."

Does anyone believe him? I don't.

However, most of the tribal leaders made a pretense of fealty to the cause, and she felt energy and enthusiasm in the room pick up. They leaned over the table and questioned her on geographic features that affected their deployment.

When we seize this treasure, he'll renege on his promise, she thought.

CHAPTER 18

Will of Iron

"There it is, Sheba's Treasure," Thiago said. "Brush off the sand and grab what you want."

He would have made a sweeping gesture, grandly taking it all in, bestowing largess on everyone, but he didn't have the energy.

Languor settled over him, exhaustion from the monumental task of turning to a whirlwind and reversing the process of hiding the treasure he'd performed months ago. He stood next to a shard of ancient ruin. The sand-blasted rock was knife sharp and stabbed up at the evening sky. He stood atop the same cliff he'd used months ago during his ambush. The wind swirled through the stony relics.

"Bright and shiny," he said, watching hundreds of Norsemen and Fire Horde warriors rush in to grab at and sometimes fight over particular pieces.

"You didn't do it justice," Lubna said. She stood next to him, staring at the piles of wealth.

"I'm just a humble poet," he said. "I ran out of adjectives."

Orm and Halfdan strode over to him followed by Ajmal, Aaliyah, and Charun. The Horde's leaders had seen it all before, but still looked dazzled. The Viking chieftains appeared stunned by the magnitude of the find.

"I thought you'd exaggerated," Orm said.

Thiago didn't pay much attention to the treasure. Instead, he stared at the surrounding escarpments. It was evening and visibility was good, but there were still places to hide a whole host of the king's forces and shadows were getting longer.

The others also looked about with the experience of warriors sizing up a potential battlefield. If an attack was imminent, it would come from the portal—or were they already here?

"Our sentries abandoned their posts," Halfdan said. "Damn their eyes. They rummage through the gold with the rest like pigs at a trough."

"Jinn warriors are no better," Aaliyah said. "They don't remember who's coming after us."

"We need to take as much as we can and disappear to the four corners of both our worlds," Thiago said. "Before the king arrives. And Lila."

"I'd like a fight, I would," Ajmal said. "We trained for it."

"Yes, what about this battle?" Orm asked. "My warriors are ready whatever comes at us."

"We trained," Thiago said. "But the best battle is the one that doesn't happen."

"But if it does," the Norseman prompted.

"If it does," Thiago said, "we have advantages. They'll be momentarily disoriented coming through the portal. And we've prepared ourselves, but things don't go as planned. That's been my life these last several months. That said, there are tactics that might help us."

He pulled his map out from underneath his chain mail shirt and spread it out on the sand.

"Let's confirm our disposition one more time. Lubna, you've read of many battles. Once we yank our warriors away from the treasure, I propose deploying them at these points."

The jinn indicated spots on the map. The Viking chieftains and the Horde's leaders nodded.

"Arab and Chinese generals would agree," Lubna said. "Except perhaps they'd recommend putting warriors on the high ground here just to the right of the portal."

"Any other helpful tactics?" Ajmal asked.

"Halfdan, I want someone who doesn't mind iron and can steer," Thiago said. "Can I borrow Njal? I'll call when I need him."

The Viking shrugged. "He's yours. Bring him back."

Thiago nodded. "So, then, we're agreed: low cunning, bad magic, fast work with a blade, and unexpected allies."

"The jinn way," Lubna said.

~

The monsters arrived.

The first one emerged from the portal in a travesty of birthing, barely squeezing itself out of the portal's opening. It was huge, as big or bigger than the creature that had chased their ship near Genoa, but this being was terrestrial rather than aquatic and had six legs ending in clawed feet. Thiago watched the portal's opening distort as the monster pushed the last of itself through, scratching for purchase in the sand.

Besides its size, the first thing Thiago noticed was its skin, greasy and iridescent like the cobra that had bitten Njal.

With a bound it freed itself from the portal's lingering grip and launched itself directly at the nearest group of Norsemen and Horde warriors. Instinctively, the jinn transformed into their most mobile forms, wind and fire, leaving the ground-bound Vikings as the most obvious and edible victims. Some Norsemen scattered, but others gamely attacked the monster with arrows and spears. This only enraged it. The missiles hit their mark and sank into muscle, but they might as well have tossed pebbles. With nimble movements, the monster slashed at its attackers, sending torn bodies in every direction. Periodically it stopped to eat one of the fallen men. Thiago heard bones and mail armor crunching.

We won't win this way, Thiago thought from his vantage point overlooking the portal. *Little iron hammers aren't saving them. This thing is sending them to Valhalla.*

He morphed into fire and swept down at the monster's head. Several of the jinn followed him in a formation of orange flame. This distracted the monster from the Norseman who grabbed the chance to push forward and hurl spears at the monster's neck and belly. Thiago saw that Njal slipped very close and swung his battle ax in wide strokes at the creature's legs. The Viking leaped under its belly and came out on the far side chopping with his ax trying to hamstring it. The monster was huge, but the ax cuts must have had an effect because Thiago saw it stumble and lick at one of its legs.

We're coordinating, Thiago thought, elated. *Will it be enough?*

"Charun, Aaliyah, Ajmal, to me," Thiago said.

"Why?" Ajmal said. "I'll burn its eyes out."

"There's a better way."

Still in fire form, he angled down to the ruins and then morphed into a whirlwind beside the long shard of ruined building he'd leaned against earlier. It was three times taller than a man and jagged. Perfect for what he planned. If he could get help lifting it.

Aaliyah joined him first then Charun and finally, reluctantly, Ajmal.

"Always it's work with you," Ajmal said.

"Pick it up and drop it," Thiago said. "Simple."

Together the four of them, all whirlwinds, tore and heaved the immensely heavy obelisk out of the sand and into the sky to fly it over the monster, now less mobile thanks to Njal's efforts to hobble it.

"To the left," Charun screamed.

"Hold it just a moment longer," Aaliyah yelled back.

"It's too heavy," Ajmal said.

Trying their best to position the rock over the creature, they dropped it spiraling downward, sending the sharp end through its skull.

The monster died a messy death, but Thiago saw at least a dozen dismembered Norsemen lying about in the sand. There were also two burned patches on the sand where jinn had met their end.

The four of them swept down and morphed back into their human forms.

"Who died?" Thiago asked. "Which jinn died?"

At this rate, the king did not need to appear himself; his beasts would do the killing for him.

"Another one!" Halfdan shouted.

He looked at the portal in time to see another enormous creature lunge out onto the desert floor. This one walked on two legs and had three red eyes. Free of the portal, it stood fully upright almost as tall as the cliff faces enclosing the valley.

How did it fit through the portal? Thiago wondered.

Norsemen and jinn alike attacked it with weapons, wind, and fire. In his fire form, Thiago flew above the horror trying to scorch it or at least distract it. Looking for weakness, burning blue hot, Kaveh flew directly at the largest eye, which burst in a fountain of blood. The creature shrieked and batted at the jinn with a massive hooked claw. From far above, an imperial eagle angled down in a steep dive at the creature's remaining two eyes. It was a fleet, brown speck against the twilight sky, and Thiago recognized the raptor he'd saved months ago over the Empty Quarter. It hadn't forgotten. And it was accurate, evading the monster's lunges, to strike both red eyes in succession, extinguishing them like campfires doused with cooking water.

The creature was now blind.

But not dead.

Enraged, it lashed around itself continuing to crush Norsemen and jinn. Lubna ran out directly before the monster screaming upward to catch its attention. The creature stamped downward with enough force to send rocks tumbling down from the cliffs. It clawed at her voice. Her mail shirt wouldn't protect her in the slightest. They were both near the cliff edge where the ruins stopped.

Does she see how close she's getting to tumbling over? Thiago thought. *No. She's fleeing for her life and it's dark.*

Thiago teetered on the verge of exhaustion and flew in a broad, slow circle in front of the creature, hoping that it would sense his heat and lose focus on Lubna. He wanted to be its target, but it ignored him. Below, Lubna sprinted for the cliff edge, continuing to scream as she ran to keep the beast's attention. She slowed barely and momentarily teetered on the edge, but rescued herself and dodged to the side. With a lunge, the beast stooped to reach for her, sensed that it hovered over thin air, flailed desperately before toppling over the edge to fall a long way down to rocks below.

Thiago landed besides Lubna. "How did you know it would fall over?"

The librarian held up her hand, signaling that she needed to catch her breath.

"Momentum," she finally gasped out. "I did a quick calculation based on mathematical treatises from the library. I estimated its weight and speed. I knew I could stop, but the creature was so massive and coming so fast that even if it had been able to see, it would have gone over."

"I'll read that text," he said.

Clusters of warriors sat on the sand all around them gasping for breath, dressing wounds, and checking their weapons. They were spent.

"That was just to soften us up," Thiago shouted to as many surviving Norse and jinn as he could see. "Their main body comes through next with the king."

And then indistinct images emerged from the portal. The figures sharpened to become masses of jinn and ifrit warriors forming into ranks and surging forward at the Fire Horde and Norsemen. Perhaps for shock value, the demons appeared as clawed, fanged, deranged, and hideous creatures. Some of them shifted into fire and flew toward the Horde and Norsemen.

"Here they are, more than I'd thought," Thiago yelled. "You've seen this before. We trained."

"They used the monsters to stretch the portal to accommodate this many at once," Aaliyah said.

"Show them your iron hammers," Halfdan bellowed to his Norsemen. "Wear them outside your armor. Use your rusty weapons. Make sure they don't shatter on the demons' shields. At them, boys!"

~

The pain was insane.

Thiago barely hung on to the lead horse among the four that pulled the iron chariot bouncing over rocks and sand and racing madly toward the main body of the king's forces. He was just far enough away from the war machine to survive, but he felt dizzy and he'd thrown up. Behind him, Njal clung to the side railings of the careening chariot periodically casting spears with enormous force at the king's formations. As best he could, Thiago gripped his horse's sides with his knees so he could shoot iron-tipped arrows at the enemy. They carved a path toward where Thiago believed the king was among his demons—Thiago had had glimpses of the monarch on a horse. He'd seen nothing of Lila.

All around them, the battle swirled and he saw members of the Fire Horde, most of whom had taken to the air, and the Vikings who fired sheets of rusted arrows and advanced on the demons behind a wall of thick wooden shields fitted with rusted bosses. Amid the savage hacking, clawing melee, he had trouble differentiating Vikings from demons. Perhaps there was no difference.

Excellent. They had divided their efforts as he'd planned, with his fleet jinn acting as cavalry and the Norsemen functioning as infantry.

"Hang on," Thiago screamed over his shoulder at the big Norseman.

He'd seen the king. He didn't know if he'd been heard, and he would have to trust that Njal could hang on and wouldn't fall to his death as they went airborne. For him, at this moment, it wasn't war, it was hunting. He goaded his mount, who leaped upward. With a surge the other horses followed and they left the ground. Though the chariot was heavy, the horses were strong and within an instant the chariot shot far above the seething fray below. The oarsman screamed curses at him. They hadn't trained for this, but Thiago had warned him to look forward, not down. He'd also told the Dane when to jump, but that time wasn't quite yet.

They soared. Velocity and altitude made the temperature plunge. The four horses snorted in discomfort. The desert fell away far below, and he saw the nighttime battle below as flashes of light and black masses of formations struggling with one another. Thiago knew the chariot was invisible to the warriors below, dark figures on black horses against a charcoal sky.

He flattened his trajectory.

"Back down," he shouted at Njal. "We'll have surprise with us. Get a spear ready. Iron is lethal to the bastard. Hold on."

And down they went, gaining speed and crushing momentum. His mounts seemed tireless and predatory, as if they'd sensed his blood lust and grown careless of their own safety. He headed toward the center of the battle, trailed by the malign iron chariot, toward piles of bodies, Viking and Horde warriors who'd tried to take on the king and died.

He banked right.

Don't overcorrect. Give Njal a stable platform to hurl his spear.

The king presided over the battle with macabre, godlike detachment, overseeing mass slaughter from a white horse, chopping and stabbing about him, lopping off an arm here and impaling a Horde warrior there. A mass of his ifrit and jinn warriors fought fanatically around him. The clamor deafened Thiago.

"Throw!" Thiago shouted.

A long dart of iron and oak flew past his head to catch the king full in the chest. No armor that Thiago knew of should have blunted this iron projectile, but the spear hit the monarch with no more effect than a sparrow hitting a stone wall.

He's immune to iron, Thiago thought.

Like no other demon. Is he also immune to a ton of dead-weight landing on top of him?

"Jump!" he screamed at Njal.

He loosed the horses' hitches and shouted at them to flee. They scattered in all directions as he leaped off his mount. The chariot pitched forward to hit the tyrant and his surrounding warriors, bouncing along before coming to a stop in a fountain of sand. Thiago landed in a pile of bodies. They cushioned his impact.

There was a red smear where the king had been.

~

Despite the king's destruction, they were losing. Thiago now fought on foot. His horses had vanished in the chaos. He didn't know where Njal was, or Lubna, or any of the Norse or jinn leaders. He fought amid a dwindling group of Vikings and a few of his outlaws who'd lost the energy to morph into fire, wind, or anything other than their bone-weary human forms.

Is this all of us? Thiago thought.

They were encircled and being crushed inward by waves of the king's jinn and ifrit warriors.

There are three of them for every one of us. Numbers are doing what their strategy didn't. But with the king dead, who are they fighting for? They're just fighting against us? Or are they fighting for the treasure?

Thiago heard a commotion by the portal loud enough to carry across the canyon and over the clash of metal on metal and screams. At first, there was no effect on his immediate situation as he fought on frantically, hopelessly, but then he noticed that his opponents begin to fall away singly and then in groups like ice melting over a fire. Suddenly they parted completely and scattered. The Vikings and members of the Horde next to him let out a weak cheer and pushed tiredly forward, attacking the backs of their retreating opponents. Flashes of fire appeared overhead to harass and incinerate the fleeing warriors, and hundreds of jinn horsemen swept over and amid the remnants of the dead king's forces, cutting them off from the portal.

The losers fled into the desert without discipline.

With no one around him left to stab or slash, Thiago stopped and leaned wearily on his sword, surrounded by bodies and smoldering patches of sand. For several moments, he focused on breathing and nothing else. Gradually, sensations penetrated his fatigue. He heard horses neighing and coins jingling. Close by, he saw Ajmal and Charun joyously, mindlessly cavorting amid the treasure, hurling gold and silver into the air. The metal fell nearby to sparkle in the moonlight.

A rider cantered up to his side. "Collect them. They're what you fought for."

Thiago looked upward at the rider.

"How are you here?" He couldn't think of anything else to say to his father.

Thiago saw that his parent still looked frail from his stay in the dungeon, but he handled his horse with confidence and carried a scimitar and lance, both bloody.

"This is the first time I've crossed the portal. It wasn't fun. I'll use it to return home, but no more after that."

"It brought you here," Thiago said.

"The air doesn't smell the same. Is all of it this dry? There's nothing growing."

"There's much more to see. Some of it is very green. Spend time here."

"I think not." Some of the hauteur that Thiago recognized so well rang through in his father's voice, but then his elder's tone softened.

"I can't sightsee. There's a lot to do in Bethinia. Civil war is a real possibility with the king suddenly gone. He was the rotten rope that tied us all together. Jinn hate ifrit, jinn hate each other, and everyone who's never gotten much out of our 'magical' world hates those who prospered. I'll defend what's ours and protect my family."

Thiago sensed an unasked question: Would he return to help his father's mission?

"I'll stay here for a while," he said. "I've adapted a little to this strange place. But I'll visit home often. I didn't do that before. If you need help, I'll be there."

His father looked happy.

"Maybe," Thiago said. "Just maybe, some new government can be formed that represents every part of the realm."

"Maybe," his father said noncommittally.

Thiago nodded, accepting political realities, but he wouldn't let that leach away elation at his victory tonight.

"How did you know to come when you did?" he asked.

"Our tribe mobilized and joined with the escapees from our dear, late king's open-air dungeon, the demons you set free. I came to know many of them in prison. We went back to let them all out. There were a lot of them and they fought well tonight. They detested the king, may he rot. Hatred and surprise carried the day, as did your own comrades. Several of the former king's so-called council of war defected to our side, too—no one believed he'd distribute Sheba's Treasure if he won—and they alerted us to his plans and timing. We got here late—there was debate about how many of us could transit the portal at a time—but get here we finally did."

"The treasure, it's everyone's," Thiago said. "Let your crew know they can help themselves. There are many fewer of my band to share it with after the fight."

There was another unasked question his father would want to put to him, but would be too circumspect to pose, so Thiago addressed it. Sometimes things could be left to fester, but not this.

"I don't know what happened to the ifrit, Lila," he said. "If she survived, she'll distress this world or yours sooner or later. So let's find out. She'd have gone wherever the fighting was fiercest."

"Your lover?"

"She's not my lover, hasn't been for a while."

Thiago scanned the canyon and spotted Orm, Halfdan, and Njal running their hands through a pile of silk. Behind them he recognized Lubna and Aaliyah and was immeasurably relieved they'd survived. Aaliyah draped herself and the librarian with royal-purple cloth.

Thiago walked alongside his father, still mounted, as they moved over to the group. He rested his hand against his father's horse. He was so bone-weary he could barely stand.

The librarian and Aaliyah looked in no better shape, with smudged faces and blackened armor beneath the silk. They embraced him.

Prostrate at their feet lay the ifrit. She looked very much alive, but her wrists were bound with an iron chain.

"The librarian has skills with a net," Aaliyah said.

"It was iron, heavy," Lubna said. "But I managed to throw it over the demon during the battle. That disabled her. I've read Latin texts about how gladiators fought. Some of them used nets to trap their opponents in the coliseum."

"Where did you get an iron net?" Thiago asked.

"I used the rusted chain mail shirt I wore into the fight," Lubna said. "I took it off and threw it on her. She wasn't expecting me to fight that way. She wasn't expecting me to fight at all."

"Surprise, the jinn way," Thiago said.

CHAPTER 19

Verses for a Librarian

"Should I kill Thiago?" the Sardinian asked.

Lila was still adjusting to the battle's outcome, so she didn't respond immediately.

"I missed the king," the executioner continued. "What's left is hardly recognizable. Your lover got to him first."

"Thiago? He's not my lover," she said sharply. "Anymore."

"I fought hard, got wounded. I'm not inclined to give back the emerald."

"You failed, but you fought well," she acknowledged. "Keep your gem. There's much more in the pile of treasure if you want it. First, get this restraint off me. My legs and hands are numb. I can't sit up. There's no one around. They posted a dozen guards on me, nasty-looking jinn, but I told them I'd make them part of my court if they looked the other way. It's an unsettled time. They don't know who comes out on top; not having me as an enemy is a good thing. At the moment, they're busy rummaging through the treasure. No one wants to be left out."

The Sardinian stooped to work at loosening the iron chain tied around the ifrit's wrists.

"Will you still need an executioner, torturer, and assassin all combined conveniently in one person?"

"Of course," she said. "I'll deal with whatever tribal leaders survived this fight when I return to Bethinia. You can help."

The iron shackles came off and the ifrit sprang to her feet with a shriek of joy.

"Should I kill Thiago?" the Sardinian asked.

The ifrit paused for a while rubbing her wrists. "I'll let you know."

∼

"You slipped your bonds and your guards," Thiago said. He stood by the portal still exhausted and soul-weary from the battle. He'd expected that the ifrit would come here eventually and he wanted to intercept her.

The ifrit rarely bothered with human gestures even when she took human form, but now she shrugged.

"Congratulations," she said. "You caught me. Want to fight? Otherwise I'm going home."

Lila moved toward the portal. She was clearly detached and didn't intend to expend energy on lost causes. It was time to return to the kingdom of jinns, ifrits, and beautiful palaces, and her shadowy tribe of demons. There would be better times to trouble mankind and perhaps trouble Thiago, too. It would be a smile.

"I'm too tired to fight," he said. He waved her toward the portal. "Be my guest. Before you go, I do have a question: Was my poem anything to you besides a map?"

"It rhymed," she said.

"Faint praise."

"I've read other verses, other poets," she said. "Your poem was stronger than most."

"Stronger than *any* others. It was a testament to our love."

"Oddly, I did love you once. Or perhaps I only liked you, but now I like the poem more than the poet."

"You mean that to hurt," he said.

"As much as possible," she said before vanishing. He felt a breeze waft past him as if a door to elsewhere opened and then closed as she transited back to the world of demons.

She was the one that got away, but in that, he was lucky.

~

Thiago watched Sheba's Treasure shrink like candy nibbled at by ants. More and more citizens of Bethinia trooped through the portal to grab whatever they could carry. The later arrivals came prepared and brought carts and horses to increase their haul back through the portal. For a while, the Fire Horde's and Norsemen's surviving warriors tried to police the pillaging, but then they gave up to focus on securing their own share. No one bothered to look at a brilliant dawn rising over the desert and the age-old ruins ruminating over the canyon below.

"I wonder how many will keep their piece of it?" he said.

"Most will lose theirs shortly," Lubna said. "Robbery, trickery, stupidity, but at least you gave them the chance to hold it for a while."

"I'm not above it," he said. With his toe, he nudged a leather bag of the finest, most portable items he'd taken from the heaps of treasure. The bag was extremely heavy.

"I'm as greedy as the rest. And I've still got this." The jinn pulled his last emerald from his cloak. He tossed it into the air and caught it, remembering standing on this same spot plotting an ambush and planning a poem.

He'd been sitting on a chest. Now he stood up. "There's something else. It's for you. Go ahead. Open it."

"A present? I've already got some pretty bracelets and a ruby necklace."

But the librarian bent down and opened the chest.

The jinn looked on. "They're from a library that mostly burned almost a thousand years ago in Alexandria during a siege, but not these scrolls. How they were in Sheba's Treasure, I don't know, but with them in your collection, your library will be unique. The caliph doesn't get a mountain of gold, but this gives him prestige he can't buy."

"You knew I'd go back," she said.

"I knew it was a hard choice after you'd seen some of your world and a bit of mine, but ultimately, you and Córdoba's library are one and the same."

"What about you?"

Thiago watched a peacock wander out of the portal as if it owned everything it saw.

"It will be chaos for the foreseeable future in my world, so if you're agreeable, I'll take you up on an offer you made to my father: become a scholar in residence in your library. I've written poems in a desert. Let's see if I can compose with wine in hand amid a pile of books while looking out on a garden in Córdoba."

"What will you write about?"

"I wrote a poem about a demon. Let's see if I can write verses about a librarian."

THE END

If you enjoyed this fanciful tale, please take a moment to rate and/or review it on Amazon, Goodreads, or other book review sites. Thanks, and I hope you'll read my other stories. I can be contacted at blaisdellliterayenterprises.com.

AUTHOR'S NOTES

Jinns (or Djinns or Genies)

*T*he *Jinn and the Two Kingdoms* has as its main character, a supernatural being known variously as a jinn, djinn, or genie. I used "jinn" throughout my novel because this descriptor appears closest to the Arabic origins of the term, though, as is often the case with archaic words in current usage, the etymology is somewhat uncertain. Perhaps this is fitting for folklore about magical creatures whose provenance is at least two thousand years old.

I also used "jinn" to create distance and minimize associations between my novel and narratives with "genies" from Disney cartoons or the 1960's era TV show, *I Dream of Jeannie*. As the gentle reader should be aware after reading *The Jinn and the Two Kingdoms*, there is little overlap between my somewhat cynical narrative laced with a blend of myth and medieval geopolitics, and depictions of blue-hued genies or blond TV starlets. Aligned with this, there are no magic carpets and only incidental references to oil lamps in *The Jinn and the Two Kingdoms*.

An enormous volume of lore has been written about jinns; a starting point for readers interested in these supernatural beings is *Legends of the Fire Spirits* by Robert Lebling.

Ifrits (or efreets, afrits, or afreets)

In this novel, one of the antagonists (and also a former lover) of the main character is a supernatural being known as an "ifrit." Like jinns, ifrits are part of Islamic folklore. However, while jinns can be good, bad, or somewhere in the middle, ifrits are usually considered malign and demonic. Certainly, in *The Jinn and the Two Kingdoms*, the ifrit are a rather dodgy crowd.

Like jinns, Lebling's *Legends of the Fire Spirits*, provides interesting background on the folklore pertaining to these demons.

A Thousand Nights and One

Any author touching however lightly on Arabic or Persian folklore, should peruse *One Thousand and One Nights*. Translations and editions of these wonderful stories are numerous and commentary on the many versions is far beyond the scope of my author's notes; one place to consider starting is *The Annotated Arabian Nights* edited and introduced by Paulo Lemos Horta and translated by Yasmine Seale.

Lubna, Abd-al-Rahman, and the Caliphate of Cordoba

They were all real, Lubna, Abd-al-Rahman and the Caliphate of Cordoba. Tenth-century Spain seemed a marvelous counterpoint to the entirely fictitious—as far as I know—Kingdom of the Demons that I invented for this novel. These form the eponymous realms of the novel's title. *The Jinn and the Two Kingdoms* only touches on the caliphate's politics and culture; it was an imperial realm under the capable caliph, Abd-al-Rahman's leadership, jockeying with contemporary powers for dominance of the western Mediterranean during a very contentious historical period. The scribe and librarian, Lubna, has been described by several sources. She appears to have been a prominent scholar in the caliphate's court who deserves additional biographical research.

ACKNOWLEDGMENTS

*T*he *Jinn and the Two Kingdoms* blends literary fantasy and historical fiction with a dash of romance. I've also included elements of portal fantasy. There are themes and motifs aplenty, but I've used the plot to propel the story along at an entertaining pace.

This novel is the first in a planned series centered on the (mis)adventures of Thiago, the jinn. The librarian, Lubna, and the demon, Lila, will also appear again.

Many thanks to Anne, Shikha, Steve F., John B., and Carolyn for insightful input. Of course, any mistakes are mine.

ABOUT THE AUTHOR

P eter Blaisdell lives in the greater LA area. He has a Ph.D. in Biochemistry and has conducted postdoctoral research in microbiology. On the literary side of his life, he has authored *The Lords of Oblivion*, *The Lords of Powder*, and *The Lords of the Summer Season*. These are fast-paced, modern fantasies centered on Bradan, an almost immortal magician and his wolf, Tintagel. Each of the three books can be read on its own or together as a series. Bradan and Tintagel make cameo appearances in *The Jinn and the Two Kingdoms*.

The Jinn and the Two Kingdoms is the first in a series featuring the jinn, Thiago.

Contact the author at blaisdellliteraryenterprises.com.

Made in United States
North Haven, CT
22 October 2022

25790982R00182